Twilight's Serenade

SONG OF ALASKA ✦ Three

Twilight's Serenade

TRACIE
PETERSON

BETHANY HOUSE PUBLISHERS
Minneapolis, Minnesota

To Morris and Pat James
with love and thanksgiving
that God made us friends.
Your faith has been an inspiration.

Books by Tracie Peterson

www.traciepeterson.com

A Slender Thread • *What She Left for Me* • *Where My Heart Belongs*

SONG OF ALASKA
Dawn's Prelude • *Morning's Refrain* • *Twilight's Serenade*

ALASKAN QUEST
Summer of the Midnight Sun
Under the Northern Lights • *Whispers of Winter*
Alaskan Quest (3 in 1)

BRIDES OF GALLATIN COUNTY
A Promise to Believe In • *A Love to Last Forever*
A Dream to Call My Own

THE BROADMOOR LEGACY*
A Daughter's Inheritance • *An Unexpected Love*
A Surrendered Heart

BELLS OF LOWELL*
Daughter of the Loom • *A Fragile Design* • *These Tangled Threads*

LIGHTS OF LOWELL*
A Tapestry of Hope • *A Love Woven True* • *The Pattern of Her Heart*

DESERT ROSES
Shadows of the Canyon • *Across the Years* • *Beneath a Harvest Sky*

HEIRS OF MONTANA
Land of My Heart • *The Coming Storm*
To Dream Anew • *The Hope Within*

LADIES OF LIBERTY
A Lady of High Regard • *A Lady of Hidden Intent*
A Lady of Secret Devotion

RIBBONS OF STEEL**
Distant Dreams • *A Hope Beyond* • *A Promise for Tomorrow*

WESTWARD CHRONICLES
A Shelter of Hope • *Hidden in a Whisper* • *A Veiled Reflection*

YUKON QUEST
Treasures of the North • *Ashes and Ice* • *Rivers of Gold*

*with Judith Miller   **with Judith Pella

TRACIE PETERSON is the author of over eighty novels, both historical and contemporary. Her avid research resonates in her stories, as seen in her bestselling HEIRS OF MONTANA and ALASKAN QUEST series. Tracie and her family make their home in Montana.

Visit Tracie's Web site at
www.traciepeterson.com.

Visit Tracie's blog at
www.writespasssage.blogspot.com.

Chapter 1

SITKA, ALASKA
January 1906

Britta Lindquist awoke suddenly from the grasp of her dream and sat straight up in bed, breathing heavily. She let her eyes adjust to the dim light and relaxed as she recognized her surroundings. After a six-year absence, she was home again—as if she'd never gone away.

Favorite childhood books lined the shelf where she'd left them. Dolls were arranged upon her dresser. In the corner, an ornately carved hope chest held years of dreaming— dreams that could never come true. Mother had once told her that if one dream seemed to be unobtainable, a person could always dream a new dream. And Britta had tried. God alone knew how much she wanted to clear her head and heart of the old and welcome in the new. Still, it seemed no matter how far she journeyed from home, no matter what new challenge she tried, nothing diminished her longing.

"Britta? Britta, are you awake?" a tentative voice whispered.

"Come in, Kay."

The door opened only enough to allow a dark-haired woman to peek inside. Kalage, or Kay, as Lydia had nicknamed her, had been with the Lindquist family for the past fifteen years. Orphaned at the age of thirteen, Kay had been called "a child of the beach" by her mother's people, though it was by no means a term of endearment. The Tlingits had shunned Kay's mother for her disgraceful behavior as a prostitute, and her white father had long since deserted them. By the time Kalage had been born, all ties to her family heritage had been severed. The shame of her mother was upon Kay as surely as if she'd acted against the Tlingits herself. Britta's family had taken Kay into their home when Aunt Zee found the child half dead from starvation.

"I thought I heard you. Is everything all right?"

Britta nodded. "I had a bad dream. You must have heard me tossing and turning. It was really nothing."

Kay slipped into the room and closed the door behind her. She studied Britta for a moment. "You in trouble?"

Kay's astute observations never failed to amaze Britta. She'd always felt close to the woman, who was only three years her senior. "I'm not in trouble," Britta assured her.

Kay, however, refused to let the matter drop. "Then what's wrong? I could see from the look in your eyes last night that you carry a heavy burden."

Britta looked up and shook her head. "I can't really talk about it just yet."

Kay went to the window and opened the drapes to let in the light. "It's almost ten. You don't always sleep this late, do you?"

Britta laughed and got to her feet. "No, though I will say I was rather spoiled when I went abroad. Europeans never seem to have the same sense of urgency that we Americans embrace. While in England and Germany, I sometimes slept late. However, we were often up well into the wee hours of the morning after a concert."

Approaching the wardrobe, Britta continued to direct the conversation away from Kay's concerns. "California was quite lovely. I think you'd like it there. It's very beautiful, and there is always something blooming. Speaking of blooms, I was in Holland last spring and could scarcely believe the fields of tulips. I wish you could have seen them. They took up positively acres and acres."

She fingered several of her dresses, glad that she'd left her more elegant pieces in San Francisco. They would hardly serve her well here. Sitka's climate might remain mild most of the year, but the lightweight muslins and silks were not appropriate for daily life. She decided on a wool jumper and cream-colored gown. "This should keep me warm." Glancing to where Kay stood, Britta quickly ascertained the woman wasn't at all interested in travel comments or fashion choices.

Britta stopped and sobered. "I can't really talk about everything just yet. In time, I promise I will take you into my confidence, but for now I need time to consider things on my own."

"You have come home to make a decision?"

With a sigh, Britta nodded. "That is all I will say for the moment. Will you help me dress?"

Kay came forward and reached for the garments. "I will pray for you."

Her words touched Britta's heart. How

long had it been since someone had offered to help in that way? "Thank you."

———

"It's so good to have you home," Britta's mother told her. "You seem awfully thin, though. Have you not been feeling well?" Lydia Lindquist had always worried over her children, but as the youngest, Britta found that she received more than her share of attention. Especially now, after such a long absence.

"I'm fine, truly I am." Britta reached for another piece of toasted bread as if to assure her mother. "I eat as much as Dalton." The reference to her brother gave Britta the perfect excuse to change the subject. "Speaking of Dalton, I understand that his boat business has expanded considerably in the last few years. In fact, Lindquist boats are all the rage in California."

"Your brother has a good eye for design. Not only that, but he's acquired some very talented employees. Most are Tlingit and were trained at the Sheldon Jackson school," her mother replied.

"What about Father? Is he working with Dalton, too?"

"Oh, on occasion he assists if there's a need. He sometimes will help with a building project, but mostly he just takes care of this place. I've encouraged him to relax more." She smiled. "But of course he isn't much inclined to sit idle."

"I can imagine. I know Dalton said they sometimes deliver boats together."

"That's right. In fact, they're going to deliver one to San Francisco together in March."

"How nice for them. Dalton really seems to enjoy Father's company, and his life here in Sitka. He seems both happy and content. Phoebe, too. And gracious, but I hardly recognized the children."

"Gordon will be fifteen next month," Britta's mother offered. "And Rachel, well she's all but grown up at the age of eleven. She never hesitates to remind me that her birthday in April will be her twelfth. Somehow, that seems to be a magic number for her."

Britta laughed. "She is quite pretty. She'll break many hearts, I'm sure."

Her mother nodded and poured Britta another cup of tea. "Alex is just like Dalton. He's not even eight years old, but he walks and talks just like his father."

"He was hardly doing either one the last time I saw him," Britta said. "And little Connie wasn't even born before I left. I feel as though I've missed out on a great deal."

"Time has a way of doing that," her mother said with a smile.

"How is Kjerstin? Does she still enjoy nursing?" Britta asked between bites of toast. "Any nieces or nephews on the way?"

Lydia shook her head. "No. Your sister is worried that perhaps she can't conceive—they've been married over five years—but Matthew tells her not to fret. As a doctor, he thinks her perfectly healthy and figures the good Lord will give them children in due time. They love working with the natives in Kodiak, and the people seem to love them a great deal."

Britta considered her sister's life for a moment, then shrugged. "Sometimes it seems that life has gone on for everyone but me."

"But you've experienced an entire world that you might not otherwise have known while you traveled and attended school." Lydia smiled at her youngest. "I hope it was everything you wanted it to be."

Britta hoped her smile would reassure her mother. "I could never have had the same education in music had I remained here in Sitka. My time spent under the tutelage of gifted teachers and as a part of several orchestras was truly a dream come true."

"I can hardly wait to hear you play the violin for me," her mother said proudly.

Britta had taken up the violin mainly to please her mother and follow in her musical footsteps. But as the years passed, Britta found the violin to be an extension of her own soul. When she pulled the bow across the strings, it seemed as though the music came from somewhere deep within Britta's own heart.

"We shall have a wonderful time playing together," Britta replied. "Just like we did in the old days."

"The old days?" her mother questioned with a raised brow. "You speak as if you're a little old woman instead of a beautiful twenty-four-year-old."

Britta pushed back her empty plate and reached for the teacup. "Sometimes I feel old—almost as if I've lived a hundred years in the last six."

Lydia's tender expression almost drew a confession of purpose from Britta's lips. Her mother's love was evident, and Britta didn't wish to keep anything from her. Still, now was not the time to explain. There were too many issues at hand. Too many ghosts that needed to be dispelled.

A knock at the front door caused mother and daughter to pause in conversation. Lydia got up and went to see who it might be while Britta gathered her wits. There was no sense in pouring out her heart. Especially when she couldn't quite figure out what her heart wanted.

That's not true. I know very well what my heart longs for. I simply cannot have it. She took herself to task silently and waited for her mother to return.

"That was one of the Masterson boys. Caleb, in fact," her mother declared as she hurried back into the room. "You remember him, don't you? I think he's nearly sixteen. Anyway, he'd just come from the Belikov place."

Britta felt as if a knife had been run through her heart. "Yuri's house?"

"Yes. Marsha is about to give birth and needs my help. I sent Caleb on to fetch the doctor, but I could use your assistance, if you can spare the time. Their little Laura is only three and will be terrified to witness her mother going through labor."

The years seemed to drop away at the mention of Yuri's family. Britta stiffened. "I'll do what I can."

"Good. I'll gather my things and then we can go."

"Should I get the wagon?" Britta asked.

"No. Yuri's cabin isn't all that far. It's just half a mile or so down the coast road. It won't take us long to get there on foot."

Britta said nothing. Her stomach churned, and she wished she'd not eaten that last piece of bread. The thought of Yuri and his wife left her sad in a way that Britta could not ever admit to her mother. Yuri's marriage had been the reason Britta had packed her things and left Sitka back in 1900. Seeing him with another woman was more than Britta could bear. Discovering he'd been tricked into marriage with a prostitute was even more difficult.

She wondered what he would look like now. She remembered blond hair that begged her touch and blue eyes that seemed full of mischief and passion. How unfair that the one man she had loved since childhood should belong to someone else. Someone who didn't even love him, to hear her brother tell it.

"I'm ready now. Grab your coat and let's be on our way," her mother announced, coming back into the room.

Britta had second thoughts about going. "Won't Yuri be there to help?"

Mother cast a sidelong glance as she pulled on her wool cape. "Yuri hasn't been around for a long time. I can't even remember the last time we heard from him."

"What do you mean?" Britta asked, retrieving her fur-trimmed coat.

Her mother frowned. "I feel bad in saying this, but Yuri has very little to do with his family. He . . . well . . . suffice it to say, he hasn't been much of a father or husband. Dalton says it's probably for the best, as he drinks too much and has little patience for anyone."

This was the first Britta had heard of Yuri's behavior. She knew he liked to have a drink from time to time when they were younger. She had even heard that he was given to drunkenness on occasion. But she'd always excused it by telling herself that this was the way of many a good man. Still, to hear that he had deserted his family . . . Britta pushed aside her thoughts and followed her mother out the door.

They could hear Marsha Belikov's screams as they neared the worn-down cabin. The building had never been much of a house, even in its conception, but now the sorry-looking collection of weathered logs looked ready to collapse at the first good wind.

Britta followed her mother into the place, wrinkling her nose at the odors. There was barely room to turn around, and no matter where Britta cast her glance, she saw stacks of dirty dishes, liquor bottles, and other piles of filth.

"Marsha?" Britta heard her mother call. She waited as her mother looked into the back room. "We've come to help."

"Help by getting this brat out of me." The woman's harsh tone took Britta by surprise.

How could anyone speak of a baby in such a way? Much less Yuri's baby?

"And bring me some more whiskey. My head is killing me."

Mother stepped back just a bit. "Britta, take Laura into the front room, please."

Unsure where the child was, Britta looked about, puzzled. Lydia pointed to the corner, where a tiny girl in a filthy gown sat cowering on a blanket. The child's matted blond hair hid her face, but Britta knew she was watching them.

"Who is that?" Marsha asked before giving out a scream of pain and a rant of obscenities.

Britta was startled by the woman's expletives. She had never heard a lady curse in such a manner. Yet from the comments she'd heard about her background, Britta knew that Marsha wasn't much of a lady. She cast a quick glance at the haggard woman. Stringy brown hair spilled out around Marsha's shoulders. She looked much older than Britta had imagined.

"This is my youngest daughter, Britta. She's going to take care of Laura while I help you deliver this baby. Britta, take Laura and then get some water heating on the stove."

"There's a pot going already," Marsha told

her. "I put it on when I sent Caleb for you. Figured we'd need it."

Britta's mother nodded. "That was wise. Now, let me check you to see how far along you are."

Uncertain how to handle the situation with the little girl, Britta moved slowly to the opposite side of the room. Kneeling, she did the only thing that seemed natural and extended her arms and smiled.

"Would you like to come play with me?"

To her surprise, the child practically leaped into her embrace. Without a word, Britta rose and carried Laura from the room just as Marsha began screaming again.

Laura reached up and patted Britta's face. "Who are you?"

Smiling, Britta glanced around to see where she might seat the child. Laura, however, had no intention of being put down and clung to Britta fiercely.

"I'm Britta, and I know you are Laura."

The child pulled back just enough to nod. "I'm hungry."

Britta lost her heart to Yuri's daughter. She looked just like him. "Let's see if we can find you something to eat." Laura tightened her grip and Britta realized there would be no putting her down. Easing her to one side, Britta freed up her right arm and began opening cupboards to see what she might find.

There was really very little. A tin of crackers and a can of sardines seemed hardly the appropriate meal for a child, but that was the best that Britta could do for the moment. She offered Laura a cracker and was trying to figure out what to do about opening the sardines when her mother appeared.

"She's having a rough time of it." Her voice was barely audible.

"Is something wrong?"

"I don't know. She's complaining of such horrible pain in her head. She's been in labor for some time now, however, and the baby is very close to being born."

"What is to be done?"

"There isn't much I can do. Hopefully the doctor will arrive soon. She's asking for whiskey to ease her pain. Have you seen any?"

Britta shook her head. "Just empty bottles." Britta bit her lip and looked at the child in her arms. "Yuri should know what is happening."

Her mother searched through the same cupboards Britta had just explored. "No one knows where he is. As I said, he's not been here in some time."

"Perhaps Dalton has heard from him?" she asked hopefully.

"If he has, he's said nothing about it to me," her mother replied.

Just then, a knock sounded on the door. Relief washed over Mother's face. "That will be the doctor."

She hurried to let him in while Britta continued to hold Laura. The child munched on her cracker and seemed no more interested in her mother's condition than she did in who might be at the door.

The doctor conversed for a moment with Lydia, and then both of them crossed the room without a word. Britta couldn't help but wonder at the seriousness of the situation. Women had babies every day. Why should this delivery be any different? But despite the fact that they'd entered a new century, full of modern wonders, women continued to die giving life to their offspring. Perhaps Marsha Belikov would die and free Yuri from the misery of their marriage.

As soon as the thought came to mind, however, Britta immediately felt guilty. She might not like that Yuri had put himself into a loveless marriage, but she couldn't wish his wife dead.

"More," Laura said, drawing Britta from her thoughts.

She handed the child another cracker and waited to see what the next few minutes might bring. She heard Marsha scream and shivered at the sound. It was unlike anything she'd ever heard. This cry sounded like something unnatural—something dark and disturbing.

When Lydia came rushing from the room, Britta couldn't help but ask, "What is happening?"

"Marsha has fainted. It's to her benefit. I must get some water."

Britta watched as her mother paid little heed to the clutter and pulled a dirty pan from beneath a stack of dishes. She quickly discarded it, however, and took up a towel and grabbed the entire pot off the stove. Hurrying back to aid the doctor, Lydia offered no other word of explanation.

Seconds seemed to creep by, but Britta busied herself with Laura and pretended not to notice. When a baby's cry filled the cabin, Britta exhaled a heavy breath of relief.

"Baby's crying," Laura said, as though Britta might have missed it.

"Yes. That will be your new brother or sister," she told the child.

"Sister," Laura echoed.

Britta smiled. The little girl was quite charming, but so poorly cared for. Even now she was shivering. "Let's see if we can get you something warm to wear."

A search of the cabin revealed little. Britta

finally gave up, figuring that whatever clothes the child might have were probably in the bedroom. She wrapped Laura up in her own wool coat and placed her on a crude stool. "Sit here while I see how your mama is doing."

Laura was none too happy to be discarded and sat in a quiet pout. Britta went to the doorway and could see from the expression on the doctor's face that things were not going well. The baby had been wrapped securely in a blanket but placed aside to cry while the doctor and Britta's mother were bent over Marsha's still body.

The doctor straightened. "There's no pulse."

"Is there nothing we can do?" Lydia questioned.

"I'm afraid not. My guess is that she burst something in her head. The pain she felt was so intense, it must have been an aneurysm." He reached for his stethoscope and bent to listen to the woman's heartbeat. He didn't tarry there long. "She's gone."

"That quickly?" Britta spoke the question without meaning to.

Her mother cast a glance her way. The sorrow in her expression left little doubt. "She passed just as the baby was born. The doctor had to work to clear the baby's airway to get her breathing on her own. By the time we turned our attention back to Marsha, she was gone."

The doctor pulled the sheet up over the woman. "I'll see to the child now."

Britta had never seen death up close. She hadn't even been home when her great-aunt Zerelda had passed away. "The baby . . . is the baby all right?" she asked her mother.

"Seems to be. It's another little girl."

Lydia came to where Britta stood. Together, the women waited for the doctor to speak. It seemed that he took forever to examine the baby.

"The child appears quite healthy. For all her delay in the birth canal, she doesn't seem to have suffered much more than a bit of skull deformity, which will pass in time," the doctor announced. He looked to Britta's mother. "Who is to care for them?"

"There isn't any family. The father . . . well, you know Yuri."

He nodded in a most somber manner. "I'll arrange for them to go to the orphanage."

"No!" Britta declared. The doctor and her mother both looked at her in surprise, but she didn't care. These were Yuri's children. She couldn't let them go to an orphanage without first trying to find their father. "I could take care of them."

The doctor appeared skeptical, but her

mother grew thoughtful. "We could take them to the house. We certainly have the room. Britta could care for them there until we are able to locate Yuri." She searched her daughter's face for a moment. "This will require a great deal from you. Are you sure you want the responsibility?"

"I must at least try," Britta said. "I could not forgive myself if Yuri returned to find his children gone and then learned that I did nothing to help them."

Her mother seemed to understand, and for this, Britta was relieved. She had no idea how she might have fought such a battle without her mother's approval.

"Very well," the doctor said, finishing his exam of the baby. "You know how to care for an infant, Lydia. I'll leave the situation to you."

Britta felt her pulse quicken as the full impact of her decision began to sink in. Had she made a terrible mistake? Glancing at the form of Yuri's dead wife, she felt a wave of guilt wash over her. Was it wrong to be glad that such a woman had passed from the earth? To imagine that she might yet have the chance to win Yuri's affection for herself?

Of course it's wrong! She hated herself for even thinking such thoughts. *What kind of woman am I that I would covet a dead woman's husband while she's not yet in the grave? A terrible and awful person—that's what.* She stiffened and turned away from the room. She couldn't stand to face the scene any longer. Worse still, she could hardly bear her own conscience.

Chapter 2

Yuri Belikov tossed back the last of his whiskey and lurched to his feet. The room swayed for a moment, and he clutched at the table to keep from falling over.

"Come on, time to get you home," someone said, coming alongside him.

Yuri recognized one of the men he worked with at the gold mine. Blinking hard in an attempt to focus, he shook his head. "Don't need help, Murphy."

The man laughed and aimed Yuri toward the door. "Of course you don't, but I do. Come on." They made their way outside and staggered toward a run-down stretch of buildings that edged up the mountain.

He couldn't remember how Murphy had gotten him into bed, but when Yuri awoke a few hours later, his head was splitting in pain. No matter how hard he tried to drink himself into an unconscious state, it never lasted long enough. Getting up, Yuri went to the chest at the end of his bed and fetched a half-empty bottle of liquor. He downed a generous portion, letting the bottle linger at his lips as he felt the liquid burn down his throat. He took another long drink, then sealed the bottle once again and placed it gently in the trunk.

"My consolation," he murmured, stumbling back to bed.

The wind had picked up and the chill in the room was enough to send Yuri under the covers without delay. He thought of how nice it might be to have a woman at his side with whom he could share the warmth. Unbidden memories of the wife he'd left in Sitka flooded his mind.

Marsha had been nice enough when he'd met her working at one of the local drinking houses, but that soon ended after she tricked him into marriage. Yuri often thought back to the morning he'd opened his eyes to find himself legally wed to the woman he'd only known on a professional basis.

"What do you mean, calling me *husband*?" he'd asked.

She had laughed harshly at his question. "You don't remember, do you?" She held up her hand to show him a small gold band. "We were hitched last night. You said it was the perfect way to celebrate a new century."

Yuri sat up and stared at the woman as if she'd lost her mind. "I wouldn't marry you. I wouldn't marry anybody."

She only laughed at him. "My cousin did us the honors last night. If you even try to annul this, he'll see you thrown in jail."

"On what grounds?" Yuri asked, trying desperately to clear his mind.

"On the grounds that I'm having your baby," she told him with a smug smile.

"You're pregnant?" He looked at her in disbelief. "Given your line of work, how in the world can you be sure it's mine?"

Pushing back her wavy brown hair, she shrugged. "One father is as good as another. You very well could be the father, and I will swear in a court of law that you are. That's all that matters."

Yuri stared up in the darkness as the memories faded. Nothing had ever been the same after that. Instead of moving on to Nome as he'd planned, Yuri found himself strapped with a wife and little else. She wasn't even grateful that he was willing to take care of her. There was no kindness in her, and she wouldn't let him so much as touch her.

When Marsha suffered a miscarriage a couple of months later, Yuri suggested they go their separate ways. That quickly changed her attitude; she poured on the sweetness, telling Yuri how much she loved him—how sorry she'd been for the way she'd treated him. She went out of her way to entice him to her bed, but Yuri wasn't interested and made no pretense of being so.

Still, it wasn't long before the demon in him turned to liquor and Marsha's seductions worked. But much to Marsha's frustration, she didn't conceive until nearly two years later, and when she made the announcement, Yuri was still not convinced the baby was his.

They left Dawson City and headed to Sitka. Yuri hadn't wanted to return to his hometown, but given their situation, he desperately needed to make a living. Dalton had promised him there would always be a job for him, and true to his word, he'd hired Yuri on the spot. No questions asked.

That had been at least a million years ago,

Yuri thought. Nothing about that time had been pleasant or good. Well, there had been Phoebe, Dalton's wife. She had encouraged Yuri to be a faithful and loving husband to Marsha. Phoebe had even insisted on having them to dinner at least once a week, and despite the fact that Marsha was always obnoxious and insulting, Phoebe continued to extend such gracious invitations.

When Laura was born at the first part of December in 1902, Yuri had marveled that anything so beautiful could be a part of him. At least he hoped she was a part of him. Given Marsha's tendency toward promiscuous behavior, he couldn't be sure. The infant managed to captivate him despite her hateful mother. Still, Marsha found a way to ruin that, as well.

Yuri rolled over and punched down the pillow. He hated himself for having deserted them, but he'd had no choice. There was something downright destructive in Marsha's nature, and he didn't like the person he became when he was with her. Marsha's harsh tongue and insulting tirades always drove him back to the bottle, and it wasn't long before he couldn't keep up with his job and Dalton had to constantly search for him.

Then there was the issue of Laura. Marsha

held her like a trump card. She'd ignore the baby and treat her miserably, but when Yuri showed the child the slightest bit of attention, Marsha would put an end to it. She had no desire to be a mother to Laura, but neither did she want Yuri being a loving father.

It baffled him, but not enough to make him stick around. Yuri figured, like everything else in his life, if he dared to love he would only come up on the short end of things. With that in mind, he left. He left Marsha and Laura, Dalton and Sitka, and struck out for no place in particular. He'd been wandering ever since.

A nagging voice told him he should go home—that he should try to make the marriage work. But that seemed more impossible than striking it rich from the gold fields. He didn't love Marsha. He never had, and he had forced himself not to love Laura, either. Sometimes he even told himself that she wasn't really his child at all—that Marsha had never been faithful to him. That always managed to ease his conscience just a little.

The thing he hated the most, however, was letting Dalton down once again. Throughout their lives, Dalton had been the only constant Yuri had known. Even his parents had moved away—returning to Russia to care for aging family members. Dalton had remained, however. No matter how often Yuri turned to the bottle—no matter how many times he failed to keep his promises to stay sober, Dalton had forgiven Yuri and given him another chance.

Just as he'd put Laura from his heart and mind, Yuri had worked with meticulous care to remove the memories he shared with his best friend. But some things couldn't be forgotten.

"I'm worthless," he whispered in the chilled air. The pain in his head was fading, and Yuri found himself falling back to sleep. "I'm not worthy of love or friendship. Not now—not ever."

Britta stared at the run-down shack and shook her head. Her fourteen-year-old nephew stood at her side. "Isn't much of a place, is it?" she murmured.

"Looks like it could fall down around us. You sure you want to go inside?" Gordon asked.

"I have to. I need to find clothes for Laura and see if Marsha had anything set aside for the baby."

Britta drew a deep breath and headed into the cabin. She had left the children with her mother and Kay, hoping that a trip to the Belikov house might reveal some much-needed supplies. Gordon had accompanied her at Lydia's request, telling him that she didn't want Britta to be alone. Who knew what kind of trouble might await her? The doctor had arranged the previous day for the under-taker to come for Marsha's body, and folks would know that the place was now deserted. It wouldn't take long for some squatter or renter to take over.

Britta left the door open, despite the cold, and walked to the only window. Pushing back the dirty draperies, she allowed light to spill into the house.

"I've never seen anything like this," Gordon told her. "How could anyone live like this?"

"I don't know," she replied. "I felt the same way when I first saw it. Now it seems even worse." She began picking through the clutter, looking for anything that might be of use for Laura or the baby. She spied a small traveling case in the corner of the room.

"If you don't mind, Gordon, check in the other room and see if you can find any of Laura's clothes. Look for baby things, as well. I'm going to open this trunk to see if there might be something kept in here." She went to the small chest and pushed aside an array of trash upon it. Tin cans fell to the floor along with wadded-up paper and moldy crusts of bread.

She knelt beside the piece and reached for the top. The trunk latches were broken, so Britta had no trouble lifting the lid. Inside she found little that would be helpful. There was an old satin gown, hopelessly stained from spills and wear. The material all but fell apart as Britta lifted it out of its resting place. Below was a stack of envelopes that bore barely legible writing but were carefully tied together. How strange. It seemed odd that anyone should have saved these things so carefully in a house that was such an abomination.

" 'Marsha Belikov,' " Britta read. " 'Sitka, Alaska.' " She felt an odd sensation as she opened the first of the letters. She told herself it was necessary to look inside in order to ascertain whether Marsha might have had family that no one knew about. Perhaps the children had grandparents who would want to care for them.

As she read the letter, she felt her heart skip a beat. " 'Here is money for you and Laura. Yuri.' " There was nothing more.

Opening the other envelopes, Britta found the same brief statement in each. So he hadn't deserted them entirely, she thought. It touched her to know that despite his leaving, Yuri had managed to continue sending money back to his family.

"This is all I can find," Gordon said, returning with one small dress in hand. "There's nothing else I can see that would be useful."

Britta put the letters back and placed the satin gown on top before closing the trunk. "Nothing here, either. I suppose I shall simply buy Laura and the baby what they need. Mother will no doubt want to help." She got to her feet. "I suppose the kindest thing that could happen to this place would be a good fire."

Gordon nodded. "I wouldn't want to have to clean it up."

"Neither would I," she said, but her thoughts went to Yuri.

They walked back to the house, not even bothering to bring the tattered dress that Gordon had found. Britta had deemed the piece too hopeless to be of any use to them. She was pondering what all she would need to purchase from the store as they rounded the bend and headed up the drive toward the house. These thoughts quickly fled, however, as she heard Laura crying at the top of her lungs.

Britta picked up her pace and all but ran

the last hundred yards to the house. She burst through the door to find her mother trying unsuccessfully to soothe the child.

"What's wrong? Is she sick?"

Mother looked up in frustration. "She keeps asking for her mama."

Laura broke free from Lydia and rushed to Britta. "Mama," she cried and wrapped her arms around Britta's legs.

Lifting Laura in her arms, Britta pushed back the child's clean blond hair. "Your mama had to go away." She didn't know how else to speak of Marsha's death to the young girl.

"You my mama," Laura said, placing her tiny hands upon Britta's face. With tears still dampening her cheeks, Laura smiled. "You Mama."

Britta looked at her mother and Kay, trying to convey her need for help. No one said a word, however. "No, Laura. I'm Britta," she finally told the child.

"No," the little girl said in an insistent tone. "Mama."

She wrapped her arms around Britta's neck and settled down. Britta didn't know what to do or say. "Has she been crying for long?"

"Ever since you left," Kay said. "We didn't

know she wanted you 'cause she kept asking for her mother."

"Apparently she has adopted you," Britta's mother said.

Britta wanted to say something to protest such thinking, but at the same time, she couldn't deny that she rather liked the way that Laura made her feel. She was needed and wanted in a way that she'd never experienced before.

"I suppose it's because I let her sleep with me last night," Britta began, "and with the shock of losing her real mother, maybe she is just pretending for now."

"Perhaps," Lydia replied. She seemed to sense Britta's discomfort. "Did you find any clothes for her or the baby?"

"No. Not a thing."

"You know, Mother probably has some of Connie's old things that would work," Gordon offered. "She saves everything. There are whole crates of old clothes in the shed."

"That's a wonderful idea, Gordon," Lydia replied. "Why don't you and I go see her right now? You can get the wagon hitched up for me."

Gordon nodded and hurried out of the house. Lydia went to Britta and gently touched her cheek. "You comfort her. Don't feel guilty or bad for that. It's obvious the child is starved for love."

Britta met her mother's eyes. "But what if we both get too attached? That might be dangerous."

"Love often is," her mother said with a smile.

The baby began to fuss, and Kay went to lift her from the cradle that had once held Britta and her siblings. "This little one is hungry, no doubt. I've fixed a bottle for her. Would you and Laura like to feed her?"

Britta tapped Laura's shoulder. "Shall we feed your baby sister?"

Laura lifted her head. "I feed the baby."

"You must sit over here, and I will bring her," Britta instructed, putting Laura on the couch. She waited patiently while Britta went to take the baby from Kay.

The tiny infant continued to fuss. "Well, I obviously don't have the same effect on her that I do on Laura."

Lydia laughed. "Give it time. Babies need to bond. By the way, have you thought of what we should call her?"

Britta nodded. "I thought Darya, after Yuri's mother, might be nice. Even if he wants to change it or call her something else, at least we'll have something to call her for now."

"I think that's a wonderful idea. Darya it is."

Settling down beside Laura, Britta took the bottle that Kay offered and held it out. "Here, you can help me feed her." She gently guided the child's hand so that the bottle nipple came in contact with the baby's mouth.

Laura squealed with delight. "She's eating it."

Britta laughed. "Well, not exactly. She's sucking the milk from it. Baby Darya is too little to eat, but she can drink her milk."

"I drink milk, too," Laura said, nodding.

"Indeed, you do," Lydia said as she took a seat in her favorite rocker. "You are a big girl and you need lots of milk."

Britta felt herself relax and enjoy the moment. There was something so comforting about holding the baby in her arms and having Laura beside her. A warning went off in her head, but Britta ignored it. Loving these babies couldn't possibly be the wrong thing. If Britta got hurt in the process . . . well, that was just the way it would be.

"I'll talk to Dalton while I'm there," her mother said, breaking Britta's concentration.

She looked at Mother in confusion. "What?"

"I'll talk to Dalton about Yuri. There has to be a way to locate him."

"I found some letters at the cabin," Britta told her. "Apparently, Yuri has been sending Marsha money for her and Laura."

Lydia smiled. "I guess we misjudged him."

"I don't understand how he could just leave them. I know people said that Marsha treated him badly, but there was Laura to consider."

"Sometimes the burden of life is just too much to face. Dalton confided in me that Yuri could not overcome his drinking and that, combined with Marsha's bad attitude and relentless complaining, made him feel violent. He never hit her, at least according to what he told Dalton—but he wanted to."

Britta frowned. The thought of Yuri hurting a woman seemed impossible. "He's a good man. I suppose leaving was the only way to keep from becoming something he didn't want to be."

"Wagon's ready, Grandma," Gordon announced from the door.

Lydia got to her feet once again. "I'll be back soon," she promised. "I'll talk to Dalton about finding Yuri. He might have some ideas— something we wouldn't know to think of."

Britta said nothing but was more than a little aware of Kay coming to take her mother's place in the rocker. Her friend stared at her for several minutes.

"You ready to talk about why you came home?" Kay asked.

"I don't think so," Britta said. Not once in the past two days had she given her own situation any real consideration. The children had absorbed her attention and time.

"I don't like it," Kay said, shaking her head. "I don't like secrets."

"This isn't really a secret," Britta said firmly. "It's just a decision I have to make." She looked down at the children and felt her chest tighten. A decision that had just become a whole lot more complicated.

She glanced up at Kay and could see the look of disapproval in her eyes. Britta didn't ask if her thoughts were of Britta's refusal to speak or of the obvious attachment she was forming for Yuri's children. Either way, she didn't think she wanted to hear Kay's comments. But Kay was never one to remain silent. The dark-eyed woman crossed her arms and leaned back in the rocker.

"You're still in love with him."

Britta's eyes widened at the bold statement. She looked down, unable to meet Kay's accusing expression, only to find baby Darya watching her with great intensity.

"You're going to get your heart broken again," Kay chided. "You just wait and see."

Britta drew a deep breath and raised her head. "It can't be broken again," she told her solemnly. "It was never made whole after the first time."

Chapter 3

March 1906

Nearly two months had passed since Darya's birth, and still no word from Yuri. Britta found herself in a comfortable routine with the children, but not a day passed without her wondering if this would be the day Yuri would be found. And once he was found, what would happen then? Would he return to Sitka and take the girls away with him? Would he refuse to come home and designate that the children go to an orphanage?

Britta couldn't bear the thought of losing her place in Laura and Darya's lives. The children seemed so happy. Laura was not only starting to talk to others around her but was allowing others to care for her for short periods of time during the day. She still slept next to Britta at night, however. It had been impossible to convince the little girl to sleep in the trundle bed beside Britta, much less to sleep across the room. Baby Darya, however, was the one who seemed the happiest. She was an easygoing infant, satisfied and content with the variety of hands that cared for her.

Phoebe had been able to provide most everything Britta needed for the girls, from tiny flannels for diapers to gowns and blankets. For Laura, there had been several perfectly sized dresses. Connie had seemed a bit hesitant to part with things she recognized, but in due time, that had fallen by the wayside and Connie had become a perfect companion for Laura. The two girls enjoyed each other's company and played well together. Life was very nearly perfect—except for the uncertainty about Yuri.

"You ever gonna talk to me?" Kay asked as she joined Britta in what had become the nursery.

"I've been talking to you ever since I came home," Britta countered, watching Laura play with a couple of hand-me-down dolls.

"You know what I mean," Kay replied. She took a seat on a wooden chair and pushed back her black hair. "You said you'd tell me about coming here and the decision you had to make."

Britta shrugged. "I guess in taking on the girls, I haven't really given it a lot of thought. I need to, however. I'm supposed to deliver an answer by June."

"It's nearly April now. That leaves just two months. What are you trying to decide?" Kay fixed her with a stare that told Britta she might as well be forthcoming with the information.

"I've been asked to join a new orchestra that a prestigious conductor is starting. I would be given the first chair in the violin section. I would have a great deal of responsibility. I might even be allowed to step in and lead the orchestra when the conductor is unable to serve."

"So why couldn't you have just said this when you first came?"

Why indeed? Britta got up on the pretense of checking Darya. She knew if she looked Kay in the eye, her friend would easily be able to see that there was something more.

"I guess I didn't want to worry Mother," Britta replied, gently tucking a blanket around the sleeping infant.

"Worry me about what?" Lydia asked from the nursery door.

Britta nearly jumped out of her skin. She turned and faced her curious mother. "Well . . . Kay was just asking me about the reasons I came home."

"And what were they?" her mother questioned with a raised brow. "I think we'd all like to have the answer to that."

"I was asked to take the first-chair violin position in a brand-new orchestra."

"That's wonderful news!" Mother declared as she crossed the room. She reached out to hug Britta. "You should have said something immediately. When will you begin?"

"I haven't . . . well, that is to say . . . I don't know that I'm accepting the position."

"But why?" Lydia cast a glance at the sleeping baby. "Because of the children?"

Of course the girls were impacting her decision. Still, how could she tell her mother and Kay the essence of her dilemma? How could she explain her return to Sitka served only to remind her of Yuri and the days she'd spent loving him from afar?

Now she was caring for his daughters and losing her heart to them. The orchestra and all that went with it seemed nominal at best, compared to the possibility that she could accomplish her first lifelong dream—to marry Yuri Belikov.

"Sit down and tell me everything," her

mother said, taking hold of Britta's arm. "I want to know all about this orchestra."

"You really shouldn't get so excited," Britta told her. "There are complications that have nothing to do with the children." At least that much was true. She wasn't yet ready to reveal all of the facts related to the matter, but she could at least discuss it in part.

She sat in the rocker and Lydia pulled up a chair. "What kind of complications?"

Britta folded her hands and looked first to Kay and then to her mother. "The orchestra is in England."

"England?" her mother questioned.

"I'm afraid so." Britta lowered her gaze to her hands. "That's why it wasn't so easy to decide."

"I can understand now," her mother said. "England is so far away."

"And the orchestra would keep me very busy. I couldn't say when I might make it home again." Britta glanced up. "I thought in coming here, the decision would be clear, but instead . . ."

"Instead you have only found it more difficult." Her mother smiled sympathetically. "Goodness, but you've always had a way of choosing complicated paths for your life."

That's putting it mildly, Britta thought. Kay got to her feet. The expression on her face made it clear to Britta that she knew there was more involved than what was being said.

"I have to go check the baking." Kay turned to Laura. "You want to go see if the cake is done? I might let you have a piece while it's warm."

Laura looked to Britta. "You come with us."

"I'll come down in just a few minutes. You go ahead."

The girl seemed to consider this for a moment—weighing the importance of warm cake against her need for Britta to be nearby. "I'll go." She put one of the dolls down and clutched the other one to her breast. "Darya go, too." Laura had named her favorite doll after her baby sister.

After she and Kay headed downstairs, Britta turned to her mother. "I don't think I can make a decision until I know what will happen to them."

"But they aren't yours to worry about," her mother reminded her. "Once Yuri is found, it will be up to him to decide."

"But who's to know when that may be? I'm confident that Marsha had no other relatives. After searching through her cabin, the only correspondence I found was from Yuri sending money to her for their care. He said nothing of where he was—probably because he didn't want her to know."

"I understand, Britta. But you should understand that if we can't find Yuri, the children will most likely have to go to the orphanage."

"Why? Why can't I continue to care for them?" she asked.

"Britta, be realistic. You have no way of providing for these children on your own."

"And you would turn us out?" she questioned.

Mother shook her head. "You know that we wouldn't. My point is that you would never be allowed to adopt them. You aren't married, and you have no income of your own. You don't even have a home of your own."

"I could take the first-chair position and . . ." She fell silent, afraid if she said anything more, she might reveal too much.

"You have to think of what is best for the children," her mother said gently.

"But I am. Laura is attached to me and Darya is thriving, as well," Britta replied. "It's obvious that Marsha showed Laura little, if any, love. I know I'm dependent upon you and Father, but I can be useful to you, as well as to them."

"Britta, it's never been an issue of whether or not you could be useful to us. You always manage to earn your keep in one way or another," Mother said with a grin. "Not that you need to. But still, these children would be better off in a family with a mother and father who could love them and see to their needs."

"But who would possibly want to take them?"

Lydia shrugged. "Perhaps Phoebe and Dalton would be willing."

"But I want them," Britta replied much too quickly.

Her mother frowned. "That's what worries me. You have grown so attached to these children that you are going to be severely disappointed when they are taken from you. Look, I know you care about Yuri. Your love for him has always been evident."

Britta was shocked. "It has?"

"Yes," her mother said matter-of-factly. "But Yuri has so many problems, Britta. You cannot hope to fix him or the problems. Only God and Yuri can do that."

She didn't know what to say. Britta wanted to tell her mother that she was confident her love for him could overcome any obstacle and heal any hurt.

"If Yuri can be found," her mother continued, "there's no way to know if he would ever be competent enough to care for the children. He would still need to earn a living, and two little girls—one of them an infant— would need more attention than he'd be able to give."

"But I could care for them while he worked," Britta replied. "That's reasonable enough. Yuri knows me. He knows I care about him, and once he returns, he'll see how much I care for the children and how they need me."

"*If* he returns," her mother countered.

———

Yuri opened his eyes to incredible pain. The last thing he remembered was a loud explosion. The ringing in his ears made him wonder if he'd ruptured his eardrums. He moved his hand to cup it around his right ear and drew it back, covered in blood.

"Just stay still, Yuri," Murphy told him in what seemed like a whisper.

Yuri tried to move, but every part of his body hurt. He glanced to his right and saw that men were being laid out beside him. He realized for the first time that he was outside of the mine. What had happened? He reached up painfully to grab hold of Murphy's shirt.

"Murph, what's going on?"

"Joe drilled into a loaded hole."

Yuri could barely hear the words above the ringing. A loaded hole made sense. When the miners were ready to dynamite, they would pack drilled holes with dynamite and fuses. Often the fuses would be connected and several holes were set off at the same time. Sometimes the dynamite didn't blow, however, and when another man came along to tamp or drill again, he'd set off the uncharged stick with a mere spark.

Closing his eyes, Yuri knew the situation wasn't good. He must have dozed off, because when he opened his eyes again, Murphy and another man were preparing to load him on a stretcher.

"I can walk," he told them and struggled to sit up. Everything went black for a moment, and Yuri fell back. He fought to remain conscious.

"You ought not to do that," Murphy told him. "You've got a bad head wound and probably a broken arm. No telling if there's injuries elsewhere."

Yuri said nothing as the men lifted him onto the stretcher. He wondered if anyone else was injured. Joe, he knew, was probably dead. Most men didn't make it through an accident like that. Yuri had been working about six or eight feet away from Joe. At least that's what Yuri thought he remembered.

They carried him to a waiting cart, where Murphy instructed the driver that he could go. "There's no one else."

What did he mean by that? Yuri wondered. Was no one else injured or was no one else alive? He didn't consider the question long as the world once again faded to shades of gray and then nothing.

Yuri heard someone talking but couldn't make out the words. He fought to open his eyes and found an older black man standing over him. The man smiled and gave Yuri's chest a pat.

"You just rest easy, young man. Don't get up on my account."

The ringing had subsided, and as Yuri's mind cleared, he could see that he was now on a bed in a small but well-lit room.

"Where am I?" he asked, his throat aching from all the dust he'd swallowed.

"You're at my place," the man replied. "I'm Morris James. Doc asked me to look after you. Seems you're doin' rather poorly."

Yuri nodded and felt white-hot pain streak through his head and down his neck. He moaned and closed his eyes. "What about the others?" he managed to ask.

"You're the lucky one. Doc tried to save one, but the man didn't make it. Four total died. You got your own problems to be sure, but Doc thinks you'll live."

He wasn't sure if that was good or bad. Yuri's life didn't really amount to much, and death might very well be the answer to all of his problems. Still, he said nothing about his thoughts. What he really wanted was a drink.

"You got any liquor?"

The man laughed and Yuri opened his eyes. "Something funny?"

"Seems strange to me that a man is laying there not so far from the pearly gates, and he asks for a drink."

"Nothing strange at all." Yuri began to feel a tingling pain down his left arm and tried to readjust it. His body seemed to protest any movement whatsoever. "I hurt."

"I'm not doubtin' it, son. The doc has something here for you to take. It ain't liquor, but I think it'll help you, just the same."

Yuri let out a groan. "I want whiskey. I have some money. Couldn't you just go buy me a bottle?"

Morris shook his head. "Liquor ain't gonna help what's ailing you."

"It'll numb the pain."

This time the man gave a chuckle, and Yuri couldn't help but frown. "You sure laugh a lot."

" 'A merry heart doeth good like a medicine,' " Morris said, pouring some liquid from a bottle onto a spoon. "The doc stitched up your head and said your arm ain't broke.

The shoulder was dislocated, but not broke. Here, take this." He eased a well-muscled arm behind Yuri's neck and guided the spoon into his mouth.

Strangling on a groan of pain as Morris placed him back down, Yuri waited for the medicine to offer some effect. "What was that stuff?"

"Not sure. Doc said it would help with the pain, though." Morris secured a cork back in the bottle. "Still, seems to me you got yourself pains that no medicine can touch."

Yuri's eyes narrowed. "Why would you say that?"

Morris pulled up a chair and sat down. Yuri could see that he was dressed in old, worn clothes, but the man was meticulously well groomed and clean. The garments had even been neatly pressed.

"I been prayin' for you since they brought you down from the mine. God's given me thoughts about you being a man who's in trouble. Trouble of the spirit. He wants me to help you."

This time it was Yuri who let out a bitter laugh. "You're mistaken. God doesn't care about me."

"I'm often wrong about things, but not this time. God's made this too clear. You're in trouble, and you need help."

"Even if I did, there's nothing you can do," he said, feeling his limbs grow heavy. Apparently the medicine was working. It felt wonderful to let the sensation wash over him. "Nothing anybody can do," he murmured. "I've made too many mistakes. Disappointed too many people, and now it's too late."

"So long as you got breath, it ain't too late where God's concerned," Morris told him. "But for now, you just rest easy. Me and the good Lord will watch over you. Just don't go dying on me. We got a lot of work to do."

Yuri closed his eyes and smiled. "You don't know the half of it."

Chapter 4

April 1906

*D*alton and Kjell Lindquist entered the restaurant and settled at a table by an open window. After ordering their lunch, Dalton picked up their earlier conversation.

"After we meet with Mr. Kirkpatrick and finalize the transfer of the boat," he began, "I was wondering if we could maybe go to the Chinese part of town. I promised Phoebe I would bring Rachel something special from San Francisco for her birthday. Li Ming at the Sitka Laundry told me of some wonderful deals you could get on jade jewelry."

His father, Kjell, nodded. "I see no reason

not to add that to our day. It would be good to pick up something for your lovely wife, as well."

Just then Mr. Kirkpatrick came rushing up to the table. "I'm sorry to be late. I had just finished inspecting the new boat when my accountant needed me to attend to other business."

"It's perfectly all right," Dalton said, getting to his feet and extending his hand. "How did you find the boat?"

"Perfect," Kirkpatrick said, shaking hands. He took a seat and smiled at Kjell. "Your son does the finest work I've ever seen. I'd like to order three more boats."

"I've always been proud of his abilities," Kjell told him.

The man motioned to the waiter and ordered coffee. "I'm afraid I can't have lunch with you, but here is my check, as well as a purchase order for the next three boats. If you take this draft to my bank, they will happily wire the money to your bank in Seattle or elsewhere."

Dalton took the pieces from Kirkpatrick and studied the purchase order. "You want the other three to be identical to this one?"

The man nodded enthusiastically. "They will serve my men quite well."

"I have other orders," Dalton told him,

"and I will need at least two months to complete them. I might be able to hire additional men, however."

"I would like my boats as soon as possible," the older man declared. The waiter brought his coffee, as well as lemonade for Dalton and Kjell. "I would be happy to increase the price by ten percent in order to have you build them before you complete the other order."

Dalton frowned. "I'm sorry, but in that case I can't accept your order." He pushed the paper back toward Kirkpatrick. "I would very much like to accommodate you, but I gave my word to complete the cannery order first. I won't go back on it."

"What if I increase the price by twenty percent?"

Dalton looked at his father and then back to Kirkpatrick. "I can't. I would like to have the order, but I'm a man of my word."

Kirkpatrick put down his coffee cup and smiled. "Which is exactly what I want in a business associate." He reached into his pocket and pulled out a folded letter and passed it to Dalton.

Dalton opened the letter as Kirkpatrick tore up the purchase order. Dalton felt a twinge of regret as he considered how important the money from those three boats might have been to his family. Even at the quoted price, they were worth nearly twice as much as the cannery order.

He didn't mourn the loss for long, however. The paper revealed another purchase order. This one requested ten boats. He looked up at Kirkpatrick. "I don't understand."

The older man finished his coffee before replying. "I have dealt with a great many men in my business. Some were honest and others were not. I've found that those who could easily cast aside their word for my benefit would also do it for someone else. I like to know that I can count on a man and his word."

The situation was still not clear to Dalton. "But I can't hope to complete this order for some months. It'll take me into next year—even if I hire additional men."

"I realize that," Kirkpatrick said. "I'm also perfectly fine with it. As you know, my fishing business is extensive. I own ships up and down the coast. As you are able to complete the boats, I will replace my poorer vessels. I find the Lindquist craft to be superior to any I've used before. You understand the needs of the fishing crew, and your vessels are solid compared to some of the cheaper boats I've used. The more efficient the boat, the less time and money I lose in repairs and other complications."

For several minutes, Dalton said nothing.

He was blessed in the way the Lord had just worked, but also humbled. He had never really thought of anyone else appreciating his strong stand to keep his word, yet here was a man who did.

"So are we agreed?"

Dalton looked up at the man. "Yes. I am very grateful and happy to work further with you, Mr. Kirkpatrick."

The man smiled. "Wonderful. Oh, and I almost forgot." He reached inside his coat and brought out two tickets. "I thought you might enjoy these. I understood after speaking with your father that your family is quite musical. These will admit you to hear Enrico Caruso next Tuesday night, the seventeenth. He's performing in *Carmen* with the Metropolitan Opera Company at Tivoli Opera House."

"Mr. Kirkpatrick, I don't know what to say. Father and I had wanted to attend but were told the performance was sold out."

"And indeed it is, but I have my connections." He got to his feet and took up his hat. "I hope it proves to be a tremendous experience for both of you." He gave a bit of a bow to Kjell and then Dalton. "I will look forward to hearing from you when you determine a schedule for the production of my boats."

"I will be in touch," Dalton told him.

After Kirkpatrick had gone, Dalton found

his father beaming with pride. "What?" Dalton asked, looking around him as if Kjell had discovered something important.

"You've made me very happy, son. You could have attempted to make promises to Kirkpatrick—hoping you might be able to get additional qualified help. But instead, you were willing to let a lucrative deal go in order to keep your word. I couldn't be prouder."

Dalton lowered his face at his father's praise. Kjell had married Dalton's mother only a short time before Dalton's birth, and while Dalton was the child of another man, Kjell had always loved him as his own.

"Thank you. It means a lot to me."

"Your work is admirable, and you are honorable with your wife and children."

Dalton looked up. "Do you ever regret not having a son who is of your own blood?"

"I have a son of my own heart, and that is far more important. No. I have never regretted a single moment of my life. Your mother is all I could have longed for in a wife, and your sisters are beautiful examples of womanhood. But you, Dalton, you have been something very special to me, and you always will be."

Yuri heard the wolves howling—screaming, really—and put his hands to his ears. Only then did he realize it wasn't wolves at all. He was the one crying in agony. His body hurt so much. The shaking only made the pain worse.

"Please . . . give me . . . a drink," he begged.

Morris came to his bedside with a wet cloth and wiped Yuri's forehead. "Now, you know I can't do that. I have some tea for you. The herbs in there will ease what ails you."

Yuri shook his head, which only caused more pain. His left arm ached from having raised his hand to his ear. "I can't . . . can't bear this." His teeth chattered. "I can't."

Pain ripped through his midsection, and Yuri grabbed at his stomach with his right hand. Morris helped him to rise just enough to take some of the tea. "I promise this will help. You got the tremors. You're far worse off now from the poison you've got in your body than the wounds you got from the explosion."

"What do you mean?"

"The demon that's got hold of you is making you sick. Your body and spirit are fighting against it."

Yuri forced down some of the tea and found it did have a calming effect on his stomach. He closed his eyes and felt Morris ease him back to the pillow. Without warning, Morris began to pray, talking to God as if He were sitting right there with them.

"Now, Lord, you see your child Yuri lying here all worn out and wounded. He needs you and your healing touch." Morris paused. "I know He needs to get right with you. He's been livin' a sinner's life like all of us. We're all of us sinners gone astray."

Morris paused again, and Yuri opened his eyes to see what he might be doing. He found Morris gazing upward and nodding as if he were hearing comments back from the Almighty.

"I know he belongs to you, Father. And I know like the Prodigal Son, he's gone astray. He's wantin' to come back home now. He's needin' to be released from the vile hold the demon of whiskey has on him." Morris looked down to Yuri. "Isn't that right, Yuri? You can tell Father God, yourself."

Yuri frowned. Was it really that simple? Pain tore through him once again. "Yes!" he cried out. "I want to be free of this." Sweat poured from his face and ran in rivulets with his tears. "Oh, please, tell me I can be free."

Morris offered him more tea and nodded. "The good Lord can set you free, son. The Good Book says that Jesus himself is truth, and that truth will set you free. You just have to ask for it."

"I want it," Yuri said, moaning. "I want to be a good man. All my life, I've disappointed everyone." He panted for breath as the pain faded once again. "I made a mess of my life. I've hurt so many people."

Nodding, Morris closed his eyes. "O Lord, I know you hear the prayers of them that seek you in honesty and truth. I know it, 'cause you heard my prayers. Please release this man now from the hold Satan has on him. Set him free, Lord. Free to live a new life. Free to make things right."

Yuri looked upward. "Please, Lord. Please save me." He didn't know what all had been in the tea, but a warmth and peacefulness washed over his body. Yuri felt himself grow sleepy and allowed the medicine to take him.

When he awoke some hours later, Yuri was amazed to realize that the worst of the pain was only a memory. His arm still ached, but not like it had before. Even the throbbing in his head had subsided. For the first time in a very long time, Yuri's mind was clear of the dull haze that usually accompanied his waking thoughts.

"You ready for somethin' to eat?" Morris asked, coming to his bedside with a plate. "I fried you some bread in bacon grease. Figured it might give you a bit of strength."

"I guess I am hungry." Yuri put his hand to his abdomen. "The pain is gone."

Morris grinned. "I think the good Lord gave you a miracle. You're even getting your color back."

"Can God really save me?" Yuri asked. "Just like that? After all the wrong I've done?"

Morris's smile only widened. "He sure can. Ain't nothin' Father God can't do."

Yuri nodded. "I believe you."

"Don't be believin' me, Yuri. Believe Him."

The afternoon of April seventeenth promised rain, but then, many days in Sitka did just that. Britta sat uncomfortably sandwiched between her sister-in-law and mother on the front porch sharing conversation and tea. It hadn't been her desire to participate in the gathering, but with Darya asleep just inside the house and Laura playing happily outside with Connie, Britta had no choice.

Kay smiled at Britta from the seat opposite where she sat. "I want to hear more about your plans. Have you decided about the orchestra?"

"What's this?" Phoebe questioned. "What orchestra?"

"Britta has been offered first-chair violin in a brand-new orchestra," her mother said proudly. "The problem for Britta is that it is located quite far from home—in England."

"And she's worried about the children," Kay interjected.

Out on the lawn, Laura and Connie were enjoying the cool afternoon with a game of tag. Laura didn't seem to care that her mother had died, nor that her father had long been gone from home. She did appear to enjoy occasional moments with the baby, but it was Britta that she cherished above all.

"Britta has always had a tender heart for those in need," her mother said in a sympathetic manner.

Kay nodded as she flashed Lydia a smile. "She comes by it naturally. After all, I benefitted from your tenderness."

Britta wished that her family would move on to another topic. She wasn't yet ready to make any decision or discuss her reasons for delay.

"Well?" Phoebe asked, whitening her tea with a bit of cream. "Tell me all about it."

Britta shrugged. "You've just heard most everything there is to tell. I was offered the position, but it would require me to move to England."

"I've always wanted to go to England. I would love to see Parliament and the palaces. Can you imagine living such a life?"

Seeing a way to change the subject, Britta nodded. "I've been lucky enough to see so many of the wonders in Europe and England. It is a most marvelous trip to make. Maybe you and Dalton could travel abroad someday."

"It might be something to consider," Phoebe replied. She put her spoon down and sampled the tea. "Still, what of you? Have you made your decision?"

"No, but I will soon," she said, deciding to try the straightforward approach.

"She's not going to go," Kay said, sitting back with her arms crossed. "She won't leave the children. She hasn't even picked up her violin since she came home. She spends all her time with the children."

"I don't blame you," Phoebe declared. "They are beautiful little girls. Darya is especially charming. You should marry and have children of your own. You're a natural mother, Britta."

Perhaps she had at last found an ally. "I had a lot of practice in helping with your children. I always enjoyed being with my niece and nephews. And Connie is a delightful companion for Laura. The two seem to enjoy each other's company." She looked out across the lawn to find the girls racing toward the forest's edge. Turning back to her family, she smiled.

"Mother, didn't you say you just received a letter from Kjerstin?"

"I did indeed. It seems there is some thought that they might head to the Aleutian Islands. If they do, she promises they will come here first for a visit. I'm torn between wanting to see them and wanting them to forsake going so far away."

"I suppose they must go where they feel God is taking them," Phoebe replied. She sighed and put down her cup. "I do wish we would hear something from the men. I checked at the telegraph office, but there was nothing."

"Kjell said they would send word when they left San Francisco. He hoped to leave no later than the twentieth. If we still haven't heard by then, we can always send a telegram to the Palace Hotel, where they are staying."

"If they don't make it home for Rachel's birthday, they will answer for it," Phoebe declared.

"Surely they'll be back by the thirtieth," Britta said. "I know Father intended to be home before then."

"Dalton did, too. He has an order to build several small skiffs for the cannery. I know he wanted to get right on them. And speaking of getting home, I should probably go," Phoebe announced. "The children will be coming home from school soon, and I need to get supper on."

She got to her feet and called for Connie. Mother rose as well and put her hand on Phoebe's arm. "Don't fret over them. They will return to us quickly."

"I'm sure you're right," Phoebe said.

With her playmate leaving, Laura quickly made her way to Britta and crawled up on her lap. Britta pushed back the child's windblown blond hair. "And for you, little miss, it's time for a nap."

"Mama take a nap, too?" Laura asked.

"Not today, sweetie." She got to her feet cradling the child. "Come on, I'll tuck you in." Laura didn't protest but instead clung to Britta's neck.

"I think we should gather these things," Mother said to Kay. "Looks like it may rain any minute."

Britta hoped her mother and Kay would back off with their questions and comments about her decision. What she most wanted was to see Yuri again. *If only I could see him and speak with him,* she thought, *then I would know what choice to make.*

She deposited Laura on the bed and untied her shoes. "Shall I read you a story about Joseph and his coat of many colors?"

"Yes," Laura said, nodding. "You read me

a story." Britta smiled and pulled the shoes from Laura's feet.

"Now you lie back, and I'll cover you up." Laura yawned and eased back on the pillow. Britta could see that she was fighting sleep but knew the story would calm her.

Just then, she heard Darya fussing downstairs. Apparently her naptime was over and she wanted to be fed. Britta almost laughed aloud. It seemed the children had a way of timing their wakeful hours to be just opposite each other. Britta seldom found a free moment unless she allowed her mother or Kay to take over, and she hated to do that. She enjoyed every minute with the girls.

"They keep me from thinking too much," she admitted as she went to retrieve the Bible. She would let her mother tend to the baby for a few minutes. It shouldn't be long before Laura was asleep, she reasoned.

Opening to Genesis, Britta began. "This is the story of Joseph. Now Joseph was a boy who had many older brothers." Laura yawned again and was just starting to close her eyes when a knock sounded lightly on the door. It was Kay.

"You need to come downstairs right now."

"Is something wrong with the baby?"

"No." Kay shook her head as if to emphasize the words. "Your mother just said to come."

Laura sat up. "Don't go."

"I'll be right back," Britta promised. "You can hold the Bible if you promise to be careful."

Laura didn't look at all pleased but finally acquiesced. Britta got to her feet and followed Kay into the hallway. "Please tell me what's wrong."

They headed down the stairs, but Kay maintained her silence. Britta was furious. "Will you please tell me what's going on? I don't like—" She fell silent when she saw who was standing by the door.

"Yuri."

Chapter 5

Seeing Yuri again . . . Britta's breath caught in her throat, her mind racing with questions. Where had he been? What had he been doing? What would he do about the children?

Could he ever love me?

"It's good to have you back in Sitka," her mother said. She was cradling Darya in her arms, and Britta wondered if her mother had already told Yuri about Marsha and the baby.

"How long have you been back?" Britta asked.

"I just got here. I saw Evie and Joshua at the dock. Apparently they just came in from Seattle. They said to tell you all that they'd drop by soon for a visit. Then I passed Phoebe on the way. She said I needed to stop here rather than go to the cabin. She said you would need to speak with me." He smiled at Britta. "I didn't know you were back in Sitka."

His comment startled her. Britta didn't realize he'd even been aware of her absence. "I've been back since January," she replied.

She considered how to tell him about his wife. It was clear Yuri didn't know about Marsha.

"Why don't we sit," her mother directed. She led the way and took her place by the fire in the rocking chair. Kay brought her a bottle for the baby, then quickly disappeared. Lydia began to feed Darya as Yuri and Britta settled on opposite ends of the couch.

"I didn't know you'd had another baby," Yuri said, looking at Lydia.

Britta exchanged a look with her mother. "Yuri, the baby doesn't belong to Mother."

He looked at her in surprise. "Yours?"

She shook her head. "Yuri, something bad happened while you were gone. I can't begin to even find the words." She threw her mother a pleading look.

"Yuri, Marsha is gone. She died giving birth to this baby."

His eyes widened as he took in the news. Britta knew from what everyone said that there was no real love lost between him and Marsha, yet still it had to be a shock.

"I named her Darya, after your mother," Britta offered.

"I didn't . . . I didn't know she was pregnant. She never said." He appeared deeply troubled. "And Laura?"

As if on cue the child came bounding into the room. "Mama! I scared." Laura climbed onto Britta's lap and hugged her neck tightly.

Britta was completely embarrassed by the situation. "I . . . well . . . I need to explain. We brought the children here and I've been caring for them. Laura has attached herself to me, and despite trying to get her to stop, she insists on calling me Mama. I'm sorry. I do not mean for her to disrespect her mother's memory."

Yuri shook his head. "She was never much of a . . ." He fell silent.

She knew what he was going to say and nodded. "Laura, say hello to your papa."

The child peeked out from where she'd

buried her face against Britta's neck. She studied Yuri for a moment, then hid again.

"What happened to Marsha?" he asked.

"The doctor believes it was an aneurysm," Britta explained.

Lydia picked up the conversation. "I was called to help deliver the baby until someone could get the doctor. By the time he got there, Marsha had been complaining of a headache for some time. The doctor said that the labor must have caused a rupture. We arranged for her to be buried in town and brought the children here. We had no way of knowing if she had other family, however. Is there someone we can notify for you?"

"No. She had no one." Yuri stared at the baby for a moment. "When did this happen?"

"January twenty-eighth. We tried to find you," Britta explained. "Dalton had inquiries out all over, but no one seemed to know where you'd gone."

"I was near Juneau, on Douglas Island at the Treadwell mine."

"Not far at all," Mother commented.

"No, not really," Yuri agreed. He ran his hand back through his dark blond hair and shrugged. "I was injured in a mine explosion or I might have come back sooner." He frowned. "Then again, I probably wouldn't have. That accident changed my life."

"How so?" Britta asked.

He met her gaze and smiled. "I could have died, and it shook me up. The doctor patched me up, but a kind gentleman named Morris James cared for me afterward. He was responsible for helping me to stop . . . to quit drinking."

Britta felt a surge of happiness at the announcement but fought to keep her emotions under control. Laura pulled away just a bit and yawned. "You still need a nap, little miss."

Lydia got to her feet with the baby. "Would you like to hold her?"

Yuri shook his head. "Not just yet. Please."

She shifted Darya to her shoulder to burp. "It's all right, Yuri. You're dealing with a lot of information all at once. Why don't I put Laura down for a nap, Britta? That way you and Yuri can sit on the porch and talk."

"Don't go, Mama," Laura said again, tightening her hold.

"Laura, we've talked about this before. You have to be a good girl and take your nap. You go upstairs and rest, and when you wake up, we'll have some cookies and milk."

The three-year-old fought back tears but climbed down from Britta's lap and let Lydia lead her upstairs. Britta felt a moment's awkwardness. Without the child between them she felt exposed, as if Yuri could see through to her heart.

She stood and motioned to the door. "Shall we?"

He nodded and followed her outside. A light rain was falling, but the shelter of the porch allowed them to sit unhindered.

"Yuri, I'm truly sorry you had to come back to face such sad news."

"I was planning a new start," he told her. "Morris helped me get right with God, and I figured it was time to try to make things work out with Marsha." He looked at his feet. "I suppose you know that we were never in love."

"I had heard that," Britta replied. She felt her nerves give way to a giggle. "Not everyone could fall in love with you from the time they were little girls." She immediately regretted her words and moved quickly to change the subject. "Your daughters are so sweet. As you can see, I adore them. I've been caring for them since we brought them home. Of course, Mother and Kay have helped, as well, but I really prefer having them to myself."

"I don't know what to do about them," Yuri said, meeting her gaze with steely blue eyes.

Britta felt her heart do a flip. She longed to reach out and touch his jaw. He needed a shave, but she found she liked the light growth of whiskers. "They're your children. You'll figure it out."

He shook his head. "Darya isn't mine."

Surely she hadn't heard correctly. "What?"

Yuri leaned closer. "She's not mine. I haven't . . . well, that is to say Marsha and I weren't . . . together . . . since Laura was conceived." He seemed to regret his words. "I'm sorry. I shouldn't have spoken in such a crude manner."

"Forget about social rules of etiquette and discretion. You can say anything to me," Britta replied. "I care about those children. Nothing you say is going to shock me so much that I would cease feeling that way." She desperately wanted the tension of the moment to subside and so got to her feet. "Why don't I get you something to eat? We just had tea with Phoebe, and I know we have some food left."

He nodded but said nothing. Britta hurried into the house, afraid that if she didn't put some distance between them, she might well throw herself into his arms.

Yuri sat, staring out at the forest beyond the Lindquist yard. Marsha was dead. How strange it seemed. Yet he couldn't work up the slightest emotion over her passing. This only served to make him feel guilty, and he pushed it aside.

I can't go back and change things now. I can't make the past right.

But maybe the past could never be made right. Maybe that power only pertained to the present and future. He thought of the two little girls in the house and shook his head. How in the world could he ever care for them?

"Here you are," Britta announced, returning with a tray. She placed it on the little table between them. "This is Mother's egg salad on bread Laura and I baked just this morning. I think you'll enjoy it. And the tea is still warm, but if it's not hot enough, I'll make you some fresh."

"This is fine." Yuri picked up the sandwich and took a bite. In the wake of the stunning news, he'd forgotten just how hungry he was. In a matter of moments, he'd wolfed the sandwich down rather unfashionably. "Thank you," he said as he selected a cookie from the tray.

"I'm glad you're enjoying it." Britta retook her seat. "Look, I'm not trying to be a pest about things, but we do need to think about the girls."

"I know," he replied. "I just feel over-whelmed."

"I'm happy to continue caring for them as long as you need me to. I enjoy the task." She looked away and settled her gaze on the lawn. "I needed the diversion, you might say."

"Why?"

She shrugged. "I was feeling rather uncertain about my future." She looked at him and smiled. "At least, that's the easiest way to explain it. The children give me something positive with which to keep my mind and hands busy."

"Laura definitely seems to love you. Then again, she probably didn't get much attention or affection from Marsha."

"Perhaps Marsha didn't know how to show her love. Then again, maybe she truly didn't know how to properly care for her child."

"Britta, not everyone is like you. You have so much love to give. I'm surprised you haven't settled down to marry with a family of your own." He startled to realize that maybe she had and just hadn't brought them to Sitka with her. "You haven't, have you?"

Her brows knit together. "Haven't what?"

"Married and had a family."

"No. I haven't." She got up and walked to the porch rail.

"I didn't mean to pry. I just wondered. You've been gone from Sitka for a long time."

Britta raised her hand to her mouth and chewed on her thumb for a moment. It was an old nervous habit Yuri remembered from when she was a child. Britta, however, was definitely not a child any longer. She had grown into a startlingly beautiful woman. How old was she now?

The thought surprised him, and he quickly brushed it aside. "So how long will you be here?" he asked, hoping to put her at ease again.

"I have no plans to leave," she told him.

It seemed she was waiting for his reaction, but Yuri honestly didn't know what to say. His mind was swimming with the news of his wife's death and the appearance of a child he knew for a fact could not be his.

"Yuri, about the children . . ."

"Maybe I should find a home for them—give them up to someone else. After all, I'm hardly equipped to take care of a baby."

"No!"

He looked up, surprised at the force of her response. "I'm not saying I don't want to be responsible for them. I just don't have the ability to work a job and care for them."

"I'm happy to go on caring for them, Yuri. I want to help you."

"But it's hardly fair to you. Soon you'll meet someone and no doubt marry. You can hardly take on the responsibility of another man's children."

"I have no plans to marry anyone," she declared. "I didn't come home to find a husband."

"I'm sure you didn't come home with the plan to be a mother, either," he countered.

"No, perhaps I didn't." She sat down and looked at him hard. "Yuri, your children have just lost their mother. Don't take away their father, as well."

"They're closer to you than they are to me," he replied. "I'd worry more about taking them away from you, truth be told. Laura obviously has replaced her mother with you." Britta started to protest, but he held up his hand. "Don't think that I'm chiding you for that. I'm glad you were there to comfort her."

She smiled. "She looks just like you."

He nodded. "I was never quite sure she was mine until I saw her today."

"But why, Yuri? Surely Marsha would have said otherwise. Besides, you were married."

"Ah, Britta, you're so innocent. I shouldn't

be this open with you, but we've been friends for a long while. You're like a sister to me."

She frowned and turned away. "You know you can say anything to me. I'm not naïve. I know all about the talk that was going around town—the stories about you being tricked into marriage."

He sighed. "It's all true. I was drunk when Marsha talked a family member into marrying us. She told me she was pregnant with my baby, but I knew she couldn't be sure it was mine. She was a hateful, bitter woman. I've never understood why she picked me. I certainly wasn't prosperous or even useful. I spent most of my time gambling and drinking, I'm ashamed to say."

"Yuri, it doesn't matter. God can forgive all of that."

"I know. Morris really helped me to see that." He shook his head. "I'm thirty-six years old, and I've wasted most all of my life. Seems a little late to be starting over."

Britta shook her head. "It's never too late."

The porch door opened, and Lydia Lindquist stepped out. She fixed him with a kind and motherly look. "Yuri, I've seen the cabin. It's hardly livable. Since Britta is caring for the children, why don't you stay here with us? We could even fix up Zee's old cabin for you and the girls."

"I need to find work," he replied.

"Well, at least stay the night," Lydia said. "You look like you could use a good meal, and we'll have plenty."

He considered her offer. "I suppose I really have no place else to go. If you're sure."

"I'm positive. Kjell and Dalton are in California. They won't be back for another week or two. It would be nice to have a man around the house."

With that, she took her leave and Yuri sat back down to finish off the cookies. The Lindquists had always been so kind to him. Even Dalton—after everything he'd done to hurt his friend, Dalton had never failed to forgive Yuri. Maybe he would even allow him to come back to work for him.

"I'm glad you'll stay," Britta said, flashing him a smile. "I'd love to hear all about your exploits and where life has taken you. You surely must have met some interesting people."

"I could say the same about you. Last I knew, you had gone abroad. Dalton told me it was almost like someone had lit a fire under you, and you couldn't leave Sitka fast enough." He chuckled. "But you were always going full speed ahead, weren't you, Britta?"

She seemed strangely upset by his words

and got to her feet. "I should probably check on the children."

She left without another word, and Yuri could only wonder what he'd said to cause such a rapid departure. Britta Lindquist was definitely a different sort of woman. She seemed all open and smiles one minute, then mystery and refrain the next.

He shook his head. "Females. What do I know about them?"

Chapter 6

"Time to get up," Kjell told his son. Dalton moaned and yawned. He stared through groggy eyes at the ceiling. He felt as if they'd only just gone to bed.

"What time is it?"

Kjell checked his pocket watch. "Five. If we're going to get things finalized and get a telegram off to your mother, we need to be on our way."

Dalton slowly sat up. "Too bad we planned to leave the day after the opera. Staying up so late sure doesn't make for an easy early morning."

"I know that well enough. I didn't want to get up, either. Having a bed this soft and comfortable is dangerous." Kjell gave a chuckle as he tossed Dalton his clothes. "If I had this at home, I might never get any work done."

Dalton nodded in agreement and started pulling on his clothes. "This is a grand place. I don't think I've stayed anywhere as nice as this since being in Kansas City with Evie."

"It is very fine," Kjell said, securing a latch on his bag. "Still, I do prefer the quiet comforts of home. The city is much too noisy for my desires."

"I agree," Dalton admitted. "Ma and Phoebe might have enjoyed it, though. Think of all the things they could find to do and buy." He thought of Phoebe and how good it would be to see her again. They'd barely been gone a month, but he missed her terribly.

"That's exactly why we left them home," Kjell replied with a chuckle. "We would still be here another month if we'd brought them along."

"But they would have enjoyed—" Dalton felt the room begin to shake. He glanced up at his father to ascertain whether the movement was just his imagination. The tremor didn't last long, however, and Dalton threw Kjell a smile. "Well, that was a surprise."

"I'll bet it woke folks up," his father replied.

"I guess they get these earthquakes all the time here."

"Probably no worse than at home," Dalton said. "So, do you have everything?"

Dalton glanced around the room to see if he'd forgotten anything. He spied the book he'd been reading on the bedside table. "Guess I can pack this. I won't have time for reading until we're well on our way home."

He picked up the copy of Jules Verne's *20,000 Leagues Under the Sea*. "This is intriguing; you really should read it some—"

The room began to shake again. Dalton lost his footing and fell as the ceiling rained plaster and the windows shattered not far from where he lay.

"Father?" he called against the roar of the earthquake.

"Looks bad," Kjell called out.

Dalton eased up on all fours and crawled away from the broken glass. "We ought to get out of here."

"I agree," Kjell said, grabbing his bag.

Dalton reached for his suitcase as a huge piece of the ceiling separated. "Watch out!" he cried, hoping his father would somehow heed the warning fast enough. But then time ceased to matter.

Yuri sat on the Lindquist porch contemplating the future. He'd awakened early, hearing the baby cry. From the hallway, he could hear Britta singing a lullaby to soothe the infant. Her presence comforted him, but he couldn't really say why. Perhaps because Britta, like Kjerstin and Dalton, were as much siblings to him as his own brother and sisters had been. Now, watching the morning dawn, Yuri wondered about his family in Russia. He hadn't heard from them in years. If they were there now, he knew they would offer him help with Laura and Darya. His sister Natasha might even want to take them on to raise with her own children.

"I thought I heard you up and about," Lydia said as she stepped onto the front porch. "How did you sleep?"

"To be honest, I was pretty restless. I couldn't seem to sort through all my thoughts," Yuri replied.

"I can well imagine. You've been given a great deal to consider." She took the seat beside him. "I hope you know how much it pleases me to see you here. You look so much better than the last time I saw you."

"I was in a bad way," Yuri said, remembering when he'd left Sitka. "To be honest, I didn't figure to live long after I left. Liquor had such a hold on me, and I couldn't think of anything but that next drink." He rubbed sleep from his eyes and eased back in the chair. "So much is different now."

"Indeed, it is. However, I hope a place to stay won't be one of your worries. You are more than welcome to remain here with us. My aunt Zee passed on about five years ago, and her cabin has been empty ever since. We could fix it up for you and the girls. It might give you a chance to get to know them and figure out what you want to do."

"Whether I keep them or find a home for them," Yuri began, "I have to find a job. Do you suppose Dalton would hire me again?"

"I wouldn't be surprised, especially in light of your reformation." Lydia smiled. "It's really all he's ever wanted for you. He loves you quite dearly."

Yuri nodded. "No brother could have been closer. I miss that—I miss him."

"He'll soon be home," Lydia told him. "He and Kjell were anxious to return once they sold the boat. They were planning to bring many supplies back with them. Dalton has a new order for the local cannery, and I know they wanted the boats delivered by the end of June. He has some good help with the boys he's hired from Sheldon Jackson's school, but I think he would always have a place for you."

"He told me that he would, long ago when

he bought the place from me—well, really, in a sense, from my father."Yuri shook his head. "What a disappointment I have been to my folks."

"But, Yuri, you can write your father and let him know how God has changed you."

"I haven't heard from any of them since Mother died. Of course, I didn't really try to stay in touch—not even with my brother." He sighed. "I don't think any of them would have wanted to talk to me. I broke their hearts."

"So let them know that things are different now. Let them know God has turned your life around and that you're a new man."

He sighed. "How can you be so sure my change is permanent?"

She laughed. "You are the proof I need. You're enjoying this new life, I can tell. Of course, you've had the shock of losing your wife and acquiring responsibility for two little girls, but even that can't deter the joy of being free from the demons that once held you captive."

"That's exactly how it feels. Remember that story in the Bible where Lazarus is raised from the dead? He was all bound up in burial cloth, and they had to free him up. That's how I see myself. I was all tied up in drink and destruction. Morris James came along and helped me turn to Jesus, and He called me out of the grave—out of my burial cloth."

"It's a sweet liberty that none of us should ever take lightly," Lydia said.

"But some folks don't have to sink as low as I did. Some folks just accept God without a struggle and they never know the misery I lived through."

"That's true. But we've all sinned, as the Bible says, and the consequences of those sins are as varied as the sins themselves. Your sins are truly no worse than mine, but perhaps the scars you bear are."

"You're a very wise woman, Mrs. Lindquist."

"You know to call me Lydia," she said with a smile. "I might as well be your auntie, for all the time you spent here as a child."

"Those are good memories. I always envied your family." He sighed. "You never seemed to struggle or have any real problems."

Lydia surprised Yuri by laughing. "You know the truth of Dalton's birth and kidnapping. You know how evil my first husband was, and how his family treated me and tried to separate us from Dalton."

"I'd nearly forgotten. I guess you have had your griefs to bear."

"We all have, Yuri. It's just that bearing them

with the Lord makes all the difference." She fell silent and looked off toward the water.

For several minutes they sat quietly, watching the morning unfold. Yuri considered her offer of a place to stay. He didn't relish the idea of returning to the ramshackle cabin he'd shared with Marsha. There was nothing there he wanted or needed.

"I suppose I could stick around here with you until Kjell and Dalton get back. I could do some work for you to earn my keep. Chop wood and such."

"That would be nice," Lydia said. "Britta and I can care for the girls while you're busy. Kay can help, too. I know you probably don't remember her too well, but she's been a great addition to our family."

"Frankly, I was usually too intoxicated to remember anything very well," he admitted. "I'll have to decide soon what to do with the children. They'd probably be better off without me."

"How can you say such a thing?" Britta questioned as she joined them on the porch. The screen door slammed into place behind her.

Yuri found himself taken aback momentarily. Britta's dark brown eyes pinned him to his chair. Though petite and angelic in appearance, Yuri could see a fiery determination in her eyes that betrayed her strength.

"They don't really know me, Britta."

"But that doesn't mean they can't get to know you. Laura is starved for affection. She needs your love. You're all she has, and even if Darya . . ." She fell silent and looked at her mother before turning her gaze back to Yuri. "Even if Darya is just a baby, she needs love and attention."

"I told Yuri that he and the girls can live indefinitely at Zee's cabin," Lydia said. "I figure we could clean it up and make it a nice little home for them."

Britta nodded. "I agree, and I could come and take care of the girls for you while you worked."

"But what about the orchestra?" Lydia questioned.

Yuri saw Britta flash her mother a look of disapproval. "What's this about an orchestra?" he asked.

"It's nothing really. I was offered a position in England, but I've decided against taking it."

"Because of the girls?" he asked, frowning.

"No," Britta replied. "It's much too far from the people I love. I don't want to move to England and leave my family again. I've been gone far too long as it is."

"I can't let the girls be the reason you give up a dream," Yuri countered. "If you've had your heart set on this, then you need to reconsider."

"I promise you both," Britta said firmly, "Laura and Darya are far more important to me than the orchestra. You're more important, Yuri, although I think you're too pig-headed to understand that." She stormed off, slamming the screen door again as she went back into the house.

Yuri looked at Lydia in surprise. "She still has that lightning-quick temper, I see."

Lydia didn't smile, and this worried him. Perhaps she felt he should have made a better effort to encourage Britta to take the position. Yuri rubbed his hands on his thighs. "I hope I didn't say the wrong thing. You seem vexed with me."

"It's not you, Yuri. There's something going on with Britta, and I can't quite figure it out. Of all my children, she's been the most secretive. After your sister Illiyana died in Russia, Britta truly seemed to close herself off."

"Well, they were best friends," he murmured.

Yuri hadn't thought about Illiyana in a long time. She and Britta had been so very close. Her death to consumption had only caused him to drink all the more as he faced the possibility of his own mortality.

"Britta's always had a mind of her own," he added, trying to forget the pain of loss.

"Indeed she has, and it hasn't always worked to her benefit. When she came to us saying she wanted to travel and attend school in the States, we thought it quite a departure from all she had voiced before. Still, we wanted to give her every opportunity, even though it meant seeing her leave Sitka."

"She left so quickly." Yuri barely remembered returning to Sitka with Marsha at his side, but he did remember hearing Dalton's news that Britta had gone. He didn't know why it stuck out in his hazy thoughts, but the situation had saddened him. Britta had always been a good friend. He smiled to himself. She had always adored him, and maybe that's why Yuri enjoyed her company so much. Britta never looked down on him. She held him in admiration since he'd saved her life when she and Illiyana had been lost on the mountain. There were so few honorable moments in Yuri's life that he was convinced this was why he'd been particularly sorry to hear of her departure.

"I'll talk to her again," Yuri announced. "I'll make sure she's certain about the orchestra and not just doing this for the children. I can always ask Natasha to take the girls. Of course, transporting them there would cost a lot of money." He shook his head. "It doesn't matter. There are other ways to see to their needs. I don't want Britta giving up an important future on account of my problems."

Lydia nodded. "You know, it's also possible Britta's sister and husband would take the children if you believe you cannot keep them. Kjerstin hasn't been able to have a child, and I know she longs for one."

"I'll think on that. It would be a good fit. I know the girls would be well cared for by Kjerstin."

Perhaps that was the answer. Then Britta could go on with her life and not worry about trying to see him through his complicated messes.

———

Britta focused on scrubbing the dirt from one of Laura's dresses while the children napped. She tried not to think of Yuri giving up the girls to someone else. She loved them. She found her life had a true sense of purpose in caring for Laura and Darya. What would she do if he sent them away?

Kay returned from hanging out clothes on the line and looked at Britta with stern resignation. "I suppose you're still not going to tell me what else is going on."

"Why do you suppose anything else is going on? You're always so suspicious of me."

The native woman laughed. "That's because you deserve suspicion. You're always hiding something, and this time is no different. I thought we were friends."

Britta sighed. "We are, Kay, and you're right. There is something else. I just don't feel at liberty to discuss it right now. I promise you, however, that I will talk to you about it. Probably before I talk to anyone else."

"When will that be?" Kay put the basket on the ground and cocked a brow. "Maybe I can help."

"Talking with you is always helpful," Britta admitted. "I just feel that this situation requires a great deal of introspection. I can't really take this to anyone else."

"You're still fretting over the girls, aren't you?"

"Of course I am. Now that Yuri's back and talking about finding someone else to take them, I have them on my mind a great deal."

"They aren't yours," Kay said matter-of-factly. She put her hands on her hips as if for emphasis. "This isn't like the time you wanted to take on caring for that orphaned bear cub."

Britta remembered the event from her childhood. Someone had shot the cub's mother and either didn't realize she had a baby or didn't care. When the cub wandered into the Lindquist yard one day, Britta had found herself completely charmed. She wanted to raise it, but her father had said it would never work. The cub couldn't live with people and no other bear would take it for her own cub. The baby bear was put down to save it from a worse fate, but Britta honestly thought that killing it was the worst that could happen. Now that she was older, of course, she knew better. That death had been quick and hopefully painless, whereas being left to die of starvation or being torn to bits by some other animal would have been cruel.

"That's not such a great example, you know. That cub had to be put to death. No one is going to put the children to death. They need a home and love."

"But they aren't yours to worry over. They're Yuri's, and no matter how much you might wish they were yours as well, they aren't. Neither is he."

Britta's head snapped up and she locked eyes with her friend. "I don't want to discuss this anymore."

"Of course not," Kay said in an unapologetic manner. "Because you know I'm right.

You're still in love with Yuri, and now that he's come back all sober and trusting God, you love him even more."

"Well, why not?" Britta raised her chin. "He's a good man. I'm the only one who has ever seen his real potential. I'm the only one who knows the real Yuri. Deep inside, he's got a great deal of love and goodness."

"But that doesn't mean he can—or should—share it with you," Kay said softly.

Wringing out the little dress harder than necessary, Brittta huffed. "I told you that I don't want to talk about this right now."

Kay shrugged. "Just because you aren't talking about it doesn't mean it's not a problem. I thought since I know what's bothering you, I'd be the likely one to talk to." She picked up the basket. "Maybe when you get done pouting about it all, you can tell me what you're thinking. But I guess I already know."

She walked off, leaving Britta to stare after her retreating form. It just wasn't fair, Britta thought. It wasn't fair that Yuri couldn't see how much he needed her—how much the children needed her. Somehow she would just have to convince him. Somehow she would have to get Yuri to fall in love with her.

Chapter 7

*T*here was nothing Zee's cabin needed that couldn't be accomplished with a little cleaning and airing out. Britta and Kay did most of the work over parts of two days while Lydia watched Darya. Laura was ever at Britta's side, trying to do her part. Britta gave her a rug to pound on the front porch, but Laura didn't want to be that far from her mama.

"Mama come wit me," Laura demanded.

"Now, Laura, you know that I have to finish cleaning the kitchen," Britta explained.

"I clean it, too," Laura said, picking up

a dish towel. She went to where Britta had pulled dishes from the cupboard and reached for a plate.

"No, Laura. Those are too big." Britta took a stack of saucers. "You wipe these." She set the dishes on the table and put Laura in the chair. "Sit right here and dust them off."

Kay bustled in about that time. "I've scrubbed down the bedrooms and made up the beds."

"Thank you. I think once I finish here, we'll be set."

"I'll head back then, to help your mother start supper." Kay looked at Laura and then back to Britta. "I think you have plenty of good help."

"Laura is a very good helper," Britta said, praising the child.

The little girl smiled and held up a dish. "I help Mama."

Kay frowned but said nothing. Britta knew what she was thinking. Laura absolutely refused to call her anything else. Not wanting to discuss it with Kay, Britta changed the subject.

"Has Mother said anything about hearing from Father? We should have had a telegram by now."

"She didn't say. I know she wants to go into town today. Maybe she can send a message and see if they've left yet." Kay looked as though she wanted to say more, but instead squared her shoulders and headed for the door. "I'll be at the house if you need me."

Britta let her go without another word. She knew Kay's opinion of the situation, and she doubted talking about it with anyone would help. Unless, of course, that person was Yuri.

She longed to speak to him regarding Laura and Darya—to help him see how important it was that he not disrupt the girls in their newfound security. Laura was finally thriving. She was learning new things by the day. Britta was reading to her every night, and Laura expressed her curiosity about what the letters meant. Mother had assured Britta that if Laura was asking such questions, it was more than right to teach her the alphabet, and so they had begun on those lessons, as well.

Laura was a bright little girl. Her lack of attention and love had only made her more determined to please those who spent time with her. While comfortable with Lydia and Kay, at least in the daytime, evenings were still a trial. Laura wanted Britta to stay with her once she went to bed and threw horrible fits if denied. Britta had tried everything she could think of to give the child comfort, but nothing seemed to work. Often she would sit in the rocker beside Laura and read until the child fell asleep. It wasn't ideal, but at least they'd progressed from Britta having to actually be in bed with Laura.

"I've brought some wood,"Yuri announced as he entered the house. "Place feels kind of chilly."

"It is," Britta agreed. She smiled at Yuri. "Why don't you go ahead and lay a fire for us?"

He nodded and knelt beside the hearth. Britta watched as he placed the wood in a crisscross pattern. "Good thing your mother had me clean out the chimney," he said. "Five years of sitting idle left the birds thinking they could nest there."

"I know Mother appreciates all that you've done. You're good to have around—especially with Father and Dalton gone. Gordon comes and helps from time to time, but he can't do everything."

Yuri straightened as the fire caught, popping and crackling. "I was hoping we might talk." He leaned back on his heels. "I want to know more about your orchestra offer."

"There's really nothing to tell. I was offered the position, but it requires more than I'm willing to give."

"Such as?"

She met his steely eyes. Britta grew uncomfortable—almost fearful that he might guess the real trouble surrounding the subject.

"I believe I stated that already. I would have to move to England. Besides, we have more pressing matters. The children are more important."

Yuri got to his feet, and Laura held up a saucer. "I help. See?"

"You're doing a good job, Laura," he told her.

She smiled and went back to work while Yuri crossed the room to Britta. "Maybe we could talk in private when Laura has her nap?"

"It's nearly that time now. Perhaps I could get Mother or Kay to put her down, and then we can discuss whatever is on your mind."

"All right." Yuri took a seat at the table. "I'll wait here."

Britta nodded. "Come along, Laura. I think Grandma Lydia has some cookies and milk for you, and then it will be nap time."

"I like cookies," Laura told Yuri.

He smiled. "I do, too."

Britta gathered the child in her arms. What was Yuri thinking? Surely if he spent enough time with his children, he wouldn't want to send them away. Of course, Darya wasn't his.

If only she could get Yuri to see how much

they needed him . . . how much they all needed him.

Yuri waited patiently for Britta's return. He liked the homey feel of the cabin and noted that the women had put it in order nicely. New heavy drapes hung at the window. They would keep out the long evening hours of light in the summer and insulate against the cold in winter.

Walking around the house, he peered into the bedrooms and found them suitable. Someone had made up the beds with beautiful quilts. He wondered if Britta had helped sew them.

She's been gone so long, he reasoned. *She wouldn't have had time.* Still, he ran his hand over the beautiful star pattern of burgundy and gold. This was a real home—nothing like the cabin he'd shared with Marsha.

He walked back to the kitchen, where Britta had been putting the cupboards in order. He smiled at the thought of Laura helping. Here, he could imagine being happy. What would it be like to stay on indefinitely? Lydia said they had no other purpose for the cabin—at least not at this point. Perhaps it was the solution to his problem.

"You are certainly deep in thought," Britta said, taking the seat opposite him at the table.

"I said your name twice and you didn't hear me."

"I have a lot on my mind, as you well know."

She nodded. "I'm glad you wanted to talk. I think it's important to weigh all the options available to us."

"Us?" he asked.

Britta blushed. "Well, I am the one caring for the children. I figured to be a part of this decision."

"I see. Well, I suppose that makes sense."

"Yuri, let me be blunt. I know you're just getting your feet under you. I know things are so awkward right now, but in time, that will pass."

"Britta, I can't have you—"

"Please, just hear me out," she interrupted.

She fidgeted in her chair, smoothing her pale green sleeves as if they were out of place. Yuri could see this was difficult for her. "Go ahead, then."

"Thank you. I just want you to be reasonable about this and not make rash decisions. I feel it's important for you to know that you have so many people who care about you. I, for one, want to do whatever I can to make life better for you and the girls."

"I can see that. You've already done so much."

"But only because I care about your well-being and theirs. I don't feel I have to do anything; rather, I want to do it. You need to know that."

"You can't throw your life and opportunities away on me and my problems."

Britta put her hands on her hips. "Laura and Darya aren't problems, they are babies. They are helpless little girls who need their father's love."

"They need a family," Yuri replied.

"Indeed they do, but with both of us helping them," Britta said, pausing to glance his way, "they would have a family . . . of sorts. My mother already loves them and has them call her Grandma Lydia. I know my father will feel the same."

"But, Britta, you deserve to have a family of your own. You can't have the freedom to court suitors and enjoy your youth with two children at your side."

"My youth? Yuri, I'm twenty-four. I'll be twenty-five in October. I'm hardly a girl anymore. I've spent the last five years enjoying my youth, and now I'm more than ready to settle down."

"Which is my point exactly." Yuri got up from the table and began to pace. "Britta, you deserve to find someone to love and have children of your own. It's not that I don't appreciate what you've done for me and for the girls."

"Then don't take it away from me," she implored. "I can't explain it, but I need this. I need the children—they make me feel . . . well, they make me feel happy. I enjoy working with them."

Yuri could see the anguish in her expression, and he hated that he was the cause of the pain. "I don't know what to do."

"Then give it time," she begged. "Get to know the children before you decide."

"But Darya isn't mine," he countered. "I don't think I want to know her. She's got a father somewhere."

"Are you suggesting you try to locate him?"

He considered that for a moment. "No. Given Marsha's penchant for promiscuity, it could be almost anyone. That's why I was never sure Laura was mine until seeing her. She looks a lot like Illiyana, don't you think?"

"I don't remember Illiyana at that age," Britta replied. "In fact, I can hardly remember what she looked like when she went away. I suppose when I heard that she had died, I tried to assuage my pain by forgetting."

"I tried that with liquor," Yuri admitted. "It didn't work well for me." He returned to the chair. "I had so much I wanted to forget. I've made so many mistakes."

"We all have," Britta mumbled.

He studied her for a moment, then asked, "Want to talk about it?"

She looked startled at the question and then shook her head. "There's nothing to talk about. I just have my regrets, as well. We all do." She got to her feet and went back to putting dishes in the cupboards.

Yuri started to say something when Kay bounded into the cabin. "Come quick," she told them. "There's bad news."

———

Lydia listened to all Evie and Josh had to say about the news out of San Francisco. Apparently, the entire place had been leveled by a terrible earthquake. Of course, given that people were given to exaggerating reports, Lydia didn't know if the situation was truly that dire.

"We heard it from the telegraph office," Lydia's stepdaughter told them, "so we don't have too many details. It happened yesterday morning."

"Perhaps we should send a telegram to Kjell," Lydia said. She didn't want to assume the worst without having proof.

"You can't. They can't receive. The lines are

down now," Josh replied. "What little information has been coming in suggests that no one is being allowed in or out. And if Kjell and Dalton were still there, they probably can't get word to us."

"I suppose not." Lydia drew a deep breath and hoped to settle the panic that threatened to rise up in her. "I guess all we can do is wait for word."

"Hopefully it won't be as bad as it sounds," Evie replied. She reached for Lydia's hand and squeezed it gently. "You know how people like to make things sound worse than they really are. I'm sure we'll hear something soon. They may already be on their way home and have no knowledge of the earthquake."

Yuri nodded. "They are in God's hands no matter, and we must continue to pray for their safe return."

Lydia met his gaze. She was glad to have him there. "Has anyone told Phoebe yet?"

"We did," Evie told her. "We stopped there first."

Lydia got to her feet. "I should go to her. She'll be quite upset."

"I'll go with you," Kay said, getting to her feet.

"We can drive you," Evie said, also standing. "I'm sure that more news will come in as it's available. Perhaps we could even contact someone elsewhere in California to see if we can get additional information."

"That's a good idea," Lydia said, taking up her shawl. "I know someone in Sacramento. I could telegraph them and see if they can give us insight." She turned to Britta. "Can you tend to supper?"

"Yes, Mother. I'll see to everything, and Yuri is here to help if I need anything else."

Lydia looked to Yuri and once again felt a sense of relief. "I'm glad you're with us." She pushed aside thoughts of how bad the situation might be. There was no sense in borrowing trouble. Kjell and Dalton could very well be perfectly fine.

Then again, they might be dead.

"I'm sorry about this," Yuri told Britta.

She nodded, still unable to comprehend the news. "I don't know what to think. Earthquakes can be . . . devastating." She looked at him, hoping he might contradict her comment. When he didn't, she continued. "But Father and Dalton are very sensible, and Mother says they were staying in the finest hotel in San Francisco. Surely that would afford a great deal of protection."

She got to her feet and turned away as tears came to her eyes. What if they were dead?

What if they were buried under the rubble, fighting for their lives? It was too horrible to think about. A sob escaped her and Britta buried her face in her hands.

Hearing Yuri's chair move, she was certain he would come to her. Even so, when he took her in his arms and turned her to face him, Britta wasn't ready for the charge that coursed through her. She cried all the harder, and he pulled her against him.

"It will be all right," he promised. "God hasn't forgotten them or us. We will pray for their safety and return."

Britta buried her face against his chest and let her tears flow. Since returning home, she hadn't allowed her emotions to best her, and now with this news, it seemed that everything had come rushing to the surface. Why did life have to be so difficult? Why were there so many painful choices and situations? She clung to him, as though letting go might forever banish her to some unknown void.

I love him so dearly, she thought. *I need him more than ever, and he can't even see how much he means to me.*

Chapter 8

Yuri tried hard to get to know the girls better. With Laura it was easy. She was his, and she was a fun-loving child. Often she would come and take his hand, pulling him along to see some new discovery.

"See, Papa," she would say and point to a bird or a rock that she found particularly interesting. Sometimes she would stop and bid him listen to the wind in the trees. With a smile as big as the sun, she would look up at him and whisper, "Pretty."

He found his affection for her growing each day. In the past, Marsha's jealousy over his interest in Laura had caused her to treat the child in a hateful, vindictive manner. She not only treated Laura poorly, but she taunted Yuri, telling him that she wasn't even sure Laura was his daughter. Yuri hadn't cared, however, and that served only to cause Marsha to treat Laura all the worse. Perhaps that was why he'd eventually stopped trying. He remembered when he'd tried to help Laura learn to walk. Marsha had been angry at the attention he'd given the child, and without warning she snatched Laura up and tied her into a chair, where the little girl sat for hours on end. Yuri had tried to intercede—to point out that Laura needed to get down and play, but Marsha told him to go back to what he knew best—his bottle.

Yuri shook off the memory. Marsha was gone. She couldn't come between him and his daughter now. He was free to love Laura, free to give her all of the attention he would have offered back then.

Darya, however, was another matter entirely. This infant—this child he knew could not possibly be his—served only as a reminder of all that had been wrong between him and Marsha. He hadn't even known Marsha was expecting. What if he had returned before Darya was born? How would Marsha have explained?

She would have laughed and thrown it in my face. She would have belittled and ridiculed me until I believed that somehow her pregnancy was my fault, even if the baby wasn't mine.

Britta had encouraged him to forget that Darya was not of his blood. She held such tenderness for both of the children and showed him daily in her actions that such love needn't come from a physical lineage. The children needed love and stability. Surely they were not to blame for the sins of their parents.

At the Lindquist breakfast table, Yuri cast an occasional glance to where Britta sat, feeding Darya. Britta smiled and cooed, talking soft and low to the infant. The baby would occasionally gurgle in response, and milk would trickle down the side of her face. It was clear that Britta was a good mother. Maybe he should just leave them with her. He could go away again and send money to her instead of Marsha.

But she deserves a life of her own, he reminded himself. How unfair it would be to leave a young single woman laden with two children. He stared at his plate and wondered what the right decision might be. Despite his fervent prayers, his path was still uncertain.

"I understand Wilford Bacon Hoggatt is to take office as the sixth governor of our district at the end of this month," Britta said, surprising them all.

Lydia looked at her daughter as if the words made no sense, but after a moment nodded. "I suppose I had heard that, as well. There will be a great many festivities."

"When I was in town yesterday," Britta continued, "I also heard that we will soon be allowed a delegate in Congress."

Yuri sensed that she was trying hard to keep the table talk about anything but her missing father and brother. Britta put the bottle on the table and shifted Darya into position for a burp.

"I think it speaks to the fact that we are slowly but surely becoming civilized," Britta added.

"We've always been civilized," Lydia replied. "At least in some sense. Of course, things have greatly improved since I first arrived." She sighed. "Sometimes it seems like just yesterday I was standing on the dock, wondering what in the world I had gotten myself into."

Yuri smiled. "Is it true you fainted right into Kjell's arms?"

Lydia gave a little laugh. "He never lets me forget it. I was expecting Dalton at the time and didn't know it. The trip and everything about my new life had overtaxed me, and I passed out. What a scene I made."

"Not as much as the one Phoebe made when she first arrived," Britta reminded her. "I remember being there on the dock when she stood up in the boat and promptly fell overboard."

"Dalton jumped in to save her without even thinking," Lydia said. She heaved a sigh and pushed back her plate. "Surely we must go to them."

Everyone fell silent for several minutes. Yuri could see the eager expression on Lydia's face, hoping for someone to agree and help her plan a rescue.

"We have no idea where they might be," Britta finally said.

Kay nodded as she helped Laura with a piece of jellied toast. "They may arrive home any day now."

"But they might be trapped in that city," Lydia countered. "They might be hurt and need help."

"We wouldn't be able to do anything," Britta said as she continued patting the baby's back. "When I talked to them at the telegraph office, they said no one was being allowed into the city. The army is keeping folks out due to the looting and fires."

"Do you suppose the city is still burning?" Lydia asked.

Yuri shrugged. "It's hard to say. The kind

of damage done by the earthquake probably caused all kinds of problems with their natural gas lines. That will only serve to fuel the fires. I think with the army in charge, however, they will have the best available help. They will know better than anyone how to get the people to safety and secure the area."

"Has anyone heard where they have evacuated the wounded?" Lydia asked him.

"No, but I'm sure news will come in time."

Yuri wished he could offer something more tangible. After talking to the authorities in town, he was convinced they wouldn't know anything certain for some time. It sounded as if San Francisco remained in utter pandemonium. How could they possibly hope that two men could be located among thousands?

"I'll ask again when I go to town today," Yuri promised. "I need to find work, so I'd appreciate your prayers." He got to his feet and smiled down at Laura. "Maybe we can go for a walk when I get back."

Laura clapped her hands and looked at Britta. "You come, too."

She smiled. "We'll see."

Laura's request was just one more reminder that the child was completely devoted to Britta. He tried not to let it bother him as he made his way from the house. At least the girls were well loved and cared for. He comforted himself with this, as well as with what Lydia had said the night before: She was grateful for the distraction of the children. It helped to keep her mind off what might have happened to Kjell and Dalton.

He tried not to think about the men as he made his way into town. The idea of never seeing Dalton again—never being able to apologize for the past—was more than he could bear. Whenever those thoughts came to mind, Yuri prayed. If not for that, he would have easily sought a drink. It was the first serious thought he'd given liquor since coming back to Sitka. Even the news of Marsha's death hadn't caused him to consider renewing his old ways. But the very idea of losing Dalton and Kjell . . . The saloons he'd frequented were ready to welcome him back. So, too, were his old friends. Misery loved company and hated the reformed.

He spied the Black Dog Saloon. It had been a favorite of his in the past. He had run into some of his old drinking buddies the day before, and all of the memories—what little he could remember—came rushing back. He had made a living off gambling, using people much as they used him. His old friends had greeted him, encouraging him to join them for a drink and a few hands of poker. Yuri told them no, saying little else, but they'd followed him to the telegraph office.

"It will be like old times," one man declared.

"That is exactly what I'm afraid of," Yuri had told him firmly.

The men were not easily deterred, but when Yuri made his way from the telegraph office to that of the local authorities, the men deserted him quickly enough. He smiled. *Perhaps I should wear a badge. Then maybe they will leave me alone.*

The presence of his old friends served to remind him that the past wasn't that distant. He'd been sober for such a short time. He had only the hope of Jesus that he could remain that way. Morris had told him it was imperative to avoid temptations.

"Folks make a terrible mistake when they put themselves in the devil's company and think they can outwit him. He's crafty and wants to eat you alive."

The words echoed in Yuri's mind. The devil had been eating at his bones for years, and all it had done was leave Yuri weak and fearful. Of course he couldn't admit his fear. What man did that?

The days passed ever so slowly for Phoebe.

She longed to know whether Dalton was all right. After hearing that most of San Francisco had caught fire after the earthquake, she'd started having fitful dreams of him being burned alive. Now that it was May and there was still no word, hopelessness shrouded her like a funeral cloth.

"There's a new ship in the harbor," Gordon said, interrupting her thoughts. "I'm going down to see if Pa's on it."

Phoebe stared down at the candlewicks she'd been braiding. She'd made a terrible mess and would have to rebraid the piece if it was to be of any use.

"You go ahead, and let me know as soon as you can," she said. She looked up at Gordon's hopeful expression and smiled. "One of these days, we will hear something." At least that's what she kept telling herself. Her biggest fear, however, was that the news wouldn't be good.

He nodded and hurried from the house, nearly knocking his sister down as he went. Rachel called after him in accusation, but he was already gone. She pouted and flipped back her long braids.

"He's so rude."

"He's in a hurry to see if there's any news of your father. Apparently, there's a ship in the harbor."

"Oh, can I go, too?" she asked, looking back toward the door her brother had just exited.

"You know I don't like you down at the docks. There are too many troubles to get into. Why don't you help me instead? I'm having a terrible time braiding this wick."

Rachel sat down beside her mother. Her nimble fingers made quick order of the thin mule yarn. "You do think they'll be all right, don't you?"

It was hard for Phoebe to face her daughter, but she forced a smile. "I know that God is with them wherever they are, and so I believe they will be fine."

Rachel bit her lower lip for a moment, then asked, "But why haven't we heard from them?"

"It was a terrible disaster, Rachel. There are so many people in San Francisco and so much area to cover. I'm sure your father will contact us the very moment he can."

For several minutes, Rachel said nothing. Phoebe got up to check on the other children, wishing she could go back to the carefree days before the earthquake. Funny, they didn't seem all that carefree then. There was still a lot of work to accomplish and sicknesses to deal with. Life had its moments of tension and frustration, but nothing like now.

Phoebe caught sight of movement near the

small garden patch. Four-year-old Connie was busy digging a row in order to plant, and Alex was fishing. How precious they were to her.

What will I do if Dalton is lost to us? How will I ever go on? How will I support our family? Gordon is only fifteen and Alex is not yet eight—who will teach them to be men?

She thought of the boat shop and all that Dalton had done to build that business. She supposed she could hire someone to take over. Perhaps Yuri could help her, now that he was sober and trying to get back on his feet. Yes, maybe that would be the answer. She could talk to Yuri about helping.

You act as though he's already dead, she chided.

But she was always the practical one. She had her candlemaking, but that couldn't earn her a living. Of course, Lydia would suggest she and the children come there to live. Maybe she would tell Phoebe to sell the shop and their house. Lydia was wealthy in her own right.

"But so is Dalton." Funny, she often forgot about his inheritance. Dalton had made such an effort to live as if there were no inheritance that Phoebe seldom considered it. This time, however, she did and breathed a sigh of relief. They wouldn't have to move.

"Mother!" Gordon called. "Come quick."

Phoebe's hand went to her throat. Was it possible? Had Dalton returned? She rushed through the house and met her son at the door. She looked at him with great expectation.

"Grandmother is here."

"Lydia?" she asked. Why would he make such a scene about that?

"No. Grandmother Robbins. She's here with Uncle Ted."

Phoebe's mouth dropped open. Her mother and brother—here? She stepped outside and saw them coming up the walk. Her mother looked lovely in a summer traveling suit of gray and navy. She smiled and opened her arms to Phoebe.

"We came as soon as we heard about the earthquake. The train took forever to cross the country, but our time on the ship passed quickly. Gordon said that Dalton is still gone. We had hoped that might not be the case, but I felt such a sense of urgency that I just knew it was God's prompting."

Phoebe had nearly forgotten that she'd written to her mother almost a month ago about Dalton's trip. She hugged her mother, relishing the embrace. "It's so good to see you both." She gave Theodore a hug but found him less receptive. At thirty-two, he had become a hard and bitter man, according to their mother.

"We've had no word from him or his father. They were supposed to have left by the twentieth, but if that had happened, they would surely have notified us or been home by now."

Her mother nodded and appeared to consider the matter. "And you've been in contact with the authorities?"

"Yes. We have sent word that they are missing and asked for information from all the hospitals that took in victims from the quake. We've also left word with the . . . morgues."

"Sensible," Theodore replied. He looked around the yard and then back to his sister. "Looks like nothing has changed."

Phoebe frowned but said nothing.

"Where are the other children?" her mother quickly interjected. "My, but I've longed to meet Connie. I can't believe she's already four years old."

"Alex is fishing, and Connie is digging in the garden. Rachel is inside. Why don't you both come in and rest. I'll put on some coffee."

They made their way inside with Gordon bringing up the rear. He came to Phoebe's side. "Mother, there was no other word."

"Perhaps you will find yourself in the same situation we did," Theodore said.

"What are you saying?" Phoebe managed.

He shrugged. "Only that perhaps Dalton won't return. Young Gordon may lose his father just as we did. Only in this situation, his father won't be dead because of the lacking of another."

Their mother was appalled. "That's a horrible thing to say, Ted."

"That may be so, but no doubt true enough. Had Dalton been more observant, our father might not have died."

"You take that back," Gordon demanded. "My father is a good man."

Theodore stared at Gordon for a moment but said nothing. Their mother elbowed him in the side. "Apologize."

He glanced at his mother. "Very well. I'm sorry that speaking the truth has caused such an uproar."

Phoebe felt Gordon bristle. "You have no right to talk like that. I remember my father telling me the story about our grandfather's death. He took his own life—probably because you were such a horrible son!" With that, Gordon ran from the gathering even as Phoebe called to him.

"Gordon! Gordon, come back!" Phoebe wanted to slap her brother. Instead, she fixed him with a hard glare. "You will mind your manners or house yourself in town. Do you understand? My husband—my children's father—is a good and loving man. He may very well be dead or dying. You have no right to say such hideous things!" He was younger than Phoebe by only a few years yet looked older. Still, instead of the anger she'd seen earlier, Ted seemed startled. Could it be Gordon's retort had actually weakened that hard façade of hatred?

"I must tend to my son," Phoebe said. "Mother, you know your way around. Please make yourself at home."

She left them and hurried down the path Gordon had taken. "Gordon, where are you?" Phoebe had a feeling she already knew the answer and made her way to the boat shop.

The shop was quiet, despite the fact that the cannery order needed to be completed in a matter of weeks. It was Saturday and that meant work stopped at noon. "Gordon, please come out and talk to me."

He stepped from the shadows. "I don't want him in our house. Why did he come here if he hates my father so much?"

Gordon looked so vulnerable. The question of his father's well-being had taken its toll on her son, who was eager to be a man.

"I'm sorry, Gordon. Ted has never been the same since losing our father. He blames himself, I'm sure. He was only your age when Father died."

"And now my father may be dead, as well," Gordon said, tears streaming down his face. "And he wants him to be dead. I know he does. I hate him!"

She went to him, and despite his age and the fact that he towered over her, Phoebe wrapped Gordon in her arms. "Ted is lost. He doesn't know the love of God. He hates so much that he refuses to see that others love him and care about him. Pray for him, Gordon, but do not become like him. Do not hate him in return."

Gordon said nothing. He clung to his mother, shaking as he cried out pent-up tears of fear and misery. Phoebe let him spend his energy, not saying a word.

O God, she prayed in silence, *please help us. We need you so.*

Chapter 9

May 1906

*B*ritta awoke to the sound of her mother's gentle voice. "Wake up, Britta. Yuri needs you."

She sat up and looked at her mother for a moment, trying to figure out what in the world she was saying. Mother seemed to understand and held out Britta's robe.

"The children woke up, and now they are crying and won't go back to sleep."

Then Britta remembered. This was the first night they were trying out new sleeping arrangements. After having put Laura and Darya to bed in their new room at the cabin,

Britta had returned to the house, leaving Yuri in charge of his daughters. They had hoped the children would sleep through the night and Britta would arrive before they awoke in the morning. It was all a part of attempting to bring the trio together as a family.

"What time is it?" Britta asked. She pulled on the robe and couldn't suppress her yawn.

"It's nearly three," her mother answered.

Britta nodded and hurried downstairs. She didn't even stop to put on her boots but made her way barefoot through the wet grass to Yuri's cabin. She could hear the children crying and worried that they might be sick.

Yuri was pacing the porch, a look of panic in his eyes. "I'm sorry to have your mother wake you, but I didn't know what to do."

"Why are you out here instead of with the children?" she asked.

He ran his hand through his hair. "I don't know how to calm them. Laura awoke from what seemed to be a bad dream. When I tried to comfort her, she withdrew to the corner of the bed and began to scream for Mama. That, in turn, woke the baby. Darya started crying, I'm sure, just to keep Laura company."

Britta considered chiding him for leaving the children alone but it would serve no good purpose. "Would you mind warming a bottle of milk for the baby while I see what else needs to be tended to?"

He nodded and opened the screen door.

Britta made her way inside and went immediately to the girls' room. She found Laura sitting on her bed, the quilt wadded up around her and her doll pressed tight to her chest.

"Whatever is wrong?" she asked, taking Laura in her arms.

"I woke up, and you were gone. You stay here, Mama."

Britta smoothed back the child's long hair. "Now, we talked about this. Your papa is going to stay here at night. I will come be with you in the daytime."

"No. I want you." Laura clung hard and fast to Britta's neck.

Darya continued to fuss and Britta knew the baby probably needed to be changed. "Laura, I want you to lie down while I take care of the baby. I'll be right here, and I'll talk to you the whole time."

Laura pulled back and looked skeptical. "You stay?"

"For a little while."

Britta went to work soothing Darya. She changed the baby's diaper and cradled her close. With everyone quieting down, Britta felt confident that all was well. Her earlier fears that perhaps they were sick passed away as she began to hum a lullaby.

"Here's the bottle," Yuri said as he came into the room. "I hope it's warm enough."

"Did you test it on your wrist the way I showed you?"

He looked sheepish. "I did, but . . . well . . . my skin is so rough. I worry that I don't have the same degree of sensitivity that you do."

Britta didn't argue with him. She took the bottle and dripped a bit of milk on her skin. It was slightly cooler than she would normally have used, but once Darya saw the chance to eat, there was no turning back. She could only pray that the baby wouldn't get a stomach-ache, or there would be no sleep for anyone tonight.

Yuri stood to the side as Britta instructed Laura to cover up. "Would you like to hear a story?" The little girl nodded, so Britta began, "Once upon a time, there lived a beautiful princess named Laura. . . ." She often put the child's name into stories to keep her attention, and this time was no exception. She wondered what Yuri might think of her practice, but continued to feed Darya and entertain Laura.

As she figured, it was only fifteen or twenty minutes before both girls were fast asleep. She yawned and got to her feet. Darya didn't so much as move when Britta placed her back in her crib. What a beautiful child—so angelic. Britta couldn't help but touch her baby-fine hair. It was darker than Laura's and had a bit of a curl to it. Britta tried to remember Marsha to gauge if the child favored her mother, but it was late and exhaustion overcame her thoughts.

She slipped from the room, finding that Yuri had already made his way out. She didn't see him and wondered if he had already gone to bed. Disappointed that she couldn't tell him good-bye, Britta made her way outside, closing the door behind her. A lighted lantern awaited her trip home. No doubt Yuri had thought of this.

"You're very good with them," Yuri said.

She startled, surprised that he was there. Britta could see him approach from the far side of the porch. "They are wonderful children, but this is an adjustment for them. Laura is used to my being there at night. She'll get over it in time." But in her heart, Britta didn't want Laura to get over it. She relished that the child needed and wanted her. It not only gave her an excuse to remain close to the girls, but it gave her a reason to be near Yuri, as well.

A breeze picked up and blew Britta's long brown hair across her face. To her surprise, Yuri reached out and brushed it back in place. He studied her for a moment, as if seeing her for the first time. Something in his expression gave Britta hope that he might love her. She longed to declare her love for him but knew it wasn't the right time. Instead, she reached for the lantern and turned to go.

"I'll be here to fix breakfast—hopefully before they wake up."

"Britta . . ." He barely breathed her name.

She turned and smiled. He was standing in the light of the lantern, a stunned expression on his face. "What?" she asked.

He stared at her for a few more seconds, then shrugged. "Uh . . . nothing. Guess I'll see you in the morning."

She hesitated a moment, then nodded. "Good night, Yuri."

———

Yuri was frantic by the time Britta arrived the next morning. It felt like he'd barely gone to sleep before Darya started crying again. He got up to find that morning's light was already casting a golden glow against clear skies. Apparently, the affairs of the night had caused them all to oversleep.

He went into the girls' room and felt a sense of helplessness. Seeing the squalling infant, he wasn't at all sure what he could do to comfort her. Against his better judgment, he picked her up and found that Darya quickly quieted.

She gazed at him with dark blue eyes that seemed intent on piercing through his well-placed walls of defense.

"Now what do I do?" he asked no one in particular.

He glanced to where Laura was already waking. She looked at him and began to pucker her lips. "Where's Mama?"

"She'll be here soon," he said. Just then, Darya's fascination with him ended, and she began to cry again.

Yuri didn't know what to think. He shifted the baby carefully and brought her to his shoulder as he'd seen Britta do. This only served to irritate the infant more. At the baby's increased howls of protest, Laura began to cry.

"It's all right, Britta . . . Mama will be here soon."

He attempted to sit down beside Laura, but she wanted no part of it. "Go away. I want Mama."

"I'm sorry, Laura. She isn't here yet," Yuri said, more sternly than he'd intended. "She'll be here soon enough, I promise."

Laura looked at him as if he'd suddenly grown horns. She began to wail in earnest, which only caused Darya to cry more. Yuri thought if Britta didn't come soon, he might well join them.

When she did arrive a few minutes later,

Yuri could see that she was still quite tired. Nevertheless, he thought her more beautiful than ever before. Funny, she'd always just been a little girl to him—a little sister. After last night, however, he found himself thinking of her otherwise. She was a grown woman— lovely and sensible—and . . .

"You certainly have a mess on your hands," she said with a grin. "I'm sorry I overslept."

"I didn't know what to do," he said, thrusting the baby at her.

Britta took Darya. "Well, you're their father, and you really should learn."

There was no real rebuke in her tone but rather an amused conciliatory manner. She gathered Laura to her side. "Now you know what you must do," she told the girl. "The bowl has water in it and is ready for you to wash your face. After that, you can get dressed. I left your things out on the chest at the end of the bed." She turned to Yuri. "Laura is a big girl and can wash up and dress herself. Can't you, Laura?"

The child looked up and nodded. "I dwess myself."

He stood amazed at how quickly order came out of chaos. Before he had fully dressed and shaved, Britta had the children secured and breakfast on the stove. When he joined them at the table, Yuri could only smile in admiration at the petite young woman.

"You make it seem so easy," he said, taking a bowl of oatmeal from her hands.

"It's just a matter of routine now," Britta replied. "It wasn't this easy in the beginning. I have to say, I relied a great deal upon my mother to show me what to do. Despite having cared for Phoebe's children when they were young, it's not the same as having full charge."

She tied a dishcloth around Laura's neck to keep food from her clothes, then took her seat beside the child. "Will you say grace?"

Yuri bowed his head and offered thanks for the meal and added silent gratitude for the quiet and order that had been restored. He opened his eyes to find Britta looking at him and smiling. It was almost as if she could read his mind.

"I'm heading into town. Do you need me to bring back anything?" he asked between bites.

"I don't think so. We stocked the cabin pretty well before you moved in. I think we're set for a little while. Mother or Kay will bring more milk for the baby after they finish with their chores."

"I heard your mother say that she's planning to sell one of the milk calves."

Britta nodded. "Yes. She has a long list of folks who want to buy them. Beef isn't as easily attainable up here as elsewhere, but folks still crave it. Whoever buys it will probably feed it until fall, then butcher it."

"And what of your family? Will they have enough meat for themselves?"

"Oh, we always do. Father smoked pork last fall and we still have quite a bit. Plus there is smoked salmon and pickled herring. He'll hunt for anything else we need. Mother and Kay always put in a garden to match no other on the island, and there are always berries. Remember when we would go berry picking? You and Dalton would come along to protect us girls." He nodded and she continued. "We will be canning all sorts of things as summer comes on. Then, too, Mother has plenty of money, and she orders in a good supply of the things she can't grow. So food is usually not an issue."

"What might be an issue?" Yuri asked. He longed to find a way to make himself truly useful.

"I can't say. I've been gone longer than you have."

Yuri continued eating. There must be something he could do to benefit the family. "I suppose I could keep cutting wood," he said after a time.

"There are always ways to help, if that's what you're looking for. Mother wants to make a better house for the chickens. Then there's a need to dig a new outhouse. Oh, and before he left, I know my father had plans to make repairs to the wood wagon."

"I could probably do those things," Yuri said as he pushed back from the table. "I shouldn't be gone long unless someone offers me a job on the spot."

"There probably isn't much available . . . except saloon work," Britta said, helping Laura to get the last of her oatmeal.

Yuri heard the hesitation and knew Britta's concern. "I can't work there," he said, hoping to put her mind at ease. He got up and smiled. "I think we both know why."

Britta nodded. "I'll be praying God brings something to you."

Yuri wanted to comment on how pretty she looked—how her hair seemed to ripple like water. He wanted to tell her that she'd looked quite alluring last night in the warm glow of lantern light. Instead, he left without another word, hoping the awkwardness he felt would pass.

He had walked nearly the entire distance to town when he spied Phoebe coming down the road. She was carrying a basket over one arm and seemed preoccupied. In fact, she almost appeared to be carrying on a conversation.

He waited as she approached, but it wasn't until she was nearly upon him that Phoebe even noticed him there.

"Oh, I am sorry," she said. "I'm afraid I was deep in thought . . . well, actually, prayer."

"That's a relief. I thought maybe you were talking to yourself," he replied. "Are you headed out to see Lydia?"

"I was hoping to see you, as well."

"Me?"

Phoebe nodded and shifted the basket. "I had hoped to talk you into working for me— for Dalton's company."

Yuri was taken by surprise. "What did you have in mind?"

"Well, if you really want a job, I can definitely use you. I have no idea of when Dalton will be home, but there's an order for three skiffs for the cannery. I don't know how long it takes to finish such an order, but I know the boys we hired from the school are already hard at work on them. I had thought to get some extra help from the school, but they are going to one of the near islands to harvest wood. They'll be tied up rafting it back to Sitka well into the summer." She paused, and a pleading expression filled her face. "Please tell me you will do it. Gordon told me the boats couldn't possibly be completed in time if we didn't get some additional help. Especially someone who wouldn't require extra time in training."

It seemed Britta's prayers were being answered rather quickly. Yuri drew a deep breath. "I know how to build skiffs."

"Wonderful." Her expression seemed to brighten. "Then you'll work for me . . . for us, I mean." She shook her head. "Sometimes I talk as though Dalton's gone for good, but I really don't believe that."

"Neither do I," Yuri told her. He could easily remember the days before Dalton and Phoebe married. A time when he, too, had been interested in courting the pretty blonde. Phoebe hadn't changed much in all that time. She was still a strikingly beautiful woman.

"Why don't you walk with me to the house, and we can discuss your pay. I'm afraid I don't even know what's fair."

They began to walk back to the Lindquists. Yuri reached out for the basket. "Here, let me carry that." Phoebe didn't protest.

"I'm taking candles to Lydia," she said, as if he needed an explanation.

"I remember you making the most beautiful candles," Yuri said thoughtfully. "They smelled so much better than those my mother used to make."

Phoebe smiled. "I didn't know your mother made candles."

"Only when necessary, and only when I was very young. Supplies were far harder to get in those days, and making your own candles was often a necessity. Of course, we used our share of candlefish, too."

"Smelly things," Phoebe said, wrinkling up her nose. "Still, those days seem like a million years ago."

"We were just talking about how you and Dalton first met," Yuri said. "Not many folks have such a dramatic introduction."

Laughing, Phoebe kicked at a rock and sent it flying down the road ahead of them. "I try to forget just how opinionated and bossy I could be back then. I've really tried to change over the years."

This struck a chord with Yuri. "Do you think God can truly change us, Phoebe? I mean, really make something new out of what we were?"

"I do. Lydia taught me to count on God for the impossible. I hated it when I came here, remember?"

Yuri did and smiled. "It was evident that you planned to leave as soon as the first opportunity presented itself."

"That's true enough. But then I lost my heart to Dalton and knew he'd never leave. So

I began to pray God would change my heart—teach me to love Sitka. Little by little, I found a great deal to love about this place. Now I honestly have no desire to live elsewhere."

"But what about me? Do you think God can truly deliver me from alcohol?" He frowned.

"Yes, Yuri. I think God can completely deliver you. I know you're probably afraid of what may or may not happen, but just keep in mind that God has already made provision for it. You will always have a way out of temptation. The Bible says so."

"I want to believe that it's true. I know Morris—he's the man who helped me after I got hurt—told me that I can overcome anything with God's help."

He heard a buggy approaching from behind and pulled Phoebe to the side of the road as it drew up beside them. Sitting at the reins was a well-dressed man who appeared confused.

"I'm wondering if you might help me. I'm looking for the Lindquist estate."

Yuri exchanged a grin with Phoebe. "I don't think I've ever heard them call it an estate, but you're on the right road. We were headed that way ourselves."

The man beamed at them. "Wonderful. Might I offer you a ride in exchange for directions?"

Phoebe looked to Yuri and then nodded. "That would be very nice. Thank you."

Helping her up, Yuri waited until Phoebe was settled before handing her the basket. Next he climbed beside her and the three of them squeezed together in the small seat.

"I'm Phoebe Lindquist. I'm married to Lydia and Kjell's son, Dalton." She paused and Yuri saw an anxious look shadow her face. "You aren't here because of them—are you? Do you have word about Dalton and his father?"

"Not at all. I only know them by name, but know nothing else. Why do you ask?"

"We have reason to believe they were in San Francisco the day of the earthquake."

"I am sorry to hear that. I was in Denver myself when word came about the quake. I once lived in San Francisco and can only wonder what remains of that dear lady."

Phoebe nodded and seemed to slump a little toward Yuri.

"My name is Brenton Maltese," the man continued. "It's nice to meet you, Mrs. Lindquist."

"This is Yuri Belikov. He's a very good friend of the family." Yuri leaned forward and gave a brief two-fingered salute.

"Good to meet you both, and very fortuitous. I was afraid I might be lost."

"It's hard to get too lost on this island. There aren't many roads, and everyone knows everyone," Phoebe countered. "So what brings you here? Do you have business with Kjell and Lydia?"

"In a manner of speaking," the man replied. "I'm engaged to their daughter Britta. I've really come here to see her."

Yuri felt as though he'd taken a blow to the stomach. He couldn't help but meet Phoebe's worried look. She seemed to question him with her eyes, but Yuri could do nothing but shrug.

"Britta has said nothing about an engagement," Phoebe murmured. By this time, however, they were approaching the turnoff for the Lindquist property. "You need to take this drive. Their house is up and around the bend."

Yuri couldn't concentrate on what Maltese said in reply. He was completely dumbfounded. Britta was engaged? Why was she caring for his children when she had agreed to marry this man? It didn't make sense.

He remembered Lydia saying that Britta had always been her most secretive of children. This encounter definitely confirmed that point. What in the world had Britta gotten herself into now?

Chapter 10

$\mathcal{B}$ritta was elbow deep in sudsy wash water when the carriage arrived. It was unusual to have anyone drive out to the property, and she feared bad news had come about her father and brother. She glanced at the porch, where Laura was playing with her dolls while Darya lay on a blanket cooing and shaking a rattle. They were perfectly happy and unconcerned about the carriage.

Britta put diapers to soak in the kettle of hot water, then wiped her hands on her apron. She glanced to the front of her parents' house to see who had come calling. At the sight of

Brenton Maltese, she froze. *What in the world is he doing here?*

She watched for a moment as Brenton secured the reins while Yuri assisted Phoebe down from the buggy. Yuri didn't look any too happy, leaving Britta to wonder what Brenton had already said. Rather than plunging herself into the midst of the situation, she briefly contemplated escaping from sight.

"You look like you've just seen a ghost," Kay said, surprising Britta. "I came over to see if you needed any help with the girls."

Britta looked to where Brenton was now chatting with her mother. Kay followed suit and noted the situation. "Is that someone you know?"

"I'm afraid so," she said with a sigh. "I suppose I should go speak with him."

"Who is he?"

"He is the complication that led me to come home. He wants me to marry him." Kay's mouth dropped open. Britta quickly added, "Don't even get started on your questions. I'll have Mother's and Phoebe's to answer in just a few moments, so I'm saving my strength."

Then all at once, she saw Yuri. He locked gazes with her, and Britta felt her knees grow weak. Was he angry or upset? She couldn't tell at all what his expression suggested.

What would Yuri think of her if Brenton had mentioned his proposal?

"Kay, would you please stay with the children?"

The dark-eyed woman nodded, still unable to speak. Britta hurried toward her parents' house, catching her mother's watchful eye.

"Ah, here's Britta now," her mother announced.

"Hello, Brenton. Why are you here?" She didn't even give pretense to propriety.

"He was just telling us that you two are engaged," her mother interjected. The expression on her face made it clear that Britta wasn't going to be able to get out of this mess easily.

"I'm afraid Mr. Maltese is mistaken. He proposed, but I have not yet agreed to marry him." Britta turned back to Brenton. "I told you I would give you my answer no later than the first of June."

"I know," he replied with a sheepish grin, "but I was growing restless in waiting. Surely you understand." He twisted his hat in his hands. "Then I thought it might do me good to see where you grew up."

"Well, it's certainly not doing me any good."

"That's an awful thing to say, Britta," her

mother reprimanded. "You should apologize for your behavior,"

The comment completely embarrassed Britta. She felt as if she were six years old again. "I'm sorry. I can't do this right now."

She turned and hurried away from the gathering. This was not at all what she had wanted. In fact, Britta had hoped the entire matter might be resolved without her having to make any decision at all. She had imagined that by delaying and maintaining her distance, Brenton would forget his proposal and simply go away. Of course, that was a childish wish.

Britta made her way to the woodshop. The scent of cedar assaulted her nose. It was a comforting smell that made her think of Father. How she longed for his return. She needed to know that he was all right, but she also needed him for counsel. She sighed and sank to a wooden bench.

What a mess. How in the world was she supposed to resolve this situation? She now knew without a doubt that she didn't love Brenton, at least not as much as she should if she were going to marry him. He was a great man. He had so much to offer a wife, but she wasn't that woman.

Furthermore, Britta knew that playing in his orchestra wasn't what she wanted. She wanted Yuri . . . just as she had when she'd left Sitka six years ago.

"Why didn't you tell us about him?" Yuri asked.

She hadn't heard him come in, and seeing him now only served to make Britta all the more uncomfortable. She shifted but said nothing.

Yuri stepped closer. "You only talked about the orchestra position."

"Well, one was pretty much the same as the other," she said with a shrug.

He eyed her carefully. "What do you mean?"

Britta gave a sigh. She might as well come clean. "Brenton is the founder and leader of the new orchestra. He was the one who arranged for the sponsors and found the musicians. He was also my violin teacher."

"I see. And you fell in love?"

Britta looked up and met Yuri's eyes. "I fell in love . . . but not with him."

Yuri frowned. "Then with whom?"

She nearly blurted out, *You, stupid!* but instead drew a deep breath. "I fell in love with the idea of living the life of a musician," she lied. "Anyway, by coming home, I realized that I didn't want that life at all."

"Because of the children?"

"Only in part."

"Why else would you stay?"

Britta turned her back to him as she got to her feet. "I don't expect you to understand. You've distanced yourself from Sitka, but I love it here. I love Alaska. Everything I've ever loved is right here." She forced herself not to turn around. If he saw her eyes, he'd surely know her heart.

Sensing the danger of continuing, Britta calmly walked to the door. "I suppose I need to talk to Brenton. Would you mind telling him to meet me at the bench?"

"All right." Yuri followed her out of the woodshop, just as she knew he would.

"I'll be there waiting for him."

She knew Yuri wanted to talk to her about the situation in greater detail, but if she said even one more word to him in this state of mind, she knew she would say all the wrong things.

Walking slowly past the garden, Britta made her way to the bench her father had built. He'd placed it in the shade of tall spruce trees near the stream that flowed through their property. It made a peaceful and secluded retreat. One could sit there unobserved to reflect upon the day or, as in this case, to deliver bad news.

A sigh escaped her lips as she settled upon the bench. Why couldn't Yuri see how much she loved him? Would she have to be the one to bare her heart first? She knew he cared for her, but perhaps he couldn't see beyond the past. She had always been like a little sister to him. Well, at least until last night.

She smiled at that memory. He had looked at her for the first time as if truly seeing the woman she'd become. And Britta hadn't seen a bit of disapproval in his expression.

"Britta?"

It was Brenton. The noise he made in his approach told her that, if not his voice. "I'm here." She got to her feet and stepped into sight.

He smiled and rushed to greet her. "Your friend told me where you were. I knew you would want to see me alone." Without warning he swept her into his arms. "I've missed you more than words can say."

She stiffened. "Please release me."

"What's wrong? What have I done?"

She maneuvered away from him and pointed to the bench. "Please be seated. We need to talk."

"That's why I've come." There was so much adoration in his expression that Britta couldn't be mad at him. "I needed to see you."

"I told you not to come. I told you I needed time to think about this," she said without condemnation. "It was important to me."

He nodded and reached out to take her

hand. "I know. I don't mean to take that from you. Please forgive me."

Britta stepped back and again motioned to the bench. This time, however, she decided to join him. "Please sit." She took her place, immediately bringing Brenton to her side.

"This is a wonderful place. I can see why you love it." He glanced upward at the tall spruce. "And the scent is just as you used to describe. So crisp and clean."

"It's my home," Britta began. "I am more attached to it than I ever believed."

"I can understand. There is great harmony here. Even a melody of sorts. Listen to how the wind hums through the trees, then the water makes a gentle rippling sound like that of trained fingers upon harp strings. I could write wonderful music here."

"I feel the same way," she replied, hoping he would begin to understand that she could not go to England.

"We would always come and visit," he said, surprising her. "We would plan lengthy trips to refresh our souls. I could make arrangements for such things. Wouldn't it be grand?" He fixed her with a smile, his dark eyes dancing.

"My father and brother are missing," she said without really thinking.

"I know. Your mother and sister-in-law

both mentioned it. I am sorry. The earthquake was quite devastating. I saw pictures in the newspaper."

"How bad was it really, Brenton?"

He frowned. "Most likely as bad as everyone says. Much of the town has burned to ashes. It wasn't enough that the earthquake took its toll, but fire swept through so quickly, there was really no hope of controlling it." He seemed to realize the heartlessness of his statement. "But I'm sure your father and brother would have had a good chance of escape."

"Then why have we not heard from them? Why are they not here?"

Brenton reached up to touch her cheek. "I'm so sorry, my dear. It seems my arrival here has done nothing but bring you sorrow."

She felt sorry for him, and for just a moment she tried to force her heart into the mold that might allow her to say yes to his proposal. He was a good man. Maybe that was enough for a decent marriage and pleasant life. Yuri would give the girls to an orphanage or her sister, and Britta could leave Sitka to travel the world with Brenton. Then, as he said, they would return here often for respite. It should be enough—shouldn't it? Yuri could go his own way and never have to come back to Sitka again if he didn't wish.

With a sigh, she stepped back. "I'm sorry,"

she said, knowing that she couldn't pretend to love him. Brenton had been a good friend to her, and she would not treat him in such a manner. She opened her mouth to speak, but he put a finger to her lips.

"There's no need to be sorry. You've endured a great deal. Let's just remain here and enjoy the quiet. Perhaps you'll find solace."

She shook her head and turned to go. "I can't, Brenton. I'm sorry. Please excuse me. I'm just . . . a bit overwhelmed."

Chapter 11

*L*ate May brought several beautiful sunny days, and Phoebe was more than happy to take her family to a picnic at Lydia and Kjell's house. It was little things like this that helped her maintain her sanity. Information about San Francisco's disaster was becoming more readily available, but not where it concerned Dalton and Kjell. The authorities assured Lydia and Phoebe that everything possible was being done to locate the men, but that did little to comfort Phoebe and her family.

Phoebe watched her youngest playing with

Laura and wondered what would happen if Dalton never returned home. How would Connie ever remember him? She touched her stomach and thought of the unborn child she carried. She had only just learned of this new baby and hadn't even had a chance to announce her pregnancy. This child might not ever know its father or grandfather.

"Everything's ready," Lydia announced. "Let's be seated."

They gathered at the large table Kjell had built out of old scarred boards. He'd taken the pieces from one of his work sites and decided to refurbish the pine for a long outdoor table. He made benches to match—three for each side—more than enough room to accommodate twenty people. Kjell was handy that way—Dalton, too. Phoebe tried not to think of how he and Dalton had built the house she lived in. She once had remembered such things with great joy, but now they only served to remind her of this nagging loss.

"You look so tired," Britta told her.

Phoebe gave a weak smile. She wasn't yet ready to announce her pregnancy. "I was going to say the same about you. Is it going any better with the children?"

Britta shrugged as she helped Laura onto the bench. "Some nights are better than others. Often I end up sending Yuri back to the house so he can get some sleep, and I just stay with the kids at the cabin."

Phoebe's brother Ted surprised them by leaning forward to ask, "Why don't you just stay at the cabin to begin with, if you are their nanny?"

Thankfully, Lydia was the one to answer. "It wouldn't be appropriate, Ted. Britta is a single woman and Yuri a single man. If Yuri had a wife, things would be different and Britta could stay with them as their official nanny. However, if Yuri had a wife, he would hardly have need for a nanny."

He seemed to consider this for a moment and then helped himself to several slices of fresh bread before turning to Yuri. "And will you take a wife soon?"

Yuri seemed startled by the question but gave a quick reply. "No. I have no plans for such a thing."

Phoebe saw Britta turn away and get up from the table. "I'm going to check on Darya." She hurried away, but Phoebe couldn't help but see that Britta was upset. Perhaps later she would have a chance to talk to Britta and see what was wrong.

"Well, you're the first sensible man I've met in some time," Theodore replied to Yuri's statement. "If the men in this family are any example, it's probably just as well to avoid such unions altogether."

Phoebe could see that her mother was mortified at the comment, while Lydia sat staring at Theodore as if he'd just grown horns. Gordon opened his mouth, but it was Kay who got the first word out.

"Especially if they're as rude and sour as you are."

Theodore shrugged. "I'm simply stating the facts. If that seems rude, then I apologize. I had no idea we were to speak anything but the truth."

It was well known that Kay spoke her mind whenever she felt it was necessary. For all intents and purposes, Theodore had thrown down the gauntlet and Kay was happy to pick it up as defender of the Lindquist men.

"We are speaking truth at this table," Kay said, "which may well be the reason you should refrain from saying anything more." She stared him down and waited for his reply.

Theodore was more than up for the challenge. "Are you suggesting that I'm a liar? I merely stated what I see to be completely true. Neither Mr. Lindquist the elder nor his son— my sister's husband—are present. In fact, no one has heard anything from either one. At best, that means they are dead. At worst, they have abandoned their families. My money is on the latter."

"You wretched man," Kay shot back.

"That really was uncalled for, Robbins," Yuri said, his eyes narrowing. "You are a guest of the Lindquist family, and thus it would be reasonable to expect better behavior and certainly better conversation."

Theodore didn't appear the least bit concerned that another man had come to the defense of the Lindquist men. Phoebe could see from his expression that he had no intention of backing down. Something had to be done.

To her surprise, Gordon was getting to his feet. He moved with methodic slowness as he folded his napkin and put it beside his plate. "If you want to discuss it further, Uncle Ted, we can take this behind the woodshop."

Theodore laughed, which was exactly the worst thing he could have done. Phoebe could see that her son was barely containing his temper. Gordon's jaw clenched and fire lit his eyes as he stepped back a pace.

"I suppose you've learned such barbaric practices from your father," Theodore stated matter-of-factly. "But I, for one, was raised with better manners."

Gordon balled his fists, and Phoebe knew the time had come to intercede. "Enough of this. I cannot believe your insensitivity. You speak of manners yet sit at your hostess's table bad-mouthing not only her son but her husband. And for what reason?"

The anger in Theodore's expression was enough to make her wilt, but Phoebe held her ground. "Answer me. For what reason do you come here today and make such a display of your bitter heart?"

"You know very well what reason. Dalton Lindquist killed our father. Maybe he didn't put a gun to his head, but neither did he take care to do anything to prevent him from jumping from the ship to his death. Our father might have lived had your husband paid closer attention to his obvious sorrow."

Gordon started for Theodore, but Phoebe put herself between them. This action brought Yuri to his feet.

"No! It's your own fault!" Gordon accused.

"Gordon, calm down." Phoebe met his contorted face with a sad smile. "This won't solve anything."

He turned and headed for the sanctuary of the forest. Phoebe longed to go after him but knew it was best to give Gordon time. She'd deal instead with her brother.

"You," Phoebe said, pointing to Theodore, "come with me right now." She glanced at

Yuri. "If he refuses, you have my permission to bind him and bring him to me."

She took off without looking back. Theodore would come of his own accord, or she knew Yuri would bring him. Either way, she would speak her mind away from the others.

It was only a matter of minutes before her brother joined her. He crossed his arms and stared at her hard. "So is this where I get my tongue-lashing?"

"No. Not at all."

He smirked. "Then what?"

"I want you to leave."

He looked at her oddly. "Leave?"

"Yes. I want you to go. I will pay for your ticket."

"Wait a minute," he said, relaxing his arms. "Are you saying you want me to leave Sitka?"

Phoebe could see that he was clearly stunned. She didn't know why it should surprise him so much. "Yes. Mother will stay, but I'm tired of your ugly comments about my husband. Dalton didn't kill our father. He had nothing to do with our father's death. You might as well say it was our fault. Perhaps we were bad children for not noticing his grief."

"It wasn't my fault!" Theodore shouted.

Phoebe noted a strange tone in his voice as he continued. "If Dalton would simply have taken notice of Father's sadness—of his desperation—he might have lived. If nothing else, Dalton should have read the letter Father penned him."

She softened her tone. "But he didn't."

"That's right. He didn't." Theodore began to pace. "He didn't realize when Father left, or he might have done something different."

"Don't you mean *you* might have done something different?"

He moved toward Phoebe. "We're not talking about me."

"Aren't we?" She watched as his face contorted. "Teddy?"

He began to pace. "I don't want to talk about this anymore. If you want me to go, I'll go."

She put out her hand and stopped him. "Teddy, I don't want you to go. I want you to tell me what's bothering you. What has caused you to become such a hardened man?"

He looked at her for a moment, and she could feel him tremble. "It's . . . I can't." He dropped his chin and shook his head. "It's too much."

"Tell me," she encouraged. "Then maybe you won't feel so alone."

For several moments he said nothing, and Phoebe thought perhaps he never would. The silence wore on as Theodore seemed to fight against his demons. He shook his head again. "You're right. I failed him. He asked me to go with him." A hoarse sob broke from his throat. "He knew he wasn't strong enough to make the trip alone."

"What are you talking about?"

"Don't you see? It was my fault. I should have gone with him." He crumpled to the ground. "If I'd gone with him, he wouldn't be dead now."

Phoebe knelt beside him. "You can't know that, Teddy." She put her hand on his shoulder.

"But he asked me to go. He came to me the night before he left and told me he thought it would be best if I went with him."

"Perhaps he only wanted you to accompany him so that you could go back and take Mother the letters, instead of trusting them to strangers. Maybe he only needed to know that someone would share the news sympathetically with Mother once he was gone."

He shook his head. "I cannot bear the thought of what might have been. I was a terrible son to him. I was more interested in my own affairs. I was nothing but a disappointment to him, and because of that, he killed himself."

"Teddy, that's not true. Father had never been able to overcome the shame of his father's actions. When Grandfather swindled their friends and neighbors out of their money— when he took off with the bank funds—he brought the whole family under suspicion. You might not remember this, but even after Grandfather went to prison, people were sent to spy on us. They were certain that Father had played some role in the embezzlement. After all, he was second in command at the bank."

"I do remember." Theodore pulled out a handkerchief and blew his nose. "I should never have come back here. It's like Father's misery and fear is all around me."

"Teddy, you have grieved for far too long. You've blamed yourself—wrongly. Now is the time to let go of the past and see God for the loving and generous Father that He is. He is there for us—despite our earthly father leaving. Where Father was weak, God is strong. Where Father had no hope, God is hope."

"I'm sorry, Phoebe. It's hard for me to believe."

"It's not easy for anyone to put their trust in someone they can't see or hear. It requires a faith that is not of our own doing. It is a faith borne of God himself—it's a gift from Him."

He looked at her with such sorrow. "I never meant to hurt you. I've made a complete fool of myself, I know. What should I do? I can go, but . . ." He grew quiet and hung his head.

Phoebe hugged him for a moment, then released him lest he be embarrassed by her action. "You don't have to go, but you do have to apologize to Lydia. She is hurting so much already."

Theodore stood and pulled her to her feet. "Oh, Phoebe, I'm so sorry."

She nodded but couldn't say anything more. The words were stuck in the back of her throat, and to force them would surely bring on her own tears.

He seemed to realize that she needed to be alone. "I'll go right now and apologize."

Phoebe turned away. She wanted to take a few moments to strengthen her resolve before she faced everyone once again. How could she help Lydia when her own heart was so heavy? How could she possibly be what everyone needed her to be?

"Mother?"

She turned to find Gordon watching her. Phoebe smiled. "What is it, darling?"

"I heard what you said to Uncle Ted." He looked skeptical. "How can you be so nice to him after what he said about Father?"

Extending her hand to him, Phoebe waited until he came to her. "Gordon, God has forgiven me of my sins and all the bad things I've said about others. How could I not forgive my own brother for his mistakes?"

"But he hates Father."

"No, Gordon. He hates himself. He hates that he couldn't save our father from taking his own life. He blames himself. Surely you must have heard that."

"Maybe he just wanted you to feel sorry for him."

Phoebe hugged him close and began walking slowly back toward the house. "That isn't Ted's way. Besides, even if that is what he needed, I do feel sorry for him. He isn't strong in the Lord. He's been angry at God for so many years that he no longer knows how to feel anything else toward Him. Love is what he longs for, but it's the very thing he can't seem to find."

Gordon considered this for a few moments. "But you always told me that God gave His love freely. It shouldn't be hard to find."

"Maybe not, but for some it is difficult to accept. Pray for him, Gordon. Forgive him and pray that he will open his heart to Jesus. He's so very lost right now, and that must surely be terrifying."

Gordon had been her most responsive child when it came to issues of faith. He often seemed wise beyond his fifteen years, and when he promised to seek his uncle out to ask forgiveness, Phoebe wasn't surprised.

"Bitterness is a terrible thing, Gordon. We must always stand guard against it, lest we fall into the same circumstance."

"I will be careful, Mother. Just as I will continue to pray for Father and Grandfather. Sometimes my faith isn't very strong," he admitted, "but then I remember Father said that walking with Jesus is a lifelong journey. You don't see or understand everything at once. It comes in steps along the way."

Her son's reminder of Dalton's teaching touched her deeply. "Indeed it does."

Yuri wasn't at all surprised to find Britta asleep later that day. She was dozing in the rocker with Laura curled up in her lap. Careful not to wake the sleeping child, Yuri lifted Laura into his arms and took her to bed. She barely stirred. Clearly the activities of the day had been too much for her. A good nap would do them all some good.

Darya was sleeping peacefully in her crib, and Yuri couldn't help but pause a moment after tucking Laura in. He watched the sleeping infant and wondered who her father might be. She was a sweet baby—well, at least most of the time. He grinned as he thought of how she would smile at him, then laugh as if she knew a secret. Lydia shared that Aunt Zee had always said that a baby's laughter had to do with hearing the songs of angels. He wondered if it might be true.

"I'm losing my heart to you both," he whispered, casting yet another glance at Laura. "But I don't see how I can keep you."

He walked back into the front room, where Britta was still dozing in the chair. She looked so content—and so very beautiful. As a little girl, she had always seemed happy and carefree. But that was only reasonable, he thought. She had grown up with good parents who loved her. But so had he. Where had things gone so wrong for him? How was it that he had ended up a drunken gambler? His mother had loved him as much as Lydia loved Britta. She had lovingly tucked him in to bed at night and prayed with him. She had listened to his dreams and encouraged his plans. He couldn't remember a negative or cross word ever coming from his mother's lips.

His father had been firm, but loving. He and Kjell were a lot alike in their work ethics and concern about family. Why had those feelings escaped Yuri? How could he have lived with such fine examples and turned toward a life of such tragedy?

How he missed his father's encouragement

and advice, his mother's tenderness and strength. His mother was lost to him now, but what of his father and sister? Were they still living? Now that he was back in Sitka, he needed to sit down and write them a letter. First and foremost, he owed them an apology for the way he'd acted over the years. They had never stopped believing in him.

Neither had Britta.

He watched her stir. Britta Lindquist had been a godsend to his children—to him. Yet she was sacrificing a proposal of marriage, and all because of his girls. Of this, Yuri was convinced.

I can't let her give up a life of happiness.

Maybe the best thing would be to give the children up to Kjerstin and her husband as Lydia had once suggested. The girls deserved to have a family—a mother and a father who were stable and could offer them love and security.

But could I bear to break Britta's heart that way?

Chapter 12

June 1906

"Britta, we need to talk," Brenton said in his usual charming manner. "You seem to avoid me at every turn."

She sat in the yard, mending one of Laura's dresses, while Darya played on a quilt at her feet. Laura was pulling her dolls in a wagon across the grass, oblivious to the tension Britta felt. Britta shielded her eyes from the sun as she glanced upward and tried to smile.

"I suppose now would be just as good a time as any." She put aside the mending and got to her feet.

"You make it sound like a chore, Britta.

Don't you remember how you used to love our discussions? We would sit for hours, conversing over coffee or tea about everything under the sun."

"I do remember," she said quietly. "Those days seem like a lifetime ago."

"Not to me." Brenton reached out to take hold of her hand. "Britta, in case you've forgotten, it's June now. You promised me an answer to my proposal."

Britta pulled her hand out of his grasp. "I can't marry you, Brenton. It wouldn't be fair."

He frowned and moved closer. "How could it not be fair?"

"I . . . I don't want to leave Alaska," she said, unable to admit to him that she didn't love him. Despite her frustration at his unexpected arrival, she hated the thought of hurting him. "Now that I'm home, I don't ever want to leave again. I was born here, and I will die here."

"And you would give up love for a place?"

He wasn't making this easy. And while at one time she thought perhaps he held the key to her happiness, she now knew she would have to admit the truth. But instead of blurting out that she wasn't in love with him— that someone else held her heart—Britta was silenced as Brenton pulled her into his arms and kissed her with great passion.

For a moment Britta really tried to muster up feelings that matched his enthusiasm, but it was pointless. Even with Brenton's lips upon her own, she could only think of Yuri. It was his face she saw, his voice she heard whispering in her ear.

"Papa!"

Britta pulled back abruptly to find Yuri watching them from across the yard. Laura ran to him, and Yuri lifted her into his arms and began closing the distance between them. Britta knew she'd done nothing wrong, but it felt as if she'd just been caught cheating.

She quickly bent to pick up Darya. "I need to change her diaper," she said and hurried to the house before either man could say a word.

Instead of going into the cabin, however, Britta hurried up the steps to her childhood home, feeling different emotions all tangled inside her. Why couldn't Brenton just leave? Why couldn't Yuri love her? What would happen to the girls? Too many questions and not enough answers.

To her surprise, Mother sat at the table as if waiting for her. Britta looked at her for a moment and sighed. She longed to tell her everything, and it seemed that fortune or God or both had presented her with the opportunity.

She sat opposite her mother and only then realized that Darya was nodding off to sleep. It seemed that everything was perfectly arranged for their discussion. Mother smiled at her gently.

"Why can't life be simple?" Britta asked.

"I used to wonder that myself. It so often seems that for every glorious moment, there are a dozen that stand in opposition."

Britta nodded. "That's exactly how it feels."

"Are you ready to talk to me about it?"

"Yes." Britta thought about Brenton and Yuri. She glanced at Darya and then back up to her mother. "I'm in love."

"I know," her mother replied softly.

"You do?" Britta questioned and then shook her head. "No, it's not what you think. I'm not in love with Brenton."

"I know."

Britta felt as if a huge load had been lifted from her shoulders. Mother had already guessed the truth. She supposed she shouldn't be surprised, but she was.

"How?"

Lydia smiled. "Because I'm in love and recognize what it looks like."

"But how did you know it was Yuri?"

She gave a light chuckle. "Britta, you have loved him since you were a child. I had thought leaving Sitka would change that for you. Hoped it, really, because he was married."

"That was my intent, as well. When Brenton proposed and then offered me the orchestra position, I thought for sure I could make it work. I thought if I just stayed far enough away from here—from Yuri—I could forget him. But I can't. It's not just the children I love, Mother. It's him. It's always been him."

"So what are you going to do about it?"

"What can I do? Yuri's heart has a wall around it. Marsha forced him into a loveless marriage and . . ." She lowered her voice. "Darya isn't even his. Yuri has struggled all of his life to feel that he belongs, and yet he feels so alone."

Mother nodded. "I've never told you much about my marriage to Dalton's real father, and that is because it wasn't at all pleasant. My husband was a very harsh man who beat me."

"Oh, Mother, I'm so sorry." Britta shook her head. "Why was he so cruel?"

Lydia folded her hands. "I never really knew. He was determined to be the best at his business and make a vast fortune, and while doing so, he viciously eliminated anyone who got in his way or threatened him."

Britta carefully watched her mother's sad face. "Why did you marry him, then?"

"I was forced into it. My father arranged the marriage as a business agreement."

"How awful."

Her mother nodded slowly. "It truly was. However, I don't say these things in order to dwell on the bad. Rather, I want you to know that my heart was just as hard as Yuri's when it came to the idea of ever falling in love."

"What changed that? How can I help him?" Britta asked.

"Your father simply loved me, and his love wore down my defenses," Mother replied. "He was so patient with me, so gentle. I'd never known that a man could be so kind and considerate until I met your father." Tears came to her eyes. "I miss him so much."

"Oh, Mama, I do, too. I pray every day that we'll hear something, but then I find myself fearing that the news will be bad." Britta longed to go to her mother and hug her close, but Darya was sleeping so peacefully that she hated to disturb her.

"At this point, it's the not knowing that grieves me. I just don't want to be without him. He's everything to me."

Britta nodded. "I've felt that way about Yuri since he saved my life when I was seven."

Her mother fixed her with a firm gaze.

"Then you must do what you can to win him over—to help him fall in love with you. Pray that God will guide you and give you the right words to say. But, Britta, don't lead Mr. Maltese on. If you don't intend to marry him, you need to release him."

"I will, Mama. I know that I need to. I guess I just wanted everyone to have a fairy-tale ending."

"And what exactly would that entail?" she asked.

"Oh, you know, happily ever after—the hero rescues the princess. Just little things like that," Britta said in a wistful tone. "I don't think that's asking for much, is it?"

"If only it could be like that on earth. But I'm afraid we will always have difficulties here. Jesus told us that much, but He also promised to always be with us. We get our happily ever after, Britta, but it doesn't truly come until we go to be with Him in heaven."

She sighed. "I suppose you're right, Mama, but you can't blame me for wanting at least a little of it now."

———

After seeing Britta in the arms of Brenton Maltese, Yuri wasn't sure what to do. The sight of them kissing had made him feel nauseous. He wanted to take Maltese by the collar and throw him aside for imposing himself on Britta. He found himself wanting to protect her, but in truth, he knew that Britta was strong enough to defend herself.

Still, he worried that Britta truly loved Maltese and wasn't able to admit it because of the children. Knowing how much the girls loved her, he considered giving them to Britta. But that wouldn't be fair to a new bride. Besides, if she married Maltese, they would go away to England, and he would never see the girls again.

"But maybe that's the answer," he murmured.

If Britta and Maltese were to marry, they could create a family for Laura and Darya. Then again, maybe Britta wouldn't want the responsibility. She had a chance at a prestigious orchestra position, at living out a dream.

Yuri remembered times when she had soloed in the little orchestra Lydia directed. Britta could make the most amazing music and emotion pour out of her violin. It was unlike anything he'd ever heard. Even Lydia had commented that Britta had far surpassed her abilities.

"But she'd throw all of that away because of the children." He shook his head. "I can't let that happen. I won't."

The next day, Yuri found himself sanding the hull of the newest skiff, still contemplating Britta's situation, when Phoebe made her way into the shop. The lack of news about Dalton had drained her of her youth. She looked tired and careworn.

"What brings you down here?" he asked.

"Gordon said you were still working. I wanted you to know that you're welcome to join us for supper, if you like."

He shook his head. "I'm expected at home. I should have left an hour ago."

Phoebe touched Dalton's workbench and bit her lower lip. Yuri could see that she was close to tears. He moved to where she stood and put down his tools. He reached out and pulled Phoebe into his arms and held her for a long moment.

"I'm confident we'll hear something soon, Phoebe. We have everyone looking, and Lydia even hired that private investigator. It won't be long now."

"I try to keep my spirits up for the sake of the children, but it's so hard. I feel so hopeless and . . ." Her voice quivered and her body shook. "Oh, Yuri, I'm pregnant. What if Dalton is dead? What if my baby never knows his father?"

Yuri was surprised by her news, but it only served to help him understand the depth of her emotions. Not only was she facing a life without the man she loved, but she was facing the reality of having another child.

He stroked her head as he might have Laura's. "God is watching over all of the details, Phoebe. He knows exactly what has happened and what will happen in the days to come. We have to trust that He will help us through this, no matter the outcome."

She pressed her face against his chest and sobbed. "I don't know that I can go on if Dalton is . . . if he's . . ."

"Shhh. Don't even think that way." Yuri held her tight.

Movement to his right caused him to glance up, and he found Britta watching him with a disapproving frown. She turned as soon as their eyes met and hurried back out the door. Yuri fought the urge to go after her. He didn't want her to get the wrong impression and think that he was betraying his best friend's trust. Still, he didn't want to desert Phoebe. There would be time to speak with Britta later.

Britta didn't know what to think. She'd come to see why Yuri had been delayed getting home. Kay had volunteered to bathe the girls, so Britta took advantage of this and walked to town. She'd wondered if Yuri had been stalled by news about her father and brother. Instead, she found him holding Phoebe in the deserted boat shop.

Jealousy ate at her all the way back to the house. *Don't rush to judgment,* she chided herself. But it was impossible not to think the worst. If her brother was dead, it would be very natural for Yuri to marry Phoebe. He knew the boat-building business and he could combine his children with theirs to make a large family. Yuri had even been in love with Phoebe before she married Dalton.

"It would all fit so perfectly," she said to no one in particular. "The girls would have a family. Yuri would have a business and a wife. And Phoebe wouldn't have to be alone."

She was practically marching now, her anger rising by the minute. "But Dalton isn't dead. At least we don't know that he is. It's not right that Yuri should be holding Phoebe. It's not right at all."

By the time she arrived at the cabin, the girls were dressed for bed and Kay was just drying out the tub.

"Mama!" Laura said as she came running. "Kay washed my hair."

Britta smiled. "Wasn't that nice of her?"

Laura nodded and thrust her head toward Britta. "Smell me! She used lab-a-dur."

"Lavender," Kay called over her shoulder.

Britta inhaled deeply the child's scent. "Lovely." Laura beamed.

Kay put the tub away and returned to take up the wet towels. "I'll hang these on the line on my way home."

"Thank you so much. I appreciate your help."

"So where's Yuri?" Kay asked.

"He was . . . uh, busy."

"I know Phoebe said they were trying to get that cannery order completed. I'll bring some supper over for him, if you like. You can keep it warm on the back of the stove."

"No, that's all right. There's enough for him to eat right here." Her voice sounded harsh even though she hadn't meant to reveal her anger.

Kay eyed her with a raised brow. "Something wrong?"

"No. There's nothing wrong." She lifted Laura in her arms. "Is Darya already in bed?"

It was obvious Kay didn't believe her, but she didn't press Britta for information. "She is. I was just about to dry Laura's hair by the fire."

"I'll take care of it," Britta said, moving

to where Kay had already lit the stack of wood.

Kay followed her and handed her a dry towel and a brush while balancing the wet ones over her other arm. "You don't make a good liar, Britta. You may be good about keeping your mouth shut where others would be spilling their heart out, but you don't hide it well."

"I don't believe in lying."

"Then you'd better stop telling me nothing is wrong when it's obvious you're upset."

Her shoulders sagged a bit, and Britta told herself it was just because Laura was getting bigger and taking more effort to lift. Still, she couldn't look Kay in the eye.

"All right, so everything isn't perfect. Life is fraught with difficulties, as my mother is always saying. Even so, I don't want to talk about it."

Kay shrugged. "I don't guess you have to. I'll pray for you all the same." She walked to the front door. "Just like I always do."

Britta felt a momentary sense of guilt. Kay had always been a good friend to her. "I'm sorry, Kay. I don't mean to . . ." She put Laura down on the stool in front of the fire and straightened. "I'd appreciate those prayers. Maybe tomorrow I'll feel like talking."

Kay smiled. "I'll be around if you need me."

"Thank you."

Britta worked out the tangles of Laura's blond hair and nearly had the long length dry when Yuri finally entered the house. She couldn't help but look up, and when she did, she saw Yuri smile.

"Don't you two look pretty tonight."

She knew he was saying it mostly for Laura's benefit. The little girl got up from her perch and ran to Yuri. "Papa. My hair got washed. Kay did it."

"And she did a very nice job." He ran his fingers though the long waves, but his gaze was ever on Britta. "You might want to pay a visit to Phoebe."

She startled. The nerve of him bringing up Phoebe! Her thoughts must have betrayed her. Yuri put Laura down and suggested she go get a book for him to read to her. Once she'd gone, he walked to where Britta sat.

"She's losing hope. She started to cry when we talked about Dalton. She's so afraid, and though I tried to comfort her, I know you or Lydia would probably do a better job."

Britta felt ashamed of her misjudgment. She looked at the fire. "I . . . suppose . . . maybe Mother and I could take the girls for a visit tomorrow."

"I know she'd probably appreciate it. But maybe you could refrain from telling her I sent you. She's proud—just like the rest of you Lindquist women." He walked away without offering anything more. Britta felt chastised just the same. She had jumped to conclusions and not only misjudged Yuri's actions, but Phoebe's.

"Will I ever learn?" she muttered under her breath.

Chapter 13

*B*ritta looked out the window at the sound of a wagon and noted the speed with which it approached the house. Her mother was already out the door, and when Britta stepped outside to join her, she could hear Phoebe's voice yelling, "They're alive! They're hurt, but they're alive!"

Soon everyone had gathered together, hugging and crying in joy and relief. The telegram from the private investigator was passed around, and almost immediately, Lydia began questioning Phoebe and Yuri. "Don't you think we should go to them? I mean, the telegram is so brief. It only states that they were injured and should be able to travel within the month. We should go to San Francisco and escort them home."

"I don't know that they would let you into town," Brenton declared. "I'm almost certain the town is still under martial law. They might be unwilling to allow you to join the men."

"That's unreasonable. They need us," Lydia replied.

"I think we should send our own telegram," Phoebe interjected. "Let's ask the private investigator what we should do."

"That's reasonable thinking," Brenton said with a nod. "After all, he didn't say exactly where the men were. They most likely have been moved from San Francisco due to the destruction."

Mother seemed hard-pressed to wait the additional time, but nevertheless nodded. "I suppose it's all we can do. After all, we wouldn't know where to go once we arrived."

"I'm just so glad to know that they're alive and well," Britta said. "At least, nearly well." She went to her mother and hugged her again.

"It's true," Lydia agreed. "I'm not taking time to be thankful for what God has provided. I need to remember that I would have been happy just for this telegram yesterday or two weeks ago."

"Or a month ago," Phoebe threw out.

Britta moved away from the gathering to check on the cake she and Laura had made. Finding it ready to come out of the oven, she took hold of the pan with her apron. The sweet scent of cinnamon, cardamom, and cloves filled the air. Applesauce cake was one of her favorites, and this one looked to be perfect.

She couldn't help but think of what her mother had said about helping Yuri to fall in love with her. Britta had no confidence in her emotions, but she was quite strong in her beliefs about God and His plan for her life. She felt certain, now more than ever, that she and Yuri were meant to be together.

"Do you need help?" Brenton asked, coming up from behind her.

"No. I have everything under control."

Brenton started to go, but Britta stopped him. "I wonder if I might have a word with you in the woodshop."

He paused for a moment, then grinned. "But of course."

"Thank you. Go there now, if you will, and I will join you shortly." She left him and hurried into the living room, where Yuri and Lydia were standing beside Phoebe as she penned their telegram message.

"Yuri?"

He left Phoebe's side to come to her. "Is something wrong?"

"No. I would like to talk to you. I wonder if you would mind meeting me in the woodshop for a few minutes."

He glanced back at Lydia and Phoebe, then nodded. "I suppose I can."

"I appreciate it greatly. Go ahead, and I'll be right there. I just need to make certain that Kay can watch the children."Yuri nodded, and Britta left him to make his excuses.

Kay was talking to Theodore Robbins when Britta found her. It amused Britta to see her friend there, arms crossed as if standing her ground about some topic.

"Excuse me, Kay, but I wondered if you would be willing to watch the girls for a few minutes. I need to talk to Brenton and Yuri."

"It's about time," Kay replied.

Britta threw her friend a smirk. "The Lord's timing is never too early or too late."

"Yes, but a Lindquist's timing can be.This talk is long overdue."

Theodore looked at the women oddly. "Is there something I can do to help?"

"No," Britta said. "This is something I have to take care of myself." Kay was grinning from ear to ear.

"So go already. I'll go see to the girls. Laura

and Connie are on the porch still. I can see them peeking over the sides from time to time." Kay pointed. "Where's Darya?"

"Inside. She was playing on the blanket by the fireplace."

Kay nodded. "I'll go right in."

Reaching out, Britta touched Kay's arm. "Thank you. You could pray for me, too."

"Silly, I've been doing that since I first came to this family. Seemed like you needed more than most."

Britta laughed. "No doubt I did." She nodded toward Theodore. "If you'll excuse me."

Making her way to the woodshop, Britta whispered a prayer for courage. The dim light revealed Yuri and Brenton standing not far from the double door entry. Yuri was leaning casually against one of the supporting posts, while Brenton was pacing back and forth.

"Thank you both for coming here," Britta said. She paused to stop in front of them, and this brought Brenton to her side.

"What is it? What is wrong?"

"Nothing. Nothing is wrong, but it is very overdue." She stepped away to put some space between them. "I should have done this a long time ago."

"Done what?" Brenton asked. "I don't think I understand." He looked to Yuri, who only shrugged.

"First, I want you to know I care a great deal about both of you," Britta said. "And, while I love music, it's not the passion for me that it is for you, Brenton."

"But I thought—"

She held up her hand. "Please hear me out. I need to say this and be done with it. Otherwise, I might not ever have another chance, and it's important."

"Go ahead, Britta," Yuri encouraged.

Brenton nodded. "Yes, please."

Britta clasped her hands together. "Brenton, I cannot marry you. I do not love you—at least not in the way I should love my husband. I tried to give your proposal honest consideration, but by coming home, I actually did the one thing that ensured I couldn't move forward to marry you."

"But why, Britta? I know you love Alaska, but I already told you we would come back often. I promise." He went to her and tried to take hold of her hand, but she refused. "In time you would learn to love me—as you do this place."

"No, Brenton, I wouldn't. And that's why it wouldn't be fair to marry you. I've given my heart to another."

He backed away as if she'd struck him. "Who? When did this happen?"

Britta looked at Yuri. "It happened when I

was seven years old and Yuri saved my life." Now it was Yuri's turn to look stunned. His eyes widened as he took a step toward her. Britta refused to look away, although the very sight of his gentle, surprised expression made her weak in the knees.

"I love you, Yuri. I always have. It's the reason I left Sitka when you returned with Marsha as your wife. I couldn't bear the pain of seeing you two together. I thought that if I went far enough away, I would forget you—forget how I felt. But I couldn't. When Brenton proposed, I knew I couldn't say yes to him without coming home first—to see you."

She turned back to Brenton. "I'm sorry. I never meant to lead you on. This is the reason I told you I needed time, and this is also the reason I must say no."

Without another word, Britta walked out of the woodshop and kept walking until she reached the porch, where Laura and Connie were still playing. Kay was sitting in the rocker at the opposite end, bouncing Darya on her knee.

"You sure were fast," she commented as Britta retrieved the baby.

"I said what needed to be said and got out of there. Let them think on it for a while." Darya squealed in delight. "I think she approves," Britta said with a laugh.

———

Later that night Britta found Brenton waiting for her on the front porch after she and Kay returned from putting the children to bed in Yuri's cabin.

"I hope you might give me just a moment of your time," he said.

There was still plenty of light in the skies to see him clearly, but Britta almost wished it was completely dark. She felt horrible for having to reject his proposal. Brenton had been a good friend to her, and she had almost been certain that she could have made their marriage work. But it just wasn't enough.

"Of course," she said, approaching the last step.

"I'll be inside if you need me," Kay told Britta.

Britta nodded and waited for Brenton to make the next move. She hoped he wasn't going to beg her to reconsider. She couldn't bear the thought of having to deal with his pleadings.

"Please, come sit with me," he said and directed her to the porch swing. "I promise to make this brief." They sat and he continued. "I just want you to know that I will honor your wishes. I'm going back to town tonight.

I will make immediate arrangements to leave Sitka."

"I wish—"

He put his finger to her lips. "I do, too, but it's not to be. I suppose I always knew it wouldn't happen. That's why I followed you here. I wanted one more chance to convince you of my love."

"I always knew that your love was real, Brenton. It was my own heart that was flawed."

"Not flawed . . . just taken," he said, his voice full of regret. "I just want you to know, however, that if this doesn't work out for you—if you ever need me—you'll always have a place in England. I would still love to have you in the orchestra."

"Thank you, but I can't," she said. "I really wanted to forget the past, but I couldn't. I couldn't lie to you and pretend that I didn't love Yuri, and I couldn't lie to myself anymore. Now the truth is out. What comes of it is yet to be determined, but at least I don't have to live a lie."

He nodded. "I only want the best for you, Britta." He took hold of her hand and kissed it before getting to his feet. "Good-bye."

She looked up and tears blurred her eyes. "Good-bye, Brenton. Please be happy."

He only gave her a hint of a smile before he turned and walked away.

Chapter 14

Yuri found sleep difficult that night. He kept hearing Britta's words over and over in his mind. She was in love with him. Her girlish fantasies of being his wife had followed her into adulthood. They had held fast through his drunken days, his marriage to a woman he didn't love, even his fatherhood.

At first light, he got up and checked on the children. They were still sleeping, so he took himself to the front porch. To his surprise, he spied Lydia walking along the drive that led to town.

"Where are you headed this early?" he asked.

"No place in particular. I'm just walking and praising God." She turned and came up the grassy hillside. "How about you?"

"Couldn't sleep. Figured I might as well start my day. That way, when Britta does come over I can head right over to the boat shop."

Lydia smiled. "Mind if I sit with you for a moment?"

"I'd like that very much," Yuri said, offering her his assistance up the steps.

She settled into the rocker. "Aunt Zee loved this chair. I used to find her out here all the time knitting or quilting." Lydia ran her hands along the well-worn wood.

"It's one of Britta's favorite chairs, too. She often rocks Darya or Laura in it." He looked at Lydia for a moment. "Did you know that Britta was in love with me?"

Lydia didn't so much as blink. "Of course. I'm her mother."

"But why didn't she say something before now?"

With a serious expression, Lydia turned to him. "You were married. Before that, you were mostly drunk. You wouldn't have heard her."

"I suppose that much is true. Still, I always

thought her feelings toward me were just . . . well, some kind of sisterly love or admiration. I mean, I was always around when your girls were little. I just kind of saw Britta as an extension of my own family."

"I can understand that," Lydia replied. "Now that you know, however, what will you do?"

"I haven't been able to think of anything else." He turned to look beyond the porch. "Do you think it's really possible for her to have loved me all these years?"

"Of course I do. Britta has always been like that. Once she gives her heart to something, she doesn't let it go without a fight." She paused. "Yuri, I want to tell you something, but I'd like it to stay between us."

He glanced up. "You can say anything you like."

Lydia nodded. "When you came back to Sitka with Marsha, Britta cried for a week. She didn't cry in front of anyone, but I knew about it nevertheless. She would often sneak off to the woodshop or hide in her room. I could hear her, but I didn't bother to let her know, because I was afraid of embarrassing her and causing further pain. Now, I kind of wish I had. She was so completely heartbroken that you had married someone else.

She had been convinced that when you were ready, you would marry her."

"But I never led her on that way, Lydia. I swear I didn't."

She laughed, surprising him. "I know that, Yuri. I've always known your actions toward my girls were honorable. Britta didn't need you to encourage it, however. She had enough love of her own for the both of you."

For a long while, Yuri said nothing. He found it impossible to comprehend Britta's feelings for him. She was young and beautiful, talented and smart. What could she ever hope to find in a relationship with him?

Yuri got up and walked back and forth for a few minutes as he tried to collect his thoughts. "When I got hurt at the mine and came to realize God still cared about me, I had planned to come make a new start with Marsha and Laura. I didn't even know about Darya. You have to believe me."

"I do. But, Yuri, it's not important that I believe anything. You've set things right with the Lord, and you're trying to do the best for your children."

"I just don't know what to do. I don't know what I'm capable of doing."

"At times like this, prayer is the best thing you can do," Lydia offered. "God has a plan and direction for you, and He will show you, if you only seek Him."

"I know you're right. I guess this all just took me by surprise. I've honestly been thinking about giving the girls away. I was going to have you contact Kjerstin to see if maybe she wanted to take them."

"What stopped you?"

He paused in his pacing. "Well, I've found I've grown attached. Even to Darya."

"What would you like to do, Yuri?"

"I honestly don't know. These last few weeks—months—have been some of the happiest of my life. They've certainly been the most peaceful, despite my accident and learning about Marsha's death and Darya's birth."

"Maybe that tells you something right there," Lydia offered. "If you've been able to find contentment amidst conflict like this, then maybe coming home to Sitka was the right choice. I think there will always be a part of your heart that belongs here."

"And Britta?"

Lydia focused her gaze on him. "What of her?"

He shrugged. "What do I do about her?"

"What do you want to do about her?" Lydia countered. "Honestly, Yuri, you have to make these choices based on what you desire—what you believe is right for you and your girls."

He came back to his chair and slumped down. "I look at the girls and I know how very much they love Britta. Sometimes I think I should give them over to her to adopt."

Lydia didn't look shocked at his comment, so Yuri quickly continued. "She shows such tenderness with them. She truly seems to love them."

"I'm certain she does. Britta has a lot of love to give."

"Even to me, eh?"

"And that frightens you, doesn't it?"

Yuri met Lydia's warm gaze. "It does. Despite how God's working within me, I don't know that I can ever love anyone that way."

"You love Laura. I'm certain of that."

He fell silent, deep in thought. "I do love her, but . . . it terrifies me. I don't want to love her only to lose her again."

"Yuri, love isn't about living in fear. It's not about controlling the hearts of those around you. It is patient and kind. It endures and believes the very best. It never gives up. Just as Britta has never given up hoping that you would love her."

"So you think I should marry Britta? Even if I don't love her?"

Lydia shifted. "I didn't say that. I have little regard for arranged marriages of convenience or business. I want my daughter to marry for love, and I know she does love you. However, I want that love returned. She's waited for years, loving you from afar. It's been to both her benefit and misery, and frankly, I don't want to see her spend any more time and effort if you have no interest in loving her back."

Yuri remembered the little girl Britta had once been. As her mother had said, she'd waited most of her life to prove her love to him. Now she was anything but a little girl. She was a woman full grown—and beautiful.

"I care very deeply for Britta. I . . . well, I would give my life for her, just as I would for Dalton. I admire her—her kindness and her gentle spirit. I watch her caring for my girls as if they were her own, and I know she loves them."

"At first she loved them because they were yours. Now I believe she loves them for themselves. She tells me about Darya's new accomplishments like any new mother might. And she shows great pride in Laura's abilities, as well. Of course, Laura has loved Britta from the start."

"I know. She adores her. That's why

it would be hard to think of separating them."

"Could you ever love Britta, Yuri?"

Her simple question took him by surprise. "But don't you see? I do love her. I just don't know that I can love her the way a husband should. I don't know that I'm capable of ever being what she needs me to be."

Lydia chuckled. "And what might that be?"

He shook his head. "I don't even know."

"Then how can you be sure you can't be what she needs?" Lydia got to her feet. "Yuri, even I don't know what Britta needs, but I can tell you what women need in general. They need respect and love. They need to be able to trust your word and to be able to confide in you. So often, we can't care for ourselves in this world, so we need protection and provision. Britta has seen her father be those things for me, so that even though I have a fortune in the bank, we try for the most part to live frugally and stay within the means of what Kjell can earn. Britta knows we talk openly through our problems and share our dreams. These are the things I would imagine she might desire in a husband."

She looked off to the mountain before returning her gaze to him. "No matter what else you do, Yuri, please promise me you'll pray. Seek the Lord first and foremost. He will answer you, although it might not be the solution you expect."

"Lydia, would you pray for me, too?"

Turning, she smiled. "I've been praying for you for longer than you can imagine. I see no reason to stop now."

———

"I've been thinking that perhaps I could help in the shop," Theodore told Phoebe. "I realize Dalton and Kjell will be home in a short time, but surely not soon enough to see the skiffs completed for the cannery. Gordon mentioned there was still a great deal of work to be done, and I'd like to help."

Phoebe looked at her brother for a moment, appreciating how he was trying to make amends with the family. He'd even gone out to Lydia's to see if there was anything he might do to offer her assistance.

"I think that's a wonderful idea." She didn't want to hurt him by explaining that many of the jobs required special skills and training. She was hopeful Yuri could find something for her brother to do. "Why don't we go down to the shop and ask Yuri?"

Ted nodded. "I'm glad to be able to do something. Mother has been so happy sewing up a storm for your family, but I feel rather useless."

They made their way out the back door and down around the path that led to the water's edge. The boat shop had been located there since Yuri's father first started the business. Rain had made the stones on the path slippery, but Phoebe was used to the rain and had to smile when she remembered how much she'd hated it when they'd first moved to Sitka. It seemed the heavens were always anointing them with everything from a light mist to torrential downpours. This time, however, Phoebe's comfortable knowledge of the land did not serve her well. The moment she placed her foot on the stone, she knew she'd make an error in judgment. She felt the ground give way as the mud shifted. Before she could so much as reach out to take hold of her brother, Phoebe fell forward and didn't stop tumbling until she reached the bottom ledge near the water.

Ted was at her side almost immediately, but she paid him little attention. Pain ripped through her stomach, and she cried out.

"What is it, Phoebe? Where are you hurt?"

"It's . . . I'm . . ." She grabbed her abdomen and doubled over. "I'm with child," she gasped.

Her brother looked at her as though she'd

just announced the start of herring season. "What does that have to do with anything? I asked if you were hurt."

She didn't want to take the time to explain. "Just help me to the house."

"What's going on?" Yuri called as he crossed the distance between them and the boat house.

"She fell," Ted explained. "From up there." He pointed up the trail toward the house.

"I need to get to the house." A moan broke from her lips as the men helped her stand. "I don't think I can do this." She slumped against Yuri.

He lifted her in his arms. "Ted, you lead the way. Let your mother know Phoebe's hurt."

"Should I tell her about the baby?" Ted asked.

Yuri looked down at Phoebe but said nothing. She nodded. "You'd better. I may very well be losing it."

A short time later, Phoebe miscarried her fifth child. Having never experienced this before, she was strangely void of feeling. She looked at her mother and then to Lydia.

"I know I should be overwhelmed with grief, but I just feel numb."

Lydia sat beside her on the bed. "You're in

shock. Things happened so quickly that the full impact hasn't had time to sink in."

"Is this how it was for you?" she asked her mother-in-law, then glanced to her mother. Both women had experienced this sorrow, and now she had joined their ranks.

"I both miscarried and had a stillbirth," her mother said, joining her daughter on the side of the bed opposite Lydia. "Both were difficult, but the birth was worse. I had fully expected the baby to be born healthy—to live. I felt so betrayed by my own body."

"I lost my babies because of my husband's violence," Lydia told them. "I learned after the first couple of times not to expect the children to live. I forced my heart to feel nothing, but of course, that wasn't possible. I was numb for a time, but always—when I least expected it—the pain came crashing down upon me."

"Dalton didn't even know about the baby," Phoebe said. "I wasn't sure when he left, and once I knew that I was pregnant, he was missing. I suppose I shouldn't even tell him."

"I think you should," her mother said.

"I think so, too," Lydia agreed. "This was his child as well, even if he didn't know about it. You both need to comfort each other—

share your mourning. Dalton would want it that way."

Phoebe nodded slowly, then closed her eyes.

———

Yuri waited in the living room with Kay and Ted and Phoebe's children. He felt such sorrow over Phoebe's loss. He knew she loved her children, and since they'd received word that Dalton and Kjell were safe, she had started to look forward to telling him about the baby. She had, in fact, asked Yuri to say nothing to anyone until she had a chance to give Dalton the news upon his return.

"Mama will be all right, won't she?" Gordon asked Yuri.

"I think so," he replied. Seeing the worried expressions of the children, he smiled. "The fall was a bad one, but your mother is a strong woman. I'm confident she'll be just fine." He made no comment about Phoebe's pregnancy, knowing that she'd said nothing to the children.

Just then, Lydia came to join them. Rachel and Connie ran to her, while Alex and Gordon looked as if they'd very much like to do the same. Yuri and Ted got to their feet, along with Gordon and Kay. Only Alex remained seated.

"Is Mama dead?" Rachel sobbed.

"Not at all, my darlings. She is doing just fine. She's resting right now, and after a few days in bed, she'll be up and around. In the meantime, I thought since school is out, you might like to come and stay with me. That way your mother can have lots of rest."

"I'll stay here and work," Gordon told them. "But the rest of you should go and stay with Grandmother."

Rachel opened her mouth as if to protest, then hugged her arms around her grandmother. "I want to go home with you."

"Me too," Connie declared. "Then I can play with Laura."

Alex gave a quick sidelong glance at Gordon and nodded. "I'll come, too."

"Good. I can certainly use the help of a strong young man. Now run upstairs and pack your things. Gordon, you can help them. You and Rachel will know what everyone needs to bring. When you come back downstairs, you can give your mama a kiss, and we'll be on our way."

The children reluctantly left to obey. Lydia looked at Yuri. "Ted drove us here in the wagon. Do you mind driving us home?"

"Not at all. I'm happy to help."

Ted reached out to stop Yuri. "Phoebe told me I could help in the boat shop. That's why we were making our way down." He ran his hand back through his hair. "I feel like this whole thing is my fault."

"It's no one's fault, Ted," Lydia assured him. "Phoebe tried to blame herself, as well. These things just happen. I took a bad fall when I was expecting Britta, and it didn't cause . . ." She fell silent, and everyone seemed to understand.

Ted squared his shoulders. "I still want to help if I can."

Yuri nodded. "Of course you can. Just come down to the shop in the morning." He paused and gave Ted's shoulder a quick pat. "This wasn't your fault. The Lord giveth, and the Lord taketh away."

"Blessed be the name of the Lord," Lydia added.

Chapter 15

When word came that Dalton and Kjell's ship had been sighted coming into the harbor, the family was beside themselves with joy. Even Phoebe, who was still not fully recovered from her miscarriage, couldn't contain her excitement.

"Gordon and Alex, run to the dock and see how soon they will start bringing people ashore." Phoebe hurried to braid Connie's hair while Lydia helped Rachel.

"I'm so nervous," Lydia said as she tried to button the back of Rachel's dress. "It feels like they've been gone forever. I do hope they're all right. The detective scarcely gave us enough information."

"Oh, Mama, he said they had healed of their injuries. That was information enough," Britta declared. "They'll soon be here, and we can ask them all about the earthquake and what happened."

Phoebe shuddered. "I don't know if I want to hear everything."

"Me either," Lydia admitted. "Sometimes it's best not to know the details. I think I would be filled with such regret that I couldn't be there to help."

"But you were filled with regret anyway," Britta teased. "So you might as well know what you missed. But no matter, I want to hear their stories." She bounced Darya on her hip, while Laura danced around the room in a new dress Lydia had made for her. Walking to the window, Britta could see Kay and Ted out on the lawn. "Looks like your brother is sweet on Kay."

Phoebe laughed. "If his table conversations are any proof of it, then I'd say he's more than a little sweet. Of course, I think Kay is the first woman who's stood up to him in a long, long time." She released Connie, who immediately joined Laura in celebration.

"Look, Connie," Laura said, "my dress is like yours."

Lydia finished with Rachel. "You two could very nearly be twins."

" 'Cept I'm taller." Connie twirled in a circle with her arms in the air as if to accentuate the fact.

Phoebe's mother clapped her hands. "And you both dance so nicely. Like little ballerinas."

"What's that?" Connie asked.

"I shall show you some pictures of ballerinas in a book," Phoebe's mother replied. "They are wonderful dancers."

"Can I be a ballerina?" Connie asked her mother.

Just then Gordon bounded into the house with Alex at his heels. "They're starting!" he proclaimed. "The passengers are coming ashore. Aunt Evie and Uncle Josh said to come right away."

Britta looked to her nephew. "Would you go down to the boat shop and let Yuri know?" Britta asked her nephew. "He'll want to come with us to the dock."

"Sure. Then I'm going back in case they come on the first launch."

"We're leaving now, too," Phoebe assured him. "Come along, children—your father has finally come home!"

Yuri caught up to Britta when they were halfway to the dock. He took hold of Laura and found that Connie immediately took his free hand. "I like you, Yuri," Connie told him.

"He's not Yuri. He's Papa," Laura corrected.

"He's not my papa," Connie countered. "My papa is on the big ship with Grandpa."

Laura seemed puzzled for a moment, then said nothing more. Britta couldn't help but chuckle. Yuri glanced over at her with a smile.

"It's a good day," he said in a barely audible voice.

Britta couldn't agree more. "It is a good day. One of the best."

The dock was teeming with activity, for the arrival of any ship was always cause for celebration. Britta stood back with Yuri and the children while Connie joined her mother and the others to draw as close to the water as possible. She fixed the moment firmly in her mind: the sun shining brightly with only a few wispy clouds to decorate an otherwise brilliant blue sky, the breeze sending only the smallest of ripples across the water and gently rocking the boats in the marina.

Putting her hand to her forehead, Britta shielded her eyes from the sun in order to see the passengers in the approaching launch.

There at the front were her father and brother. "There they are," she announced.

Yuri nodded. "I see them."

"I can't see," Laura said.

Yuri lifted her and pointed to the boat. "See. There they are."

"Can't see," she insisted.

"I'll take her down with us if you like," Kay said, coming up from behind them with Ted at her side.

"Would you like to go down to the water with Kay?" Yuri asked his daughter.

Her enthusiasm was evident. "Yes! Yes!"

Britta laughed and Kay held out her hand. "Come along, then. The boat will soon be here."

Laura fairly danced along as Kay and Ted took hold of her hands. Britta put Darya to her shoulder and couldn't help but smile at the sight before her. It was only when Yuri began to speak that she turned and forgot the others.

"I've thought a great deal about what you said—that you love me—that you've loved me all these years."

She met his gaze, feeling rather nervous. "And?"

"Well, I have to tell you that I was surprised by it. I mean, I knew you cared about me, but I figured it was like a sister for her brother."

Laughing, Britta only uttered one word: "Hardly."

Yuri gave her a quizzical look. "You're unlike anyone else I've ever known."

"I feel the same about you."

"I don't know why. I've been nothing but a mess most of my life. And you can't begin to understand how I'm hardened by all that I've endured. And frankly . . . well, I don't think I'm at all what you need in a husband."

"Why don't you let me be the judge of that?" Britta replied as casually as she could muster. She didn't want to appear overly excited by the fact that Yuri was finally speaking of marriage.

"I just can't imagine that you know what you need, either."

She fixed him with a stern expression. "I've loved you since I was seven. I've watched you practically destroy yourself and then recover; you think I don't know my own heart?"

"Britta, you don't know what the past has done to me," he said honestly. "I don't want to love anyone, because I fear I'll only make a mess of it again."

"Liar. You're afraid you'll be hurt. Well, welcome to life. It's full of hurts but also full of pleasures, and you don't get the latter without risking the first."

He considered her statement for a moment.

"I just don't know, Britta. I think if I were to ever fall in love with anyone, it would be you." She couldn't keep from smiling, but before she could get a word out, he added, "But I just don't know how long that might take. How long are you willing to wait?"

"I'm not," she said, surprising him. She could see in his expression that this was far from the comment he'd expected. *Good,* she thought. *Let him be shocked—confused.* She shifted the baby and waited for him to speak.

After what seemed an eternity, he finally asked, "What do you mean by that? Have your feelings changed?"

"No, but I'm done waiting. I've waited for seventeen years. I think that's long enough—don't you?"

"But I didn't know you were waiting for me. I can hardly be blamed for that."

"No, but you can remedy the situation. I believe you will fall in love with me," she said with more confidence than she felt. She hoped she could gain his love—prayed he might fall passionately in love with her. But she wasn't exactly sure it would happen. Was she being naïve?

"Well, that was sort of what I was saying. Maybe in time—"

"We don't have a lot of time. The girls need a family now. They need us."

"What are you suggesting?"

Britta knew there was no going back now. "I want you to marry me, and I want you to do it right away."

His eyes widened. "What?"

"Yuri, I don't want to wait anymore. I want to marry you. If you feel you can't love me right away, then fine. We'll live platonically. We'll be good parents to the children."

"That's hardly fair to you. You deserve a husband who is madly in love with you. Britta, you're a beautiful young woman. You could have anyone."

"I want you." Her words were straight to the point. She was determined to fight this battle and win the victory. "You said if you could ever love someone, it would be me. So marry me, and let's stop wasting time."

"What if love doesn't come?"

Britta felt a momentary flash of fear. What if it didn't? Could she spend the rest of her life in a loveless marriage?

"I have to believe it will. As time passes and you see the benefits of true love, you'll let down your guard and learn to trust me." She met his blue eyes. "Yuri, I'd rather at least try than to lose you forever. If you're unhappy, then I'll let you go. I'll return home to live with my parents and raise the girls, and you can go your way. But I'll never stop loving you."

Britta left him to consider her declaration and made her way down to where her father and mother were locked in a tight embrace. "Father!" she cried as she drew closer.

He looked up and smiled. Mother pulled back, revealing the tears that stained her cheeks. Father took two awkward steps toward her and opened his arms to her. "Britta . . . oh, you're a sight for these eyes."

He hugged her, careful not to squeeze Darya too tight. "My, but this little one has grown. Look at her."

"We've missed you so much. Are you all right? How were you hurt?"

Kjell laughed. "I promise to answer all of your questions later. Right now, I just want to look at you all and enjoy the sight."

"And what a sight," Dalton said, leaning over to give her a peck on the cheek. "You are looking as ornery as ever, little sister."

"Might I say that your new scar gives you a distinguished look?" She eyed the three-inch mark across his forehead. "If you grow your hair out a bit, no one will ever notice it, and you can go back to looking like the mischievous fellow I know you to be."

They all laughed at this. Yuri joined them and he and Dalton embraced in a hearty hug.

"I didn't know you'd come back," Dalton told him.

"There's so much for us to discuss," Yuri replied. "I'll look forward to catching you up."

"Yuri has changed a great deal," Phoebe threw in at Dalton's questioning expression.

"She means I got off the hooch and got right with God," Yuri clarified.

Dalton laughed and gave him another hug. "Well, that's the best news you could ever tell a fellow." He sobered all at once. "I was sorry to hear about your wife, Yuri. Real sorry."

"It's all right. God taught me a great deal, even in that."

He turned to Kjell. "Good to have you home."

"Thanks, Yuri. I guess I owe you a great deal for taking care of my gals. Lydia said you were a godsend."

"I like to think I blessed them, even in a small way. They've been more than good to me and the girls."

"Well, you let me know if there's anything I can do for you," Kjell said with a pat on Yuri's back.

To Britta's surprise, Yuri immediately said, "There is one thing."

Everyone fell silent and looked at him.

Apparently no one had expected Yuri to seek a reward for what he'd done.

"What is it, Yuri?" Kjell asked without a hint of condemnation.

"I'd like your permission to marry Britta."

Britta's mouth dropped open. She had hoped for this but hadn't figured it would happen—at least not this soon. She flashed her stunned father a smile. "Well, do say yes. I've been waiting for this since I was seven years old. We have plans to make."

Everyone laughed, but Britta could see the concern in her father's and mother's eyes.

Chapter 16

July 1906

Amidst Fourth of July celebrations, Britta and Yuri were quietly married on her parents' front lawn. Britta had never been more pleased about anything in her life. She finally felt whole—like there had always been a Yuri-sized piece missing in her life and now it was complete.

"You may kiss your bride," the pastor declared.

Yuri looked hesitant—almost fearful. Britta smiled. She wasn't going to let him off the hook. If she was going to win his love, she needed to start now. "Well, are you going to kiss me, or am I going to have to kiss you?"

Friends and family who heard her question laughed, but Britta kept her gaze fixed on Yuri. He bent as if to give her a quick peck on the cheek, but Britta wrapped her arms around his neck and pulled him to her lips. She kissed him with seventeen years of pent-up passion, and when she pulled away, she could see the surprise in his eyes. She smiled again.

"See there . . . you lived through it."

The family came forward to wish them well, but Britta could sense her parents' apprehension. She especially hated the worry in her mother's expression. Her mother had suffered a horrible loveless marriage, and Britta was certain that she feared the same would befall her daughter.

"I pray you will be happy," Mother told her. Taking hold of Britta's hands, she held them tightly for a moment. "It seems just yesterday you were but a little girl, and now you're a bride." She shook her head and released Britta's hands as she turned to Yuri. "Please take good care of her."

"Goodness, Mother. It's not like we're going anywhere," Britta declared. "We'll just be living in the cabin down the hill—not even five hundred feet away."

"I know," her mother replied, "but things are different now."

Britta tried not to betray her concern. Mother was right. Things were very different now. She found herself wondering for just a moment if they'd done the right thing, but just as quickly, she pushed her worries aside. Of course they'd done the right thing. It was exactly what she had hoped for—prayed for.

"The food is ready," Kay announced.

"We should eat before it gets too cold," Britta said. "Come on." She took hold of Yuri's hand. "Hungry?"

He looked at her oddly for a moment. If she didn't know better, she'd almost believe it was a look of desire mingled with confusion. "Yuri?"

"I could eat," he said in a barely audible voice.

She laughed to keep from showing how nervous she suddenly felt. "Then let's not keep our guests waiting."

The picnic supper was the perfect way to end the day. The family was together, sharing not only the joy of the wedding but the return of Kjell and Dalton. Only Kjerstin and her husband were absent. There had been no time to get word to them, but a letter had come just the day before with wonderful news: Kjerstin was pregnant, and they had decided to remain where they were rather than take the mission in the Aleutians. Britta heard her mother already talking with Father about arranging a trip for when the baby arrived.

"I want to offer a blessing," Father announced as they gathered around the long plank tables. "If we could all join hands."

The party quickly fell into order, and even the children seemed to understand the importance of the moment. Britta felt Yuri's warm fingers close around her hand, and she realized how she longed for his love, his touch. She could only pray that his trust and affection for her would soon follow.

"Father, I thank you for this day and for the blessings you have bestowed upon this family. I thank you for the children you have given us and for the joy they have been. I pray you will surround Britta and Yuri, Laura, and Darya and make them a strong, loving family. Give Yuri the wisdom he needs to be a godly husband and father. Help him to seek you in all that he does. Let Britta be a godly wife—obedient and loving—always fixing her heart first on you and then on the things of this earth. Bless these children and watch over them as they grow. May Yuri and Britta always be a light to them—a light that shines your love and hope. In Jesus' name, amen."

Britta looked and saw tears in her father's

eyes. She couldn't help but drop her hold on Yuri and reach out to embrace him. "Thank you," she whispered in her father's ear. "And please don't worry."

He held her close for a moment. "I won't worry. I will pray, however."

She nodded. "I should hope so."

———

Dalton found a moment to be alone with Phoebe, away from the celebration. Standing there, looking out at the distant harbor, he couldn't help but thank God for another day with her. He hadn't talked much about San Francisco and what had happened, but now he felt the need.

"How I feared I'd never see your face again," he said, pulling her back against him. He leaned his chin on the top of her head, catching a whiff of the sweet floral scent of her perfume.

"I know," she whispered. "I feared the same thing. I was so desperate to know you were all right. I wanted nothing more than to get aboard a ship and come find you."

"That is a nightmare I'm glad you did not have to endure." He continued to hold her tight. "I didn't know the half of it myself for weeks afterward. When I saw even the briefest glimpse of the devastation, I knew that I was only alive because God clearly had ordained it. He had something yet for me to do."

"He knew I needed you—that we all needed you. Oh, Dalton, I could not even imagine how I would get by without you. The very thought sickened me, and I had to push it aside."

"You would have found a way," he said, turning her to face him. "You are stronger than you know, Phoebe. I would want to know that you could go on—that you would be strong for our children."

"Don't ask me to tell you that I would," she said, tears coming to her eyes. "Because I just don't know. I can't make that promise."

He reached out and wiped the tears that fell upon her cheek. "Phoebe, I love you with all of my heart, but I would hate to believe that you get your strength only in me. God is the one who will always be there for you. You can't expect me to do His job." He smiled and pulled her close once again. "He is your stronghold—a mighty fortress."

"I know," she admitted. "But I cannot bear the thought of being parted from you. I love you so dearly, Dalton. When I lost our baby, it was like I had lost a precious part of you. I felt I had failed you."

"Oh, my darling, you could never fail me." He took her face in his hands and gazed into her blue eyes. "I am so sorry that you had to go through such a painful experience. I'm sorry for the child we've lost, but I thank God you are all right. You didn't fail me or anyone else. I don't know why it had to happen, but I know that God will be with us. He'll see us through this sad time."

"He's given us rejoicing even in the midst of sorrow," she murmured. "You are here, and all is well." She hugged him close and gave a sigh.

In that moment, Dalton had never known greater peace. He let the minutes pass without thought of the future or the past. There was only now, only the moment.

———

"But how did you get out of the hotel?" Britta asked her father, who was surrounded by family and guests. He had been telling them about the earthquake and the aftermath.

"The hotel itself was in pretty decent shape right after," he explained. "A piece of the ceiling had come down on Dalton, which was how he got the scar on his forehead. We managed to get out of the room and make our way downstairs, but there was such pandemonium. People were hysterical. I found that opera singer I told you about—Mr. Caruso. He was clad in his robe, clutching a framed picture of President Roosevelt, trying to find his way to safety."

"Why did he have the picture?" Britta questioned.

Her father shrugged. "Who can say? Many people were clinging to items that made little sense to me. I saw one woman cradling a hairbrush and single boot in her arms. It certainly didn't seem like the kind of thing one would worry about when trying to flee, but panic causes folks to do strange things."

"So what happened next, Grandpa?" Gordon asked, intent on the story.

"Well, your father and I made our way outside, but that wasn't as good of an idea as you might think. There were so many buildings that had been weakened by the quake and pieces were constantly falling. People were running around, scared. The air was filled with dust, and at times, it was impossible to see where we were going. We had no idea what to do or where to go. I knew Dalton would need to see a doctor eventually. His head wound was pretty bad, and while I had stopped the bleeding, I knew it would have to be stitched. However, the town was in complete chaos, and there was no one who could help us."

"It sounds so terrible," Mother said, giving a shudder. "I can hardly bear to think of it."

Father leaned over and patted her hand.

"God was certainly busy that day. And the days that followed."

"But how did you get hurt?" Gordon pressed.

"We were walking around, trying to find a doctor or the hospital when an aftershock hit the city. The weakened buildings around us began to crumple and fall. It was like nothing I'd ever seen. They might as well have been made of sand. Dalton and I found ourselves buried under debris. I was knocked unconscious, and when I awoke, I knew I was badly hurt. We were blessed to have been spotted so quickly. We were only trapped for about ten hours, according to our best estimate."

"Ten hours? How awful," Britta said. "Were you in terrible pain all that time?"

"I can't lie. Both of my legs were broken, and I didn't know where Dalton was. I called to him, but he never answered. It was a terrible and fearful time for me. When they finally dug me out, I wouldn't allow them to take me away until Dalton was at my side. They found him not ten feet from where I had been, but he was so buried in debris I hadn't been able to locate him, and he was unconscious and couldn't call out. We were then moved to a place outside of the city. Someone had set up a tent hospital. Later we moved to another town. It was a long, arduous trip and I don't like to think back on it."

"But why didn't you let us know that you were all right?" Kay asked.

"I did. I gave money to a man and asked him to wire my family. He assured me he would, and I presumed he had, as he came back to see me. He even told me there had been a reply and that the family was relieved to know that we were recovering. I sent him on this errand twice more, but apparently he was only taking my money and doing nothing. I am so very sorry about that. I can't begin to imagine how you felt."

"We heard that fire destroyed a lot of the town," a neighbor interjected. "What of that?"

"The fires were bad. We were very nearly consumed by flames at one point. Remember I told you it took ten hours to get us free of the debris. Fires were engulfing the area due to broken natural gas mains. We were told that twenty-five thousand buildings were consumed by fire."

"Twenty-five thousand!" Gordon exclaimed. "I can't even imagine a place having that many buildings to begin with." He shook his head. "Just think of that."

"It's true," Father continued. "But as sad as that was, the loss of life was so much more devastating. The officials are only reporting that about four hundred people lost their lives, but the detective told us it is more likely to be in the thousands."

"Oh my," Mother said. "How tragic."

"Coupled with that was the fact that so many people were left without homes. Hundreds of thousands of people who survived the fires and the quake itself were left without a roof over their heads. All of their possessions were lost: clothes, tools, furniture, photographs. Everything."

"We must do something to aid them," Mother announced. "Surely there are charitable groups working to help the people."

Father smiled. "There are. In fact, I knew you'd want to help, so I found out about it before we left. We can arrange it as soon as you like."

Britta saw her mother give Father a tender gaze. For a moment, no one said anything, and then Mother motioned to the table. "Enough of sad stories. We are celebrating. Now, there is still plenty of food. Let's not let it go to waste."

———

Dalton and Phoebe made their way back to the party only to be stopped by her brother.

He smiled apologetically. "I wonder if I might have a word with you, Dalton."

Phoebe seemed to sense the matter's importance and pulled away from him. "You two go ahead and talk. I want to get back and check on the children."

She slipped away without another word, and Dalton found himself missing her almost instantly. He turned to his brother-in-law. "What can I do for you?"

"I've come to apologize. I don't know if Phoebe told you about the things I said or did prior to your return, but I feel I owe you an explanation."

Dalton shook his head. "No one has said anything to me."

"I figured they wouldn't. They're a good bunch, that family of yours. My sister included. I can only hope to one day be even half as good, but the truth is, I came here bearing you a grudge."

The admission took Dalton by surprise. "Me? But why?"

"I blamed you for my father's death." He held up his hand. "I know it was foolish—at least now I do—but then I was bitter and filled with hate. I had told myself all these years that if only you would have been more observant, if you would have read your letter sooner, my father might have lived."

Dalton shoved his hands into his pockets and nodded. "I blamed myself for those very things. I can't tell you the time I spent reliving every moment, wondering if there wasn't some sign I'd missed."

Ted frowned. "Truly? I had no idea." He paused and shook his head. "Well, Phoebe did mention something to that effect, but at first I paid it no heed. I am sorry, Dalton. I never realized the misery that others were going through because my own was so fierce."

"It must have been hard to lose your father at such a young age," Dalton sympathized.

"The pain haunted me for years. But I hope you will forgive me now for blaming you. It was never your fault."

Dalton sensed the man's deep regret. He reached out and took a firm hold on Ted's upper arm. "I forgive you. I also hope you will forgive me. If there was something I overlooked—something that might have made a difference, something I didn't see—I hope you will forgive me for not realizing it."

"You have nothing to be forgiven for," Ted replied. "You've only ever done the utmost for my family. I'm grateful for that, and I hope now, with this behind us . . . well, I'd like very much for us to be friends."

Dalton smiled. "Of course we're friends. But even better, we are brothers."

Ted clenched his jaw and appeared to fight for control of his emotions. Dalton didn't want to embarrass the man, so he dropped his hold and patted his stomach. "I'm still hungry. What say we go get some dessert and coffee?"

"I think I could put away a piece of pie. Or two."

Chapter 17

August 1906

Yuri watched Britta bathe Darya and marveled at her patience. They had been married a little over a month, and never once had she lost her temper with the girls—or him. In fact, despite the fact that they lived platonically, with Britta sleeping in his former bedroom while Yuri slept on a cot just off the kitchen, she actually seemed happier than before.

If only I could say the same thing.

He turned away. His life there was good, and he had no complaints where Britta was concerned. No, the fault was all his. He was the problem, just as he'd always been.

Frowning, he left the house to bring in more wood before work. His mind battled with his heart. He cared deeply about Britta—even loved her in his own way—but memories of Marsha and her trickery haunted him. Britta was nothing like his first wife; even so, he had once again married for reasons other than love.

But Britta knows the truth, he told himself. But it offered little comfort. She knew he had married her more out of a sense of obligation toward the children.

The children.

He shook his head and hoisted several pieces of wood. Laura had won his heart, to be sure. She reminded Yuri of what he'd been like as a boy. Happy, carefree, and so affectionate. His mother had once said he had been her most loving child, and he definitely saw that trait in Laura. Now that they were all living under one roof, she no longer had the nightmares or difficult bedtimes. That alone made him believe his decision to marry Britta had been a good one.

So while things were working well with Laura, Darya was another story. Try as he might, Yuri couldn't quite allow himself to love her, at least not the same way he did Laura.

It was no fault of the infant. She was a pleasant baby with bright eyes and an infectious smile.

"But she's not mine." He hadn't meant to speak the words aloud and glanced around quickly to make certain no one had overheard. He felt guilty for his thoughts. He knew it wasn't Darya's fault. Marsha had been the unfaithful one.

He couldn't help but wonder who Darya's father might be. He would probably never know. Since his arrival home, his old cronies had been more than happy to share information on Marsha's activities while he'd been absent. Perhaps they did so to entice Yuri to drink away the injustice done him, but he wasn't even tempted. He had ruined his youth with liquor. He'd hurt so many people—people he couldn't make it up to, like his mother.

With his arms straining under the weight of the firewood, Yuri made his way back into the cabin. He deposited the wood by the stove, then turned to find Britta dressing the baby.

"I'll be going now," he told her.

"Don't forget, it's Friday and we're going to have supper with Phoebe and Dalton tonight. Kay's coming with us." She grinned. "I think Ted might actually ask for her hand."

Yuri nodded. He'd heard Ted talk about it at the shop, where he'd been quite useful as Dalton's bookkeeper. "I kind of figured it was coming."

"Well, don't sound so enthusiastic about it. Some folks actually enjoy being married."

He was surprised by her comment, but quickly realized she'd spoken in a good-natured manner. "I wonder if they'll stay here on the island," he said, trying to accommodate her mood.

"I hope so. I wouldn't want to see Kay go. From my experience in the States, I doubt folks would be very accepting of Ted marrying a woman who is half Tlingit." Britta finished buttoning Darya's gown and lifted the baby to her shoulder as Laura came into the room.

"This is too hard," she declared, holding up her pinafore apron.

Yuri gave her a smile and reached out to help her position her arms. "You hold still, now, and I'll put it over your head."

Laura did as he told her, and he maneuvered the apron into place. "Now turn around, and I'll take care of the tie."

By the time he finished, Britta had secured Darya in the high chair, padding her with dish towels to help her keep upright. She gave the baby some toys to play with and was rewarded with Darya's squeals of delight as she slapped at the tray. Britta laughed and kissed the infant before turning back to the small tub of water she'd used for bathing the baby.

"Would you mind toting this out to the garden for me?" she asked Yuri. "Laura is going to water the vegetables today."

"Are you really?" Yuri asked his daughter.

Laura nodded enthusiastically. "I get to help, and you can, too."

"Your papa has to get to work," Britta said, flashing Yuri a smile.

"He's going to make boats," Laura announced as if this fact were unknown.

Yuri couldn't help but laugh. He picked up the tub and inclined his head to the right. "Why don't you open the door for me?"

Laura danced away, jabbering about something he couldn't quite make out. He glanced over his shoulder at Britta. "I'll see you later."

She nodded, but he saw a hint of sadness in her eyes. He wished he could say something to change that, but he couldn't. He didn't know how to make things different, so he walked away.

Later at the boat shop, Yuri couldn't keep

his mind on what he was doing. Thoughts of Darya, Laura, and Britta piled up one on top of the other.

"You're gonna sand that right out of existence," Dalton said, coming up alongside him.

Glancing down, Yuri could see that he was making a mess of things. "Sorry. Guess my mind is somewhere else."

"I can see that."

Yuri put the piece aside. Turning to lean against the workbench, he pushed back his hair. He wasn't sure what else to say. There had been a time when he and Dalton could tell each other anything, but now Yuri felt the distance of years and poor choices standing between them.

Dalton seemed to understand. "Yuri, I'm blessed to have you back in my life, you have to know that." He took a seat on one of the nearby stools. "Phoebe said you were very supportive in my absence. I suppose I should be jealous, but instead, I'm just grateful."

A smile spread across Dalton's face, and Yuri returned it. Other men might take umbrage at the comment, but Yuri knew Dalton meant it only in jest. Phoebe was completely devoted to her husband, and Dalton knew his trust was well placed.

"I'm glad I could help," Yuri said. Sobering,

he looked at his feet. "I appreciate that you took another chance on me."

"Speaking of which, when you feel ready to discuss it," Dalton began, "I'd like to talk to you about coming back on as my partner. I've always felt that this place should be half yours."

Yuri looked up in surprise. "How can you say that?"

"It was your birthright. After all, the place belonged to your father before me."

"But I sold my birthright."

Dalton nodded. "And I want to see it brought back to you."

"Is this because I married your sister?"

"No," Dalton answered without hesitation. "It's because it's the right thing to do."

Yuri felt overwhelmed. "I don't know what to say. I feel like such a . . . well, I don't know what to say."

"I know something is bothering you, Yuri. Why not talk to me about it?"

He could see the concern in his friend's eyes. For reasons he couldn't understand, Yuri felt compelled to let his guard down. Dalton had a good head on his shoulders and a heart for God. Maybe he was exactly the person Yuri should talk to.

"I don't know how to be a father or a husband," he confessed.

247

Dalton nodded. "I don't think anything prepares us for the task."

"I know I wasn't prepared for it with Marsha." Yuri shook his head and was silent for a time. "Marsha was never happy, and part of that was my fault."

"But she's gone now."

"Yes, but Laura is still here. Darya too, but . . ." He fell silent and stalked to the open door. "Darya isn't my child."

Dalton joined him at the door. "I guess I figured that much."

"You were always the smart one. I didn't even know Marsha was expecting again. She never told me. You can imagine my surprise when I showed up and found out that Marsha had died in childbirth."

"I can't even imagine."

For a moment, Yuri toyed with the idea of dropping the entire conversation. How could he possibly hope for Dalton to understand? Here he was, married to Dalton's little sister and father to two daughters. He should be happy. He should be quite content and willing to go forth in this new life and make the best of it.

"Do you love my sister?"

Yuri was taken completely by surprise. "That's . . . well, of course I love her. She's been a part of my life since she was born.

She's a wonderful woman and a good mother."

"A wonderful woman. Not a wonderful wife?"

"Look, just forget about it." Yuri went back to the workbench and gathered his tools. "I should finish up. We're having supper with you tonight."

Dalton put his hand on Yuri's shoulder. "Marsha was wrong for what she did, but she's gone. Your daughters need you. Both of them. Darya may not be your flesh and blood, but you are all she has."

His comment made Yuri stop and turn. "But what if I can't be what she needs?"

"Are you asking about Darya or Britta?"

He started to tell Dalton that it was none of his business, but the truth was his friend had hit a raw nerve. "I don't know, Dalton. I just don't know."

———

Britta could see that her husband was uncomfortable. He shifted several times at the table and ate very little. She wished she could know what was on his mind, but with so many people around them, it was not the time to ask.

"I hate to dampen everyone's spirits," Phoebe's mother announced, "but I suppose it's time for us to return home to the States."

"You know, Phoebe and I have been discussing that very subject," Dalton said. "We were hoping maybe you would consider staying. Both of you."

Britta exchanged a look with Kay, who was beaming. "I think that would be wonderful," Britta declared. "I know Phoebe would love having you here."

"I would, indeed," Phoebe replied. "Oh, please say you will."

Her mother looked to Ted. "I don't know what to say. I think I would like that very much, but I would never ask Ted to go home alone."

"Truth be told, I was hoping to stay," Ted said, glancing at Kay. "You see, I have something to announce. I've asked Kay to be my wife, and she said yes."

Britta clapped her hands. "That's wonderful news!"

"Oh, Kay, Teddy, congratulations!" Phoebe flashed them each a smile. "I hope you'll let us help you with the wedding plans."

Kay giggled. "Of course. I haven't any idea of what to do first."

"You've already done the best thing," Ted said, giving her a wink. "You fell in love with me." Kay blushed while everyone else laughed. Everyone but Britta.

The initial joy of the announcement faded from Britta's thoughts. Kay and Ted were obviously in love—happy at the idea of spending the rest of their lives together. She looked at Yuri, but he didn't see her. He was busy slathering butter on bread and seemed oblivious to everything else.

Britta's stomach began to sour, and she was almost happy when Darya began to fuss. "If you'll excuse me." She got up from the table and lifted the baby from the high chair. Without another word, Britta escaped to the front room. Why did such a happy occasion have to bother her so much?

"Are you all right?"

She looked up to find Dalton watching her closely. "I'm fine." She turned back to the baby. "She's wet."

"Britta, something is bothering you. You haven't seemed yourself lately."

"I'm fine, really." She focused on Darya's smiling face. "I've just been so busy lately."

"Mother told me you gave up an important position playing violin in England."

"It wasn't right for me. I didn't want to go so far away." She finished changing the baby and straightened. "I'm happy with the choice I made."

"Truly? You used to be happy playing the violin, too." He seemed to look deep into her soul. "Mother says you haven't played once since your return to Sitka."

"Children take time, and I find that I prefer caring for them to sitting alone playing a serenade." She lifted the baby. "I love being home, and I adore Darya and Laura. They make me very happy."

"And Yuri?"

Britta raised a brow. "What about him?"

"Are you happy with Yuri?"

"Of course. You know I've loved him most of my life." She tried to sound matter-of-fact, hoping Dalton would let the subject rest. "Honestly, Dalton, you worry too much."

"I just want you to be happy," he said softly. "I care about you."

Britta felt her breath catch. If she wasn't careful she'd start to cry. "I care about you, too. Just stop worrying. Now, come on. We should join the others."

He reached out to stop her. "Britta, ignoring a problem won't make it go away."

"Neither will dwelling on it," she snapped back. She handed Darya to him. "Here, would you have Kay watch her while I put this diaper to soak?"

Dalton took the baby in his arms but refused to leave. "Britta, I can see that there are problems between you and Yuri."

"Why? Has he said that?"

"No, but you two are hardly very affectionate with one another. You don't seem happy."

Britta let her guard drop just a bit. "Marriage is hard work. You know that. We're still trying to adjust to each other and to having a family."

"Is that all?" Darya reached up to pull on his lip, and Dalton pretended to bite at her hand. The baby laughed and grabbed for his ear.

"Look, I don't want to talk about this. Yuri and I have to work through some things, but it's no one else's business." She turned back to retrieve the diaper. "Please just let the matter go. I'm sure in time, everything will fall into perfect order." At least, she prayed it would.

She was glad that Dalton didn't offer any other thought on the situation. It was hard enough to keep her own disappointment at bay. Thinking about how difficult her marriage was—how unloved she felt, how much she longed to be Yuri's true wife—was enough to destroy any hope Britta had at happiness.

She'd made her choice—had practically forced Yuri to marry her. For the sake of the girls, she had to make this work. She just had to.

Chapter 18

*B*ritta found it impossible to sleep that night. She tossed and turned and finally gave up just as she heard the clock strike two. *What if I did the wrong thing? What if marrying Yuri went against God's will for me?* She couldn't imagine how that could even be possible. She loved Yuri, and he did care for her. Laura and Darya needed them. How could it be wrong?

Yet ever in her mind was the example of Kay and Ted marrying for love. They were giddy, and everyone knew how much they enjoyed each other's company. Britta pushed back the covers. She and Yuri acted more like business associates than lovers.

"But that's because, in Yuri's eyes, it is nothing more than an arrangement to care for his children," she said, pulling on her robe. The very thought pierced her heart.

She went to check on the girls and found them sleeping soundly. There was a definite chill to the room, however, so Britta stirred up the embers in the stove and added more wood. She checked once more on Darya. Such an innocent. Britta gently touched the baby's brow. One day she hoped she might have her own baby. Not that she wouldn't treat Darya and Laura both as her own. Hugging her arms to her body, Britta tried to imagine just for a moment what it would be like to carry a child in her body. The wonder of it caused the aching in her heart to increase.

She tiptoed from the room and started to head back to bed, then decided instead to step out for a breath of fresh air. The wooden floor creaked as she made her way to the front door. She hoped Yuri would sleep soundly and not notice that someone was moving about.

Outside, the cold damp air did nothing to ease her loneliness. A misty rain fell, making it impossible to leave the porch. Not that she would have wanted to venture far. There was no telling what might be lurking.

Leaning against the porch rail, Britta couldn't shake a strong sense of guilt. Dalton must have known more than he was letting on. Yuri probably had told him how unhappy he was. Maybe he'd even said that Britta forced him into marriage just as Marsha had.

Of late, that thought had started to bother Britta a great deal. Had her insistence to wed been any different than that of his first wife? They both were after something they wanted. Britta tried to soothe her conscience with proof of how her desires had all been self-less, but she knew it wasn't true. She'd had her motives, just as Marsha had.

The previous Sunday their pastor had spoken on not making a promise to God that you didn't intend to keep. He quoted a Scripture that had drawn Britta's attention. She couldn't remember where it was from or exactly how it went, but it had something to do with how it was better for a person not to make a vow to God at all than to make one you didn't intend to fulfill.

She had made a vow to God, along with Yuri, when she'd married. She had pledged to them both that she would love and honor and obey. Was she miserable and lonely now because of such a false promise?

"But I meant the words I pledged," she

murmured. Maybe Yuri hadn't, but that wasn't her fault. Or was it?

"Is something wrong?"

Yuri's voice startled her. She turned to find him standing in the doorway. She couldn't see his face, but his voice bore concern.

Britta tried to sound nonchalant. "I just wanted some air."

"Kind of cold out here."

She nodded. "Sometimes that clears my head. I'm sorry if I woke you."

He came to stand beside her. "Britta, if something is wrong, I would hope you could talk to me. After all, we were friends long before we . . . married."

What could it hurt to talk? But just as she considered that, a horrible thought came to mind. What if in talking about her feelings of loneliness and longing, Yuri decided they should have the marriage annulled? It would be just like him to want to set her free to pursue love.

"Britta, do you regret our marrying?"

She was surprised that he would ask such a question. It was as if he had been hearing her restless thoughts. "I could never regret marrying you, Yuri. However, I fear that you regret marrying me."

"I suppose I have some regrets," he admitted.

Her heart sank. She chided herself for ever getting out of bed. If she'd just stayed in her room, she wouldn't have to face this conversation now. The feelings of hurt spread out and wrapped around her like a blanket.

"I figured you did," she said. "I suppose I shouldn't blame you. After all, I'm no better than Marsha."

"How can you say that?"

He sounded almost angry, and Britta backed away a step. "I imposed a marriage on you that you didn't want. I used the children to convince you of the merit, just as she did with the announcement of her pregnancy. You didn't want to marry her, and you didn't want to marry me." Britta was glad the night was dark so Yuri couldn't see the tears that flooded her eyes and slowly slipped down her cheeks.

"But I also regret making you so unhappy," she continued.

"You have nothing to do with that," Yuri countered. "I've made a mess of my life, but it had nothing to do with you."

"But I'm only adding to that mess."

"Britta, you're the only semblance of order in my life. I just feel bad that you're struggling to make this work, and I'm completely clueless as to how I can help. I don't even know my own mind very well, much less my heart.

I have so many regrets. I did a lot of things to hurt myself and others. I can't just pretend that I didn't."

" 'All have sinned, and come short of the glory of God,' " she countered. "Your sins are certainly no worse than mine. Oh, the consequences might be different, but without Jesus, we're all wretched messes."

"But some of our messes are more public than others, and people have long memories."

"Don't worry about what others think, just work on your own heart. That's what my mother always said."

Yuri shifted and eased back against the rail. "I miss my mother. I hate how much I ended up hurting her. She knew I was suffering, but she never stopped caring about me—or loving me."

"Then we have that in common," Britta said without thinking. "I've never stopped loving you."

"Britta . . ." He fell silent.

"Yuri, I know this situation is difficult for you. I won't pretend it isn't hard for me at times," she began, "but I want to make it work."

He said nothing, and Britta didn't know what to do. If she continued talking, he might not speak his heart. But if she said nothing, he might leave, thinking she wasn't interested.

But then, almost as if her body didn't need her permission, Britta drew closer to Yuri and reached her hands up to his neck. She let her actions do the talking and pulled his head down so that her lips might touch his. Britta had only intended a brief, heartfelt kiss, but instead she found herself lost in a passionate display. By the time she realized how much she'd betrayed in that single action, she was too shaken up to say another word. Instead, she hurried back to her room and locked the door behind her.

Yuri felt the strange sensation of desire stir through him at Britta's kiss. He found himself wanting to talk with her, but she left before he could find his voice. He wanted to go after her—to kiss her again and see where things led, but he couldn't move.

"What do I do?" he asked the night air.

How could he risk his heart when he'd never understood love to begin with? His parents had loved him unconditionally. He'd grieved and hurt them, but they continued to love him. On his mother's deathbed, her thoughts had been of her love for him and her hopes that he might realize God's love, as well.

"But it makes no sense. How can I be loved when I've done so little to deserve it? In fact, maybe I've done nothing at all."

It was at times like this that he missed Morris James the most. If the wise man could be with him now, he might explain in full all of the questions that rose up to haunt Yuri. Questions that seemed to stand as sentinels, guarding against feeling or thinking too much.

"God, I don't know what to do. I don't know how to feel without hurting, and I'm tired of getting hurt and hurting others."

He pushed the hair back from his face and felt dampness on his cheek. At first he thought it was rain, but then he realized it must have been Britta's tears. Why was she crying?

Staring at the house, Yuri remembered her saying she felt guilty. Did she honestly think she had forced him into marriage? Didn't she know him well enough to realize he was strong enough now not to be forced into anything?

"What's wrong?" Kjell asked, lighting the lamp.

Lydia turned from the window and shrugged. "I'm just worried for Britta and Yuri."

"Why?"

"Because they're struggling," she said matter-of-factly. "They married for the wrong reasons, and I fear it's catching up with them."

"They'll have to be the ones to work it out," he replied. "All we can do is pray for them."

"But I wish she would talk to me about it," Lydia admitted. "I know she's hurting. But she's much too proud. She's convinced herself that she can deal with it alone."

"Hmmm, sounds like somebody I know."

Lydia smiled. "I might have been that way once, but not anymore. You know that I talk to you about everything."

Kjell edged up in bed to lean against the headboard. "You're a strong woman, Liddie, but you have to let go of Britta and let God have her. He'll work the details out."

"What if Yuri never loves her? What if he begins to blame her for making him marry her?"

He laughed. "Do you honestly think that's what happened?"

"Well, I know it wasn't a passionate love affair that brought them together. Britta was worried about the children, and since she cared deeply for Yuri, it seemed only fitting to suggest marriage."

"And you think Yuri just went along with it because there was nothing else to be done?"

"Well, I suppose I do. It wasn't like he had a lot of options; after all, there were the children to think of."

"I thought you told me that Yuri had considered letting Kjerstin and Matthew have the girls. You even mentioned telling him that they could remain with Britta."

"That's true enough."

"So, he had options. He didn't have to marry Britta."

"I suppose not." Lydia considered this for a moment longer. "But they're living platonically. They aren't intimate. It's as if they've constructed a thick wall between them."

"Then they will have to be the ones to scale it. You can't do that for them. We had to scale our wall, didn't we?"

She smiled. "I suppose we did. I guess I would like to keep my child from experiencing the same misery I had in my first marriage."

"But Yuri isn't Floyd Gray. He's nothing like him, in fact. He's good to Britta and the girls. Give it time, Liddie. Give them time to get to know one another and realize that love is sometimes borne out of the strangest moments."

"Like being rescued from the side of a mountain ledge?" she asked.

He nodded. "Or taking the responsibility for someone's children."

Lydia came to Kjell's side and sat beside him. "When did you get to be so smart?" she asked, reaching up to gently touch his weathered face.

"I've always been smart," he declared. "I'm a Swede."

"You're also Russian," she teased.

"That just means that I can dance." He grinned and pulled her into his arms.

———

Britta awoke late the next morning. A moment of panic filled her as she considered all that would need to be done in starting her day. She dressed quickly, then pulled on her boots and began to secure the laces.

Through the closed door, Britta could hear Laura laughing and Yuri talking. Why hadn't he come to wake her? Perhaps he figured her late hours the night before had done her in. Then again, maybe he was embarrassed by the kiss they'd shared.

She frowned and went to the door. If he was ashamed that his wife had kissed him . . . well, that was just too bad.

In the kitchen she found Yuri and Laura making flapjacks. Darya was secure in the high chair, completely intrigued by a pair of wooden spoons she had been given to play with.

"Good morning. You should have gotten me up," she said in greeting.

Yuri glanced up from the stove. "We decided to make breakfast."

"Mama!" Laura jumped off the chair where she'd been helping her father. "Come see. I made you food."

Britta laughed at the child's enthusiasm. She allowed Laura to pull her to the table. "See?"

The plate at Britta's place was covered with several rather sorry-looking cakes. She smiled. "They look . . . wonderful."

Yuri shrugged with a grin. "It's my one and only contribution to the world of cooking. Used to eat these for every meal of the day when money was really tight."

"I'll bet they taste great." Britta took her seat. "Looks like you have everything well under control."

Yuri brought the last of the flapjacks to the table and joined her. Laura climbed up on her chair and folded her hands together as she always did at each meal. Britta bowed her head and breathed a sigh of relief. Yuri seemed just fine this morning. He didn't appear embarrassed or concerned about what had happened the previous night.

"Amen."

Britta looked up rather sheepishly to realize she hadn't kept her mind on the prayer. "So what are you planning today?" she asked Yuri.

"Fishing. I hoped you might come along with the girls."

She hadn't been fishing for a very long time. "That sounds like fun. I can pack us a picnic, too."

"Your father and mother are planning to join us. In fact, it was your father's suggestion. He was over here just about twenty minutes ago. I told him yes. I hope that's all right."

Britta nodded but said nothing. She had been avoiding private moments with her mother, for fear she would feel the need to pry into Britta's well-being. Perhaps with the girls there, as well as her father and Yuri, Britta's mother would refrain from getting too personal.

I hope.

Chapter 19

September 1906

The fall was bringing many changes to the island. With the government and capital moving to Juneau, many Sitkans worried that it would sound the death knell of their little town. Other citizens were happy to see the government eliminated from their community, hoping the loss would prove to bring more freedoms.

Of course, legal authorities would remain in place. The navy would keep a force at the coaling station on Japonski Island just across the harbor, and the marines would continue on Baranof Island for protection purposes, but daily life was bound to change. Some said that supplies would be harder to get as the ships were bound to forgo stopping at Sitka and move right on to Juneau. Lydia hoped that wouldn't be the case, however. Perhaps she and Kjell would have to look into starting their own shipping company.

She couldn't help but remember Kjell chiding her to not fear change, but she couldn't help it. Change usually brought about some kind of discomfort, and even in good situations, there were bad moments of adjustment.

For Lydia Lindquist, it seemed she'd watched a lifetime of changes. When she'd first arrived in Sitka, the city was barely three years under American rule. The Russian influence was still quite heavy, despite many of the Russian families having departed. Now, though the Orthodox Church remained, other Russian effects were gone.

She had seen the coming of Sheldon Jackson and his school for the Tlingit natives. She'd watched the various missionary battles for the souls of the native peoples, as well as an influx of Americans who had come in search of yet another gold rush. A lot of factors had gone into shaping Sitka into what it had become.

Lydia couldn't help but think of Aunt Zerelda. Her aunt had been such a dynamic woman, coming to Sitka long before the

American purchase to act as a nurse to a local family. She was the bravest woman Lydia had ever known. It was hard to imagine leaving everything behind for an unknown island. But Zee's love of Sitka easily dispelled fears and concerns. It was her love of the island that had drawn Lydia to this place—had allowed her to dream of one day being free of Floyd Gray and his children. She had found peace there— peace that had allowed her to heal from the horrors of her past.

"You look happy," Kay said, coming into the kitchen. "What's going on?"

Lydia laughed. "Nothing, really. I was just thinking about my life here and how much I've enjoyed it." She looked at the young bride-to-be. "So how's the dress coming?"

"It's nearly done. Good thing, too. There's only a week left before we marry." Kay picked up a scone and nibbled at the edge. "Phoebe and her mother are helping me with the wedding lunch, but otherwise I just want to keep everything simple."

"I think that's a good idea," Lydia replied. "I hear that Ted is planning a little trip to Mount Edgecumbe for your wedding holiday. I thought it too cold, but Kjell assured me you'd find ways of keeping warm."

Kay giggled. "I have a few ideas." The clock chimed the hour, and Kay turned to go. "I promised Britta I'd take care of the children while she went to town. I'd better get a move on."

"Have fun. I know that Laura will probably expect you to give her another sewing lesson. She ranted and raved all about the last one."

"Today we're going to sew buttons onto cloth. Should be fun."

"Just make sure she doesn't decide to eat any of the buttons."

Kay nodded. "I will."

Lydia finished cleaning the kitchen, then hurried upstairs to put clean linens on the bed. She had barely managed to strip away the old sheets when a knock sounded at the front door.

Making her way downstairs, Lydia pulled open the door without even bothering to glance through the window at who might be visiting. To her surprise, the image of her dead husband, Floyd Gray, greeted her.

"Hello, Lydia. I would imagine you are surprised to see me."

"Marston." Her heart pounded. He could have been his father's twin. She felt her heart skip a beat at the horrifying memory. "What do you want?"

He took off his hat to reveal a head of white hair. "I've come to make amends."

"I'm not interested." Her voice was without emotion. "Please go."

Marston smiled. "Lydia, I'm nearly seventy years old. I certainly can do you no harm. Won't you please just hear me out?"

She narrowed her eyes. "For what purpose?"

"The purpose of letting an old man set things right before he meets his maker."

Lydia shook her head. "You cannot make the past right. There is nothing that will change what you did to me—to my family." Her hand went involuntarily to her shoulder, where her high neckline hid the scar that she'd received that night, so long ago.

"I realize I cannot undo the things I did; however, I would like you to know how very sorry I am."

"I don't believe you, Marston. You've never done anything without a deliberate reason—a reason steeped in selfish ambition."

"I haven't seen you in over thirty years, and you can't find it in your heart to allow that I might have changed?"

She considered this for a moment. The man was certainly no threat to her—that much was right. He looked as though a good wind might knock him over. He was leaning heavily on a cane, and his clothes hung on him as if he'd recently lost a great deal of weight.

"I will allow you to come inside and tell your tale," she finally said. "But then I want you to leave the island and never return."

"I want to apologize to Dalton and Evie, as well."

Lydia met his eyes. She nearly shivered at the memories of Floyd's anger and Marston's betrayal. Forcing herself to be strong, she nodded. "Very well." She knew her son could take care of himself, and Josh and his boys would never let anything happen to Evie.

"What a lovely fire," Marston said, plodding methodically toward the hearth. "I fear I'm chilled to the bone." To Lydia's frustration, he took a seat in her rocker. "Ah, this is much better."

For a moment, she thought of offering him tea, then decided against it. Such an invitation would only prolong his stay.

"How did you get here?" she asked, taking the chair opposite him, where Kjell usually sat.

"A man named Dober-something was heading out this way and offered me a ride."

Lydia knew Carl Dobermeier well. He worked at the Sheldon Jackson school. "Very well. Will he return for you?"

"I don't think I have the luxury of that," Marston said. "But I can walk, so do not fear that I will impose on you."

She said nothing. Memories flooded her mind—things that she had thought to have buried long ago. Why couldn't the past stay at rest like those who had died?

"Your operating team has done a good job with the casket company," Marston offered.

Perhaps he thought flattery would put her at ease. "It is none of your concern, and certainly no reason for your visit." Lydia's words were firm. She folded her hands in her lap and fixed him with a stare. "I have other things to do, so if you wouldn't mind getting to the point, I'd be grateful."

"Liddie, I'm going to take the dresser in to Dalton," Kjell announced, bounding into the house. He stopped at the sight of the old man. "I'm sorry; I didn't know we had company."

"Kjell, Marston Gray has come to make amends," she said, relaxing at the sight of her husband. Although he was a year Marston's senior, he didn't look it. Kjell was still well muscled and quite healthy, whereas Marston looked to be wasting away.

"Gray," Kjell said. He came to stand beside Lydia's chair.

"Mr. Lindquist. I wish this could be under better circumstances," Marston began. "I know I'm not welcome here, but I felt I had to come. You see, the doctor believes I will be dead in six months' time. He suggested I get my affairs in order, and this seemed to be the only thing I'd left undone."

"You're dying?" Lydia asked. "Of what?" She still didn't believe a word that came out of his mouth.

"It's a cancer," he replied. "But that isn't important. What is important is that I show you my humble apologies and make restitution for the pain and suffering I caused."

"I don't want your apologies or your restitution," she snapped. "You certainly have gall coming here. You try to murder my aunt and me, and then take my son. You left me . . ." She fell silent, not wanting to give him any power over her. The truth was, she had spent far too much time looking over her shoulder, wondering when he might reappear.

Kjell put his hand on her shoulder to comfort her. Lydia tried to calm her spirit. Marston could no longer hurt her. He was nothing more than an old ghost.

"I know the things I did were awful. You must believe, first of all, that I never intended for either of you to be killed. I simply wanted time to escape with Dalton. It was wrong, I know now, but then it seemed reasonable."

"Reasonable? How could such an act ever be reasonable?"

"I thought you were quite mad and feared

Dalton could be in harm. You left a comfortable situation where you were well set and could get the medical care you needed for your pregnancy; yet you headed to an isolated island in the northwest. What was I to think?"

"Please don't pretend to have been concerned with my health or well-being. We both know you wanted to take Dalton so that you could somehow keep your father's fortune."

Marston lowered his face. "Of course, that is true, I'm sorry to say. Greed drove me to despicable choices. Still, I reasoned that I was doing a good thing for Dalton. I honestly thought he'd be better off being raised by his father's sons. He deserved to know about his heritage."

"A heritage of merciless beatings, betrayal, and murder? That's not exactly the kind of life I wanted for my son," Lydia countered. "Your father was evil—plain and simple. Do not insult my intelligence by suggesting otherwise."

"I do not mean to insult anyone," he replied. "I came here to apologize. You are right; I cannot undo what has happened. But I do want to make restitution. I have amassed a small fortune of my own. I never married, and I want to leave it to you and Dalton and Evie."

Lydia didn't know what to say. This certainly

wasn't the heart of the man she'd once known Marston to be. "I don't need your money. It doesn't change what happened."

"I didn't mean to imply that it would. I thought I already said that."

"Then you've had your say. . . ."

For just a moment, Lydia thought she saw anger in his eyes, but it passed in a flash and was gone. Marston once again seemed nothing more than a contrite old man, settling his earthly affairs.

"I suppose then I will make my way back to town to speak with Dalton and Evie. I was rather hoping we could go together. I didn't want to frighten my sister."

Lydia got to her feet and looked to her husband. "Perhaps Kjell could take you, but I want no part of it."

Marston struggled to stand. The cane kept him balanced, but he briefly seemed to totter. The years had taken their toll. Then again, perhaps it was the sickness.

"I'll go with him," Kjell said. "There is no sense in Evie having to face him alone, in case Josh and the boys are off cutting logs."

"I have a better idea," Lydia interjected. "Why don't you take him to the hotel? Then you can speak to Evie and Dalton alone. We can send word back to you, Marston, when they are ready to meet with you. That seems the kindest thing you could do."

Marston nodded. "I suppose it would be." He took up his hat and shuffled to the door.

"I believe I will come to town with you," Lydia told her husband. "It's only right that I be there for Evie."

———

Yuri was surprised when Dalton approached him. "I wonder if you would take a walk with me," his friend asked.

"Sure." Yuri took off his work apron. "Is something wrong?" He could see by Dalton's expression that he was upset.

Neither one said a word as they moved away from the shop. Yuri couldn't imagine what had happened to disturb his friend on such a beautiful day. A crisp morning breeze blew over the water, while sunlight danced on the surface. It was a perfect morning. When they were well out of earshot of the other workers, Dalton stopped.

Yuri could see that his friend was upset. "What's wrong?"

"Do you love my sister?"

"Why are you asking this again?"

"Do you love Britta?" Dalton's tone grew irritated. "It's not that hard of a question, Yuri."

Taking a deep breath, Yuri sat down on a nearby rock. "Please tell me what this is all about."

"Phoebe told me that you two married out of nothing more than convenience for the children. I want to know if that's true."

"In part, it is. Britta felt that the girls needed a mother and father under one roof. She suggested we marry, and eventually I agreed."

"Eventually? What's the matter? Isn't my sister good enough?"

"She's too good. That's the problem. She deserves much better than me." This seemed to dispel Dalton's initial anger. "Look, Dalton, the arrangement is between Britta and me. You don't need to be in the middle of it."

"Maybe not, but I care about my sister's happiness. You made a pledge before God to also care about it. You promised to love her, and I want to know why you don't."

"I never said I didn't love her."

Dalton looked at him in disbelief. "You let her cook and clean and care for your children, but you offer her no tenderness—no comfort. How lonely she must be."

"I'd like to make things better for her, but I don't know what's best. Do you suppose I should annul the marriage and set her free?"

Dalton's expression was one of shock. "I

do not. What's wrong with you? How can you even suggest such a thing?"

"I want her to be happy."

"And you don't think she can be happy with you? Good grief, man, she loves you. She lost her heart to you long ago. Phoebe said she's never seen anyone so completely devoted to another person. Britta would stay married and loveless for the rest of her life if it kept her close to you."

"But I want better than that for her."

"So do I," Dalton said, coming to stand in front of Yuri. "That's why I'm here. Why can't you allow yourself to love her?"

Yuri shook his head. "I do love her. Maybe more than I even realized. Still, I'm afraid. I don't want the past to repeat itself in this marriage."

"Then don't let it. My sister isn't Marsha. She didn't trick you into marriage. She may have initiated it, but she didn't force you to do anything you didn't want to do. There had to be a reason it appealed to you."

He considered that for a moment. "Britta never turned against me for my mistakes or expected too much of me. She accepts me just as I am. She doesn't try to change me, but rather encourages me."

"Who could ask for more in a wife?" Dalton

said with a smile. "And she is pretty. You have to admit that much."

"I never said she wasn't. Her beauty isn't the problem. I am. I have all these doubts that I can be what she needs me to be."

"Well, so do I—with Phoebe. I always worry about being what she needs. That's just the way it is. Those doubts cannot rule our hearts, however. You know what you need to do, Yuri?"

He shook his head.

Dalton grinned. "You need to court your wife. You need to let go of your fears and give her your heart."

"What if it's too late? What if she decides she doesn't want it?"

Dalton laughed heartily. "You really don't know my sister at all."

Chapter 20

D alton stared at his mother in disbelief. "Here? My brother is here?"

"I'm afraid so. We went to tell Evie first." Lydia glanced at his sister. "I didn't want Marston surprising her as he had me."

"Why has he come?"

"He says he's dying. He has come to make restitution." Her words were flat and lacked the compassion she so typically held for others. Lydia could see the disbelief in her son's eyes. She couldn't blame him; she felt it herself. Could Marston be telling the truth? Was it that simple?

"Where is he?" Dalton questioned.

"Kjell said he took a room at the hotel," Evie offered.

"Well, I suppose I should go and speak with him," Dalton said, getting to his feet.

"You don't have to do that," Lydia told him. She got up as well, but not nearly as fast. The ache in her hips brought on by the rainy weather caused her to move more slowly. She straightened and met Dalton's blank expression.

"Dalton, it's not necessary. He can't possibly expect you or any of us to believe him. He's caused this family too much harm. Just because he says he's changed—that he's here to make things right—doesn't mean we should listen to him."

"While it is difficult to believe that Marston could have changed," Evie began thoughtfully, "I know God is capable of working to recreate anyone. I will go and hear him out. He can't hurt me anymore."

Dalton nodded. "I'll go with you. The sooner we hear what he has to say, the sooner he will leave. I can't imagine he'll want to remain in Sitka any longer than is necessary. Once we hear him out, hopefully he will depart."

"I think you're both making a mistake," Lydia said, crossing her arms. She didn't want her son to have anything to do with the man, but she could hardly stop him. "Marston Gray may be old, but mark my words: He hasn't changed. I can feel it when he speaks to me." She turned to her husband. "You once told me that such uneasiness was often the Holy Spirit's way of helping us to recognize evil."

"That's true enough, Lydia, but I agree with Dalton. If you go to him collectively and stand up to him, perhaps he will say what he has to say and return to Kansas City."

Lydia felt as if they'd all turned on her. Though she knew that what her husband said was probably true, she didn't like giving Marston even that much room to maneuver.

"I'll do whatever you suggest, but I won't trust him," she finally said.

"Nor will I," Dalton agreed. "I didn't suppose we should trust him, Mother." He reached over and gave her shoulder a squeeze. "He cannot hurt you anymore."

She met her son's gaze. "He can if he hurts you."

Dalton smiled. "He can't hurt me—not if I don't let him. I am not a fool."

"He says he wants to leave us his fortune," Lydia said.

"We don't need his money," Evie said. "We'll tell him to leave it to Jeannette or

Mitchell. After all, they're likely to be the ones who'll oversee his funeral expenses. That would be the appropriate way to manage the matter."

An hour later, they were suggesting just such a thing to Marston. He looked at them and shook his head. "My funeral has already been arranged and paid for. Jeannette's husband would only drink my money away and waste it on those drunkard sons of his, and Mitchell agrees with me that the money should be given to you three."

He eased back in his chair. "I realize this makes you uncomfortable, and that was never my intention. My lawyer had suggested I simply leave the money to you in my will, and he could send a letter of explanation. I suppose that might have made it easier, but you know me. I was never one to do what was easy."

"Yes, we do know you." Evie's voice dripped with sarcasm, but Marston took it in stride.

"I know that I don't deserve your kindness—"

Dalton raised his hand to interrupt. "No one here wishes to remember the pain of the past. However, that doesn't mean we are inclined to forget and trust you again."

"Nor would a reasonable man expect you to," Marston said, nodding. "That would be completely irrational—even foolhardy. No, I don't come seeking trust or kindness even. I merely wanted to extend the olive branch. To do what I could in the sight of God and man to make restitution."

Watching his older brother carefully, Dalton tried to figure out what he was really doing in Sitka. Like his mother, Dalton didn't trust Marston Gray. There was something that just didn't seem right.

"Tell us about your sickness," Dalton requested. "What exactly is wrong?"

"The doctor believes it to be cancer of the stomach," Marston replied without blinking. "It has caused me a great deal of weight loss and much pain." He glanced at Lydia and Evie. "I'm sure that news must please you."

"Stop it," Dalton protested. "No one here wishes you such a fate."

Marston shrugged. "I don't hear either of them saying so, but I'll take you at your word. Anyway, the disease is progressing quickly. Every day I find myself weaker than the day before. Realizing my time is short, I felt it important to seek you out. Whether you believe that or not, it is the truth."

"Well, now you've come and shared this

with us," Evie stated. "You know how we feel about your money, so take it and go back to Kansas City."

Lydia nodded and got to her feet. Kjell and Dalton did likewise, but Marston remained seated. He looked at her apologetically. "You will forgive me for not rising. I'm afraid my strength is played out from visiting you earlier."

She turned away without a word. Dalton could see that his mother was deeply troubled by the encounter. He hoped his father would take her home and get her as far from Marston as he could. It was obvious the man still had the power to hurt her.

Evie rose and turned to Marston once more. "You really should return to Kansas City. At least there Mitchell's family might care for you in your final days."

Dalton saw his brother's face contort as if he were wrestling with her comment. "You know, I spoke of this with several people before coming here. I did not make this trip without great reservation. It was not my intention to bring my unwelcomed presence back into your life as much as to show my contrite and spiritually renewed heart. I suppose like Judas in the Bible, however, there shall be no peace for me."

"Judas never sought peace," Dalton's

mother snapped back. She glared at Marston, her anger burning bright. "He sought his own way—a way to prosper his coffers even though it cost Jesus His life." She drew a deep breath, and Dalton knew she was attempting to still her anger.

"I honestly do not wish you harm, Marston. And believe me, it took a great many long years for me to come to this place. Therefore, if you have no peace in your life, then I suggest you reconsider your spiritually renewed heart and seek the Scriptures for what's missing. I can assure you, for my part, I simply no longer want to be bothered with you."

She turned and took hold of Kjell's arm. "Please take me home."

Dalton exchanged a glance with his father before watching his parents leave the room. His sister followed but paused at the door.

"I agree with Lydia. I would rather be left alone after this. I have no desire to share in your fortune. My memories of you and my life before Sitka are all sad and marred with pain. I prefer not to think on them at all."

With that she was gone, leaving Marston to look to Dalton. "Well? Will you also leave me now?"

Folding his hands on the table, Dalton

narrowed his eyes. "Why are you really here?"

———

The following day, Britta heard all the details regarding Marston's surprise visit. She had never seen her mother more irritated when discussing a topic than in watching her react to the arrival of Marston Gray. Twice she'd seen her mother take refuge in her bedroom, pleading a headache. Obviously this man was the cause.

Britta considered the past and all the stories she'd heard about Marston Gray as she rolled out a pie crust. What a strange and violent history in their family background. Watching Laura rolling out her own tiny pieces of dough while Darya slept, Britta couldn't imagine enduring all her mother had lived through.

"Hello? Britta?"

"I'm here in the kitchen, Kay."

Kay popped her head around the corner. "What are you doing?"

"Making a pie." Britta held up the rolling pin.

"I'll finish that for you. Yuri is waiting outside."

Britta put the rolling pin aside and dusted

flour from her hands. "What are you talking about? Waiting for what?"

"For you, silly." Kay gave her a grin. "He asked me to watch the girls so that he could take you on a walk. Now, take off your apron and go."

For just a moment, her stomach did a flip. Yuri wanted to go for a walk? What was he planning? "Laura, you play nice for Kay, and Mama will be back in just a little bit." Britta put her apron aside and headed for the door. She took up her coat and went outside.

Yuri stood at the bottom of the steps. As she came through the front door, he reached up to take hold of her hand. "It's much too pretty to stay inside all day. I thought perhaps you would accompany me."

She hesitated. "There's a chill in the air."

"Then it's good that you brought your coat. Here, let me help you into it." Yuri took the garment and assisted her.

Britta looked up at him, hesitant. "What . . . did you have in mind?"

He gripped her hand tighter and drew her closer. "I thought we could take a long, leisurely stroll."

She glanced skyward. "Looks like it could rain." She offered him a smile. "But then, when doesn't it?" She picked up the side of her skirt and allowed Yuri to lead the way.

A million questions rushed through Britta's head, but she didn't utter a single one aloud. She couldn't imagine what had come over Yuri to cause this change. She glanced up and found him actually smiling. This caused her to look away quickly. Something was going on, but she didn't know what.

They walked up the mountain trail she knew so well. Since she was a small child, this had been a place she had played and sought refuge. The spruce and cedar forest seemed to extend its boughs to embrace them—to muffle the sounds of all but their breathing. The heady scents of earth and moss blended with the trees. It was like an aroma of memories—pleasant, welcome memories.

For just a moment, Britta closed her eyes. She loved this man—her hero. She had dreamed all of her life about moments like this.

"You're going to fall if you don't open your eyes," he teased.

Her lashes fluttered open. "Not if you're holding on to me. I trust you."

He stopped and looked at her for a moment. "And what makes your trust in me so absolute?"

She shrugged. "You didn't have to do anything in particular. You're a good man, and that's enough."

"I wasn't good to Marsha."

"Yes you were. I saw the letters." She met his gaze. "You sent her money all the time. You supported your wife and child. That was honorable."

"Britta, I appreciate your esteem, but it wasn't right. If I left now and sent you money every week or two, would that be enough for you?"

"No. I suppose it wouldn't be enough. But Marsha didn't love you. She couldn't have loved you and still treated you the way she did."

"You're right. She didn't love me, and I didn't love her. If I hadn't gone, it would have turned ugly, and Laura would have been caught up in the middle of it all."

"So doesn't that make you a good man for putting her needs first?"

He shook his head. "No. A good man would have changed his attitude and stayed. A good man would have stopped drinking and found a way to live with his child's mother. A good man would have done things differently."

Britta finally recognized the truth of his words. She'd allowed herself to think of Yuri as blameless for so long that it was difficult to accept. "So you made mistakes. We all have."

He nodded. "I just want you to see it like it really was, Britta. I'm not the hero you make me out to be. I may have helped save you that day so long ago, but that one act wasn't enough to redeem my entire life."

"Maybe not, but Jesus' one act was. You've given your life to Him. That changes everything."

"I agree, it does. And I do want to move forward instead of live in the past."

Britta cocked her head to one side. Only then did she realize Yuri was rubbing his thumb gently over the back of her hand. It caused her to shiver.

"Are you cold?" he asked.

She shook her head, never looking away. "I'm fine."

For a moment, neither one said another word, and then Yuri began walking again. He led them to a small clearing where a low rocky wall made a good place to rest. Sitting, he pulled her down beside him.

"I had a long talk with your brother."

"Is something wrong?"

"Well, he thinks there is." Yuri smiled. "I guess I do, too."

"What is it?" Britta couldn't keep the concern from her voice. "Is Phoebe all right?"

"Everyone is fine. Everyone but you and me."

Britta realized he was still holding her hand. She felt as if she couldn't breathe. What was he about to say? Had he given up on the idea of being her husband? She jumped to her feet, and Yuri dropped his hold.

"You aren't going to suggest we end our marriage, are you? Is that why you brought me here?" Britta began to pace. "Is that what this is all about? You want an annulment?"

"No, that's not what this is about."

She stopped and fixed her eyes on his. "Then what?"

"I want to make this work, Britta. I've done you a great disservice, and like Dalton pointed out to me, I lied to God."

"What?"

"I promised before God to love you, to cherish you, and I've done none of that. I didn't even intend to do it when I pledged it. That makes me a liar."

Britta was consumed with her own guilt and looked away. Hadn't she worried about the same thing? She had pursued marriage with a man who didn't feel for her the things she felt for him. Their marriage was a lie.

"I want to change things," Yuri continued. "I want to court you. I want to let my heart love again. We already share a strong friendship. It seems a good foundation upon which to build a marriage."

Her heart skipped a beat. She was afraid to even face him. "Do you mean it?"

"I do, if that meets with your approval. I won't promise that it'll be easy. Your brother tells me that marriage is the hardest work there is."

She glanced over her shoulder to find him grinning. "I'm a hard worker."

"I've heard that about you."

Turning, Britta began to move toward him. "I'm very determined, also."

"I've heard that, as well."

"And I speak my mind."

"Do you ever," he said, laughing.

Britta maneuvered closer, and instead of returning to the rock, she pushed his hands aside and took her seat on his lap. His eyes widened in surprise, but he didn't rebuke her. Instead, he sat without moving, without speaking.

Reaching up, Britta pushed back an errant strand of hair from his face. "I'm also told that I can be very persuasive."

His blue-eyed gaze penetrated deep into her soul. Britta didn't give him a chance to speak but instead kissed his forehead lightly. She trailed kisses along his face until she reached his lips. Giving him a gentle kiss, she pulled back. "Very persuasive."

"I can see that now," he murmured.

Britta had never thought of herself as much of a seductress, but as Yuri wrapped his arms around her and caught her in a passionate kiss, she thought, *Maybe I'm better at this than I give myself credit for.*

As if reading her mind, Yuri gave a low throaty chuckle and wrapped her in his arms. "I think loving you may be the easiest thing I've ever done."

Chapter 21

*B*ritta watched her family commence dinner at her parents' table amidst an awkward silence. No one seemed anxious to disturb the thread of normalcy in their actions. Ever since Marston Gray had come to the island, the family dynamic had been off. Britta knew her parents were upset by the man's reappearance, but Britta wasn't entirely sure why Gray continued to hold such sway over her mother's emotions.

Phoebe passed a ceramic bowl to Britta. "I'm sure glad we were able to get some decent potatoes."

"Yes." Britta helped herself to the potatoes and passed them to Yuri.

Her mother continued to look at her plate, downcast in spirit. As far as Britta could see, there was to be no peace for her mother while Marston remained in Sitka. Her mother and brother, as well as Aunt Evie, were wary of the man and wanted nothing to do with him. Britta couldn't help but wonder what needed to happen in order to see peace restored. She hated seeing her mother like this.

"I've talked to him on two occasions," Dalton said as if someone had asked about Marston. "I believe I may well go along with one of his ideas, simply to see him leave the island."

"What idea is that?" their father asked.

Dalton put down his fork. "Marston suggested we could give him a letter of transaction for our bank in Seattle. He could go there and arrange deposits in our accounts and be done with it. We'd not have anything else to do with him, and he promises he would not return to Sitka."

"I do not want his money," Mother said, slamming her fist to the table. Everyone turned at this. Britta had never seen her mother so angry. "I told him I didn't want his money, and I meant it. You do as you like, but I do not want anything more to do with that man.

The Grays have caused me enough trouble." She got up and left the table, not even touching her food.

"I didn't mean to upset her," Dalton told his father. "I thought maybe this would be an amicable solution. I even wired the bank to ask the manager's opinion."

Father got to his feet. "I'll talk to her, but honestly, Dalton, it might be best if you just let him deposit the money into one account instead of three. Then you can decide at a later date what to do with the money. If this is what we need to do in order to see Marston leave, then I suggest we do it quickly."

With that he was gone, and Dalton turned to Evie. "Do you have any objection to that? I could have the manager open a single account and give Marston the ability to deposit into that. We can always donate the money to charity."

"I suppose that would be acceptable," Evie said. Her husband, Josh, nodded in agreement. "I can't see that any harm could be done that way."

Britta wished fervently that they could speak about something else. To her surprise, Yuri changed the subject.

"I hope Ted and Kay aren't regretting their trip to Mount Edgecumbe. It looks like snow at the higher elevations."

Phoebe laughed. "I'm sure my brother will keep Kay warm enough."

"I thought they had a lovely wedding," Britta joined in. "I've certainly never seen a happier bride."

"Nor I," Phoebe admitted. "Mother said Ted has become a completely new man. He needed someone to stand up to him, and Kay seems to have little trouble."

"How is your mother?" Britta asked. "I heard she was under the weather."

Phoebe nodded. "It's just a cold, but she wanted to stay home and nurse it. The children are with her, so if she needs anything, she'll be well cared for. Rachel made her soup, and Connie already considers herself Mother's personal nurse."

Britta smiled, imagining Laura would be the same way. She looked over at her daughter and saw her wolfing down her salmon. My, but the child did love to eat. Darya was already finished with her tiny bits of finger food, but she was playing with the spoon she'd been given, chewing and drooling in contentment. It was hard to believe the baby was already eight months old. She was pulling up to everything and crawling about. How quickly time passed. Mother said it wouldn't be long before she'd be off and running.

Thoughts of her mother once again gave

Britta concern. She put her napkin aside. "I'll be right back," she told Yuri, then announced to the others, "If you'll please excuse me a moment."

She left the table and immediately headed for her parents' bedroom. She could hear her mother and father talking in low hushed tones. Knocking lightly, Britta called out, "May I come in?"

Her father opened the door. "Is everything all right?"

"Yes, but your food is getting cold. I thought maybe I could talk with Mother for a moment."

"Please go eat, Kjell. I'll be fine," her mother said from where she stood across the room.

He seemed torn, but Britta insisted. "Go. We'll be fine. I have something I need to discuss."

Finally he gave up. "If you need me, you'll send Britta?"

Mother nodded. She looked so weary. In that moment, the years made themselves quite evident. Britta had never thought of her mother as old, but now she could see the changes—the frailty.

Britta closed the door behind her father. "I'm sorry that this has been so difficult to bear."

Her mother shrugged and crossed the room

to sit by the fire. "I don't mean to let it bother me so much, but that man has caused this family so much pain."

She nodded. "Why don't we sit? You can tell me what is worrying you the most."

They took the seats by the hearth, but Lydia surprised Britta by asking, "What of your worries, Britta? Are things working out at all?"

The firelight reflected the concern in her mother's eyes. Britta thought of Yuri's decision to court her and smiled. "Things are much better, Mother. I've not had a chance to tell you, but Yuri wants this marriage to work out. He wants to be a proper husband and father, and he's been . . . well, courting me."

Her mother's brows knit together. "Courting you?"

Britta folded her hands and smiled. "Yes. He's taken me on walks and has brought me little gifts. We sit together in the evening and share Scriptures and talk about the future."

"Are you still . . . well, that is, how are your . . . sleeping arrangements?" her mother asked. It was clear she was trying to be delicate.

Britta laughed. "We're just taking small steps at this point. We have to build trust between us. I trust Yuri implicitly, and I think it's just a matter of time before he trusts me—and himself—as well."

"He's been hurt."

"That's true for all of us," Britta replied. "As you once told me, you cannot let the pain of the past destroy the happiness of the future."

Mother looked at her for a moment and nodded. "It's a battle I have not yet overcome. I still allow Marston Gray to wreak havoc with my happiness."

"I wish you wouldn't, Mother. I fear it is making you old before your time—even sick. You don't want him to have that kind of power over you."

"I hadn't thought of him having power over me," her mother replied, shaking her head. "But it's clear that he does. I have to find a way to diminish his capacity to trouble me."

Britta reached out and took hold of her mother's hand. "Mama, you are the strongest woman I know. I've always been amazed at your ability to do what must be done. I know that you rely on God for such strength, and it has inspired me to do likewise. Things aren't perfect for me with Yuri and the girls, but I know that God has a purpose for this. Just as He has a purpose for Marston coming to Sitka."

"You're right, of course. Daily I give this to God and then wrestle it back from Him. I have to learn to let it go once and for all. I just can't bring myself to trust that Marston Gray is honorable."

"No one said you needed to. I don't believe he can expect that, either. Let him do his good deeds and assuage his conscience. Like Dalton said, the money can be given over to charity. You needn't even handle it. He can get one account, and Mr. Gray can leave his fortune there. Dalton will take care of it all, and you can be free."

Mother met her gaze. "I hope that is true."

———

Yuri and Britta sat in front of the fire as a gentle rain fell outside. The girls were asleep, leaving the couple time to themselves. Britta was focused on sewing, as Yuri had often seen her in the evening. He wondered if she missed her old life—the life of excitement and opulence that she'd enjoyed prior to moving back home. She had once told him a story of performing in an orchestra for Queen Wilhelmina of the Netherlands. Her violin solo had made the woman weep with joy. He couldn't imagine giving up such a life to rear his children and live in Sitka. Did she regret her decision?

A part of him wanted to ask her, but he didn't want to break the companionable silence between them. Yuri thought back to his first memories of her. He remembered

Kjerstin and Britta being close friends with his sisters, Natasha and Illiyana. He and Dalton had joked that the girls would probably grow up to live in one big house together. Then his family had moved back to Russia. He knew it had devastated Britta and Illiyana, especially. That's why they had run away that night so long ago. The night he and Dalton had rescued them from the side of the mountain.

"You are very quiet tonight."

Yuri looked up to find Britta had abandoned her sewing and was now just watching him. He smiled. "I was just enjoying the evening. Sometimes quiet is good for the spirit."

"I can stop talking if you'd prefer."

"That's all right. I don't mind at all."

"What were you thinking about?"

Yuri drew a deep breath and let it out in a sigh. "The past."

She nodded.

He tried to put his thoughts into words. "I can't help but wish I'd done things differently."

"What would you have done?"

Yuri considered her question for a moment. "Maybe I would have taken you more seriously when you told me you were going to marry me."

Britta giggled. "I suppose it's hard to believe a seven-year-old knows her own mind, but I did."

"It certainly appears that way." He shifted and looked at her for a moment. "I don't have the best memory, but I recall a time you were running wild through the yard, your hair flying out behind you. You were chasing something or someone." He laughed. "I remember your father saying the man who married you was in for a reckoning."

"That's an awful thing to say. I wasn't that bad. Just high-spirited. At least that's what Aunt Zee used to say."

"You are, indeed, high-spirited," Yuri agreed. "I suppose that's what fascinates me most."

"But why?" Britta looked at him oddly. "It hardly seems to be a trait that would make a woman valuable to a man."

"But of course it makes her valuable. Especially in Alaska. Your high-spiritedness will help you to endure anything that comes your way. You are stronger than you give yourself credit for, Britta Lindquist."

"Belikov," she corrected.

He nodded. The firelight cast such a warm glow on her face that she seemed to practically shine from within. "Would you do me a favor?"

"Of course."

"Take down your hair."

She didn't ask him to explain or bother to protest the idea; instead, Britta immediately pulled the pins from her hair. Brown waves rushed down like water over a falls. The firelight picked up tiniest hints of red. Yuri had never wanted anything more than to run his hands through the long, lush bulk.

Britta seemed to understand and moved closer. Kneeling by his feet, she smiled up at him. "Is that better?"

He held out his hand, hovering it just over her head. He felt charged with anticipation. Letting his fingers touch her ever so gently, Yuri closed his eyes and ran his hands through her hair. He tried to remember if he'd ever felt this way about another woman but knew he hadn't. There was no other experience, no other moment in his life, that had prepared him for what he was feeling.

"It's like silk," he whispered.

She took hold of his hand and drew it to her neck. "So is my skin."

His eyes opened in a flash, and he tried to pull back his hand, but Britta would have no part in that. He met her gaze and easily recognized the passion in her dark brown eyes as a reflection of his own. "Britta." He barely breathed the name.

She rose to her feet, pulling him upward with her. Yuri stood only inches from her. He could smell the sweet scent of the soap she used. He wanted to hold her—to make her his wife in full. But nagging, lingering doubts began to flood his mind.

What if I fail her as I did Marsha?

What if I'm never able to be the man she needs me to be?

What if . . .

"Yuri," she whispered. "I'm tired of the walls between us. Can't you trust me just a little?"

He inhaled slowly. "I trust you, Britta. It's myself I don't know."

She drew his hand to her lips. "Then why not let me help." She kissed his hand. "You see, I know Yuri Belikov very well. I can tell you just about anything you'd like to know."

"Tell me, then, that I won't make a mess of this. Promise me that, and I'm yours."

Britta dropped his hand and gave a light-hearted laugh. "You're already mine, Yuri."

For a moment he did nothing, said nothing. She was right. Somehow, somewhere along the way, he had already given her his heart.

Chapter 22

October 1906

*B*ritta rolled over in bed and stretched. Life was better than she could have hoped for. She was content in her role as wife and mother and could not imagine being happier anywhere else in the world.

Yuri had already gone to work, but the place beside her still bore the proof that he shared her bed. She pulled his pillow to her face and breathed in. His scent lingered there, and she reveled in the closeness they shared. Things were really changing between them. Yuri was starting to relax, to trust. She could see daily how his confidence was growing, and it pleased her more than words could say.

Realizing she couldn't afford to waste any more of the day, Britta got up and began to make the bed to begin her morning routine. Her mother had once asked her if she missed her life abroad and in the States. Britta could honestly tell her no. That life had been filled with parties and people, all with the purpose of keeping her from dealing with the real feelings that haunted her. She hated being alone in those days, always afraid of what she might have to face down deep within. Now she was happy to live quietly. She no longer feared what might surface.

With the bed made, she quickly dressed in a serviceable blue wool skirt and long-sleeved blouse. She made mental notes of the projects she would need to complete that day. She was thankful that her mother had already promised to fix supper for everyone. That made one less chore. Still, there were numerous other tasks that vied for her attention.

"Laura?" she said, softly opening the door to the girls' room.

She found Laura sitting up in bed looking at a picture book. The child was positively engrossed, examining each page.

"Good morning, my darling." Britta went

to the edge of the bed and waited for Laura to crawl into her lap.

The little girl put the book aside and quickly maneuvered into her mother's arms. "Kisses." She wrapped her arms around Britta's neck and gave her a wet kiss on the mouth, then just as quickly pulled away. "I was reading."

"I saw that. It won't be long until you will be able to go to school and learn all of those words for yourself. But for now, we have chores to do. I put your clothes out last night, so wash your face and get dressed."

Laura scooted off Britta's lap and hurried to the washbowl. She was happily splashing water when Britta went to ready the baby. Darya was still sleeping, looking ever so content. For a moment Britta just watched her. It was such a peaceful sight.

She ran her finger along the baby's cheek and froze. The infant's skin was cool, almost cold to the touch. Britta put her hand to the baby's face, then quickly pulled the quilt from her body. She lifted the child's limp body in her arms.

"Darya! Darya!"

Britta patted the baby's back and then tapped her cheek, but the baby didn't move. A steel-like band tightened around Britta's chest. Panicked at the sight of the lifeless infant, Britta looked in panic to Laura.

The girl was clueless as to what was happening, however. She was just starting to strip away her nightgown.

"Wait," Britta practically screamed. "Go get Grandma—right now. Go. Hurry!"

Laura looked at her mother with a curious expression and then gazed down at her gown. "You said don't go outside in my nighty clothes."

"Laura, just do what I ask. Tell Grandma it's . . . tell her . . ." Britta barely contained a sob as she pulled the infant to her chest. "Tell her the baby is sick."

Finally sensing the urgency, Laura didn't ask another question. Instead, she hurried out the door. Britta could hear the screen door slap against the frame as the child flew across the threshold.

Nothing in her life felt worse than the weight of the dead child in her arms. Britta knew in her heart it was too late to do anything, but until her mother declared the situation hopeless, she had to believe there might be a chance.

She looked at the baby and shook her head. "Please breathe. Please, Darya. Please."

The shock of the moment held her tears at bay; it also blurred her ability to reason. What had happened to cause this? Had she fed the baby something that didn't agree with her?

"Didn't agree with her?" Britta said with a touch of hysteria. Such a thought seemed almost nonsensical. It wasn't a matter of not agreeing with her—something had killed her baby.

It seemed forever before Lydia appeared with Laura—and Kay—in tow. "Mama, we comed back."

Britta met her mother's worried glance. Her mother seemed to understand and came forward to take the baby from her arms.

"She's . . . I . . ." Britta shook her head over and over. "No. No. No." She couldn't stop saying the word.

"Give her to me." Her words were soft but insistent. "Kay, dress Laura, then take her to Phoebe. She can play with Connie. Then bring the doctor and Yuri back to the house."

"Here's my dress," Laura said, holding up the red plaid material.

"Get your shoes and socks, and we'll get dressed in the front room, where it's warmer," Kay told the child.

Everything seemed to happen in a matter of seconds. Lydia examined the infant for a moment, then tore away the tiny gown and pressed her ear to the baby's chest.

The room began to spin, and Britta made her way to the edge of Laura's bed. This wasn't happening. This was just a bad dream. Any moment now she would wake up. She watched her mother move to place Darya in the crib. When she turned to face Britta, there was no doubt as to the child's condition.

"I'm so sorry, Britta."

"No!" Britta jumped to her feet, ignoring the dizziness. "She's fine."

She rushed to the baby's bed, but her mother took her hand before Britta reached Darya. "Britta, stop. She's gone."

Mother's gentle but firm statement was enough to halt Britta's movements. She looked to her mother for strength—reassurance.

"Why? What did I do wrong?" Still the tears would not come. Britta felt as if her body had stopped all normal function. She could no longer feel herself breathe. She couldn't feel the beat of her heart. "What did I do wrong? Tell me."

Lydia led her daughter to the kitchen table. "Sit here."

Britta did as she was told, but only because she didn't know what else to do. Her mother went to the stove and lifted the coffeepot. It was only another moment before she returned with a cup of cold coffee, urging Britta to drink.

"I can't. I can't." Britta clenched and unclenched her hands. "Tell me what I did wrong."

"Sweetheart, you had nothing to do with Darya's death. This happens sometimes. I lost a child after Dalton."

"No. I . . . no, you didn't."

Her mother sat beside Britta at the table. "I did. He was just a few weeks old. We never talked about it much. Babies are fragile. They sometimes die for what seems no apparent reason."

Easing against her mother, Britta found it impossible to speak. Nothing about this made any sense at all. How could a baby be living one moment, happy and healthy, then be dead the next?

After what seemed an eternity, Yuri and the doctor arrived with Kay. Britta watched her mother take charge. She went and spoke to Yuri and the doctor in hushed whispers while Kay came to her side.

The two men disappeared into the back room with Mother, while Britta tried to rationalize the moment. Her stomach churned and bile rose in the back of her throat. Yuri would blame her. He would think that she killed the baby—his baby. No, Darya wasn't his child. Would that matter? Would he think Britta unfit to raise Laura?

"Are you all right?" Kay asked.

Britta looked at her friend as if she'd lost her mind. "Darya is dead."

"I'm so sorry, Britta." Kay reached out to touch Britta's shoulder. "I feared that was the case."

"It doesn't make sense." Britta surprised them both by jumping to her feet. "I can't understand this. I can't." Her voice rose. "It isn't supposed to be like this. I don't know what I did wrong. I don't know why this is happening."

"There are no easy answers," Kay said, reaching out again.

Britta pushed her away. She turned to go, knocking over the chair as she did. "It has to be a mistake. I won't let this happen."

She headed back to the girls' room and stormed inside. "She isn't dead. Give her to me."

"Britta, you have to calm down," Lydia said, coming alongside her.

"No. This isn't right. She wasn't sick. I'd have known if she was sick. I'm a good mother."

The doctor pulled the stethoscope from his ears. "I'm sorry, Yuri, Britta. She's been gone for some time. Probably passed in the night shortly after falling asleep."

"No!" Britta tried to rush forward, but Yuri stopped her. He held her fast, but Britta fought him. "She's not gone. She can't be gone. She's my baby."

As her hysteria mounted, Britta felt all

reason and control leave her. She pummeled Yuri with her fists. "Let me go to her. She needs me."

Yuri pulled her tight against him. He tried to calm her, but Britta could only think of Darya. They were keeping her from her baby. They knew she could help, but they were keeping her away.

"Britta, it was crib death. There's nothing you or anyone else could have done," her mother explained.

She began to flail all the harder at her mother's comment, but Yuri wouldn't let her go. His arms felt like steel vises around her, but Britta wasn't deterred. "You have to let me go to her." A wailing sob broke from her throat and tears began to flood her eyes. "I have to help her."

"You can't help her now, Britta," Yuri whispered.

"Let me give you something," the doctor said, reaching for his bag.

Britta shook her head again but felt the strength drain from her body. "I don't need something—Darya needs it."

"Darya is gone."

Britta stilled for just a moment. "No. She's just sleeping."

He shook his head sadly. "Sweetheart, she's with God."

Yuri watched Britta sleep and wished fervently he could undo the events of the day. He felt consumed by guilt. He had never given Darya the love she deserved. Because she wasn't his, Yuri had kept himself from getting too close. Now she was gone.

Could a baby die from a lack of love?

Well, it wasn't that she hadn't enjoyed love. Britta had adored Darya, as did most everyone who came in contact with her.

"Why couldn't I love her?"

Of course that was the age-old question for him in regard to so many people in his life. He had always pushed people away. Only Britta had found a way to break down his defenses.

Well, there was Laura. Lydia had arranged for her to stay with Phoebe and Dalton. She had no idea that her baby sister was dead. He couldn't help but wonder how it might affect the child. Would she miss Darya?

Britta moaned in her sleep, and Yuri put aside thoughts of his daughter and turned to his wife. He climbed into bed beside her and pulled her into his arms, finding that he needed her comfort as much as he imagined she needed his.

Nothing in life had prepared him for the

death of a child. Even a child that he couldn't quite accept.

"It wasn't her fault," he whispered.

Darya had done nothing wrong. It was all his stupid way of looking at things. His anger and frustration over what Marsha had done. Now they were both gone, and he could either let that anger continue or let it go. He seemed to be standing at a crossroads . . . and thankfully, God was standing there with him.

I can go on feeling this fear, this rage, he told himself, *or I can leave it here and move on without it.*

He sighed and felt Britta stir in his arms. How in the world would they ever get beyond this moment? Things were just starting to look up for them. He and Britta were finally able to open up to one another, to enjoy marriage the way God intended. And now this.

Yuri hadn't realized that he'd dozed off, but when he awoke, he found Britta sobbing softly in his arms. He pushed back her damp hair and stroked her cheek.

"I'm so sorry, Britta. I'm so sorry you were alone. So sorry Darya . . . that she . . ." He couldn't say the words.

"It's not fair. She did nothing wrong."

"No one did anything wrong. Not you or Darya."

"I must have. I must have missed something.

She needed me and I didn't know it. I should have known."

Yuri lifted her face so he could see her eyes. "Britta, you don't control life and death. Not for yourself or for the children."

It was then that she seemed to remember Laura. "Where is she? Where's Laura?"

"She's with Phoebe and Dalton. She doesn't know yet about Darya. I thought we'd wait until you were feeling better."

Britta tried to sit up. "She must be upset. She could see that something was wrong. We need to go to her."

Yuri pulled her back down. "Your mother and father just saw her. She's fine. She's having a lot of fun. Phoebe is keeping her busy."

For several minutes, Britta said nothing, and Yuri thought she'd faded back to sleep. He eased his chin against the top of her head and closed his eyes.

"What if this happens again?" Britta asked in a barely audible voice.

"What do you mean?"

She pulled away and looked at him. Her eyes were swollen from crying. "What if I have a baby and that baby dies, too?"

He hadn't considered them even having children. For some reason, it hadn't been uppermost on his mind. They had been intimate for such a short time that the concern had not been real before this.

"I suppose . . . well, it's possible. Life is so fragile."

"Everyone dies," she said almost flippantly. "Illiyana died. Aunt Zee. Marsha. Darya. I'll die . . . you'll die." Her voice broke. "Everyone dies." She fell back against the bed in a fresh flood of tears.

Her pain pierced Yuri's heart. He had mourned so much of his life that death had never frightened him. Until now. Britta was right. Everyone would die sooner or later. The thought filled him with sorrow. Laura would die someday—and hopefully he would be long gone before that happened. But it would happen.

Britta would die. In fact, what if she died in childbirth as Marsha had? The thought terrified him more than he wanted to admit. If she died giving birth to his child, how could he not blame himself? And then he would be alone again. Alone without anyone to turn to—to love.

For the first time in a long while, Yuri wanted a drink. He wanted to forget what had happened, and he wanted to forget what might happen.

O God, I'm so weak. I cannot bear this alone. Please help me—help us.

Chapter 23

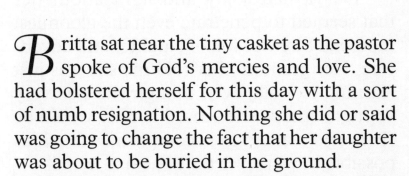

*B*ritta sat near the tiny casket as the pastor spoke of God's mercies and love. She had bolstered herself for this day with a sort of numb resignation. Nothing she did or said was going to change the fact that her daughter was about to be buried in the ground.

Yuri sat solemnly beside her, looking rigid and awkward in a suit he'd borrowed from Dalton. Everyone else stood nearby, while Laura moved back and forth between Britta and Lydia. Britta's mother and father had explained Darya's death to Laura. She seemed curious, but not overly grieved. It was impossible for Laura to understand the full implication of the situation or even to be afraid, and for that, Britta was thankful.

"It is never easy to say good-bye to a loved one," the pastor began, "but even harder when that loved one is a child—an infant." He opened the Bible and recited several verses about Jesus being the resurrection and the life, but Britta found no comfort in them.

"Little Darya Belikov was only eight months old, but in observing her at church I have to say she was one of the happiest children I've ever known," the pastor continued. "And I've had the pleasure of watching a great many children in my years as a minister.

"Darya had a joy and light about her that seemed to penetrate even the gloomiest moment. She was full of laughter and adventure. Her grandmother told me she was just learning to walk, even though she was very young. Perhaps she sensed her life would be short and wanted to accomplish as much as possible in whatever time she had here."

Britta twisted a handkerchief around her fingers until she felt pain and slowly released the tourniquet again. Such action kept her from weeping or thinking too much on the words that were said. It was the only way she could make it through the funeral.

"Sometimes we face situations like this and

we can't help but ask ourselves, 'Where was God? Why did He not keep this child from death?' "

Yes, Britta thought. *We ask those questions, but we get no answers. God is ever so clear on a great many things but strangely silent when bad things happen to the innocent.* She looked up, almost afraid she'd voiced her thoughts aloud. No one seemed to notice, however, and the pastor continued.

"Many folks will ask these questions, and often we will hear things like, 'This is a fallen world. Adam and Eve brought sin into it and because of this, death.' And while that's true, it offers little comfort."

Britta could vouch for that. She didn't want to hear all the well-rehearsed Christian answers. The pain she felt could not be eased by remembering that the world suffered because of sin. The rest of the world's pain was not hers to contemplate when her own was eating her alive.

"Sometimes it's hard to believe that God is good and compassionate when something like this happens," the man went on. "Some would even call God cruel for having robbed a mother of her child."

Or a child of her mother, Britta thought. Of course, she hadn't felt that way when Marsha passed away. The woman hadn't cared properly for Laura, so there was no reason to believe she would have been a decent mother to Darya. Still, Marsha's death had been nothing but relief to Britta. Her death had freed Yuri.

Maybe that's what this is all about. It felt as if Britta's heart had tightened into a knot. Was this some kind of divine punishment for having coveted another woman's husband?

But I didn't, Britta reasoned. *I loved him first. I went away when I learned he was married. I tried to fall in love with another man. I didn't sit around, pining for Yuri. I loved him— that's true enough. But I've always loved him. I'll always love him.*

Surely God wouldn't take Darya as punishment for having loved Yuri. She sat staring at the tiny casket.

"The psalmist says in Psalm 116," the pastor said, turning in his Bible, " 'I love the Lord, because he hath heard my voice and my supplications. Because he hath inclined his ear unto me, therefore will I call upon him as long as I live. The sorrows of death compassed me. . . .'

"We have found trouble and sorrow here on earth. The sorrows of death compass us and leave us with the pain of hell's hold. But there is release—there is hope beyond this moment of misery. I speak here today to those left behind, those who mourn the passing of this infant girl. God has not left you to bear this sadness alone. He has not abandoned you."

Then where is He? Britta looked skyward. *Where are you, God?*

She thought back to those exhausting nights when both Darya and Laura had been trying to adjust to life at the Lindquist house. Some nights she had begged God to help the children sleep—to give them peace and let them feel safe. Rest had been so important then; now there seemed to be no rest, no peace.

As if on cue, the pastor continued reading from the Bible. " 'Then called I upon the name of the Lord; O Lord, I beseech thee, deliver my soul. Gracious is the Lord, and righteous; yea, our God is merciful. The Lord preserveth the simple: I was brought low, and he helped me. Return unto thy rest, O my soul; for the Lord hath dealt bountifully with thee. For thou hast delivered my soul from death, mine eyes from tears, and my feet from falling. I will walk before the Lord in the land of the living.' "

Britta refused to hear anything more. How could her soul return to rest? How could she call upon the Lord for deliverance when she felt He had turned away from her? The psalmist might have found comfort in those words, but Britta wondered how she could possibly feel the same way.

Then she remembered that David, too, had lost a child. That child had been the result of his sin with Bathsheba. God had taken that child, just as He had taken Darya. Why did the innocent suffer?

But in this case, the innocent didn't suffer, she thought. The innocent babies were whisked away from the pains and sicknesses of this life. Those children were spared the grief that life on earth could bring. The innocent didn't suffer . . . but she did.

I wasn't innocent. I made a vow to God and pressed Yuri to do the same, not knowing whether it would ever be fulfilled. I'm paying the consequences of my own sin.

She buried her face in her hands and bit her lip so hard she tasted blood. The pain did nothing to take her focus from the accusations in her heart. Yuri put his arm around her shoulder and pulled her close. Britta didn't try to stop him. She needed the warmth of his touch, even though there was little comfort to be had.

Her only thought was to endure to the end of the service and then go home. Home to sleep and forget the pain of her loss. Home to hide away from the questions and pitying glances of her loved ones.

The pastor continued to speak, but Britta refused to listen. She waited until the final prayers were said, until the men lowered the tiny coffin into the small grave beside the spot where Marsha Belikov had been buried eight months earlier, before hearing so much as the breeze blowing through the trees.

"I'll take Laura back with us," Phoebe said, coming to Yuri and Britta. "She can play with Connie, and then we'll bring her home for supper."

"Thank you," Yuri replied.

Britta nodded but could scarcely meet her sister-in-law's eyes. Instead, she glanced to where her father was helping her mother into their carriage. They had ridden there together as a family, but all she wanted now was to be left alone.

"I'll walk back," she said, nodding toward the carriage. "You go ahead with them."

Yuri didn't argue. He seemed to understand that she needed some time to herself. She hated closing him out of this moment in her life, but Britta couldn't deal with the guilt that consumed her. Somehow, all of this was her fault and she had to figure out a way to make it right.

One by one, the funeral-goers left and Britta stood by herself at the grave. She let the grief pour over her as she remembered losing Illiyana, Aunt Zee, and now the baby. It hurt so much to have loved and lost them. Their passing left holes in her heart that would never be filled.

"Only God can fill the empty spaces of our hearts," her mother had once told her. *"Whether those empty places come about because of death or betrayal, God is the only one who can make broken hearts whole again."*

Britta shook her head. God seemed so far away.

"I didn't want you to walk home alone."

Britta turned and found her father standing only a few feet away. She suddenly felt like a little girl again—scared and confused. Britta rushed into her father's arms as she might have done twenty years earlier.

"This hurts so much," she said, letting her tears escape.

"I know." He held her close and stroked her back as he had when she'd been young.

For several minutes, she stood there crying—desperate to find solace and hope. Her father had always been such a pillar of strength for her.

"I don't understand," she said, finally pulling away. "Where is God in all of this, Father? I just don't see how He can possibly be here—how He can still care."

Her father put an arm around her and led

her from the grave. They walked toward the road, leaving the cemetery behind them.

"I can't give you answers I don't have," he said softly. "But I can assure you that God is still here. He still cares."

She wanted to believe him. "How do you know?"

"Because He said He would never leave us or forsake us."

"I feel forsaken. I feel betrayed. God has taken the life of that baby and left me to bear the guilt of my sins."

"And what sin would that be?"

She hung her head. "Yuri and I made a vow to God and to each other when we married, and yet we were not honest about it. Yuri didn't know if he could ever fulfill that vow, and I forced him to pledge it anyway."

"And you think God is punishing you by taking Darya?"

She looked up and met her father's look of disbelief. "Well, why not? God disciplines His children. You told me that long ago. You said the Bible says that He disciplines those He loves."

"Discipline and the death of a child are two different things, Britta. It would be a great injustice to suppose they were one and the same."

"But what of David and Bathsheba, Father?

They sinned, and God allowed their child to die."

He thought on this for a moment. "I don't pretend to know all the answers, Britta. You're right, God did take David's child. Such a punishment seems harsh, yet He later gives David and Bathsheba another son. Solomon becomes an even greater, wiser king than his father. God's people were blessed under his rule."

"I don't understand. God is all-powerful. He has the power of life and death in His hands, isn't that true?"

Her father nodded. "God is omnipotent."

"So God didn't have to let Darya die."

"No. I suppose He didn't."

Britta looked back at the ground. "But He let her die all the same."

"Just as so many have died before her."

"Yes. So many people I've cared about." Britta stopped and turned to her father. "I can't see the love in that. I can't see the mercy or the promise of never being forsaken. I feel alone and hopeless. My pain is so great that I can scarcely breathe."

"I know. I've felt that pain many times. When Dalton was taken and your mother nearly died; when your brother died; when my first wife died."

"Mother told me about the baby—my

brother. Why did no one ever speak of it before?"

He shrugged. "I suppose that pain you're speaking of caused us to hide it away. Dalton was too little to remember, and the baby lived only a very short time. He's buried up in the mountain behind the house. Your mother used to walk up there from time to time, but she preferred we not speak about it, so we didn't."

"I don't want to be that way about Darya. She was such a good baby. I loved being her mother." Britta wiped at the tears with the back of her hand. "I'm just so afraid."

Her father again opened his arms to her, and Britta stepped into his embrace and let him hold her. "What if it happens again?" she whispered.

"Britta, you can't live life in fear of death. Death will come to each of us. It's a part of our world. If you live in fear—if you spend your days watching for death at every turn—you'll never know happiness again. And sweetheart, you have so many reasons to be happy. Laura, for one."

"I know she needs me. She doesn't understand why I've been so sad. I tried to talk to her about Darya and how I miss her, but she just patted my hand and said that Darya was safe with Jesus. She trusts God more than I do, I suppose."

"She's a child. It's easy to trust when you're little. Remember how you felt as a girl? You weren't worried about much of anything. I think you were pretty carefree and easygoing."

"Until Illiyana had to move away," Britta said, looking up.

"But even then you weren't afraid. You and Illiyana went up across the mountain to try and get the help of a Tlingit shaman."

She smiled ever so slightly. "I was afraid when I fell over the side."

"But even then you were brave. You have to be brave now, as well. I'm not going to tell you it will be easy, because it won't. I won't promise you that if you get through this you'll never have to go through such things again. I can't make those kinds of promises."

"I wish you could."

"So do I, darling." He smiled and took hold of her hand. "If I could, I would do just that. If it were in my power to see that nothing bad would ever happen to the ones I love, you would never suffer again."

They started walking again and Britta clung to her father's strong grip upon her hand. It was all that kept her from feeling as though she might sink down into the mud and be lost forever. She was so very tired. So weary of the day and all that it represented.

Father seemed to understand, as he always did. He dropped his hold and put his arm around her shoulder instead. "I'd carry you if I could—just like when you were little."

"No one can carry me now." Her voice betrayed great sorrow.

"God can," her father offered, hugging her close. "God can."

Marston Gray stood at the banker's desk and extended his gloved hand. The check he held was for ten thousand dollars. "I would like to deposit this amount in the account number I gave you. I would also like you to give me a balance on the account afterward."

"Very good, sir. If you'll take a seat, I'll be right back."

Marston sank into the leather chair and rubbed his aching knee. The weather had turned damp and cold. Not exactly a novelty for Seattle, but it seemed to cut Marston to the bone.

When all of this is settled, he told himself, *I will head to a warmer climate.*

The banker returned and handed Marston a piece of paper. "I have made the deposit and have written the information you requested on the back of this paper. Please know that your funds will not be available until we are able to clear the check with your bank in Omaha."

"Yes, I understand." When everything had started falling apart in Kansas City, Marston had moved his money to several other cities, Omaha housing one of his larger deposits.

Getting to his feet, Marston glanced down at the ten-thousand-dollar figure written on the paper. He turned the sheet over and saw the bank's deposit information. "I don't understand," he told the man. "I asked to know the full balance of this account."

"Yes, sir. Ten thousand dollars is the full amount—the amount you deposited today."

"But I thought this account was an open account owned by my brother, Dalton Lindquist."

"Yes, sir, it is."

"I know for a fact he has a vast fortune. As do his mother and sister. I hardly understand how this can therefore be the sum total of what is held in the account."

The man smiled. "I can see your concern, but fear not. Mr. Lindquist opened this account especially for your transactions. His other accounts are separate."

Marston clenched his jaw and tried hard to look unmoved by the man's statement. "I see. Thank you for that clarification." He picked up his hat and cane. "I will check back with you to confirm that the funds have been released."

He turned without waiting for the man to comment. He pushed his hat down firmly and nodded as the doorman opened the nearly floor-to-ceiling door. "Good day, sir."

"Good day."

But it wasn't a good day, and Marston was beginning to feel a deep annoyance at the situation unfolding before him. Dalton was smarter than he'd given him credit for . . . or perhaps it was just plain dumb luck. Either way, Marston would have to rethink his plan— and quickly. It was only going to be a matter of time until his house of cards began to collapse, and he intended to be long gone before that occurred.

Chapter 24

*B*ritta's birthday fell on a Wednesday that year. It was exactly two weeks after she'd found Darya dead, and still the pain was as intense as the day it had happened. Despite her family trying hard to rally her spirits with gifts and attention, Britta longed to simply crawl back into bed and forget everything. She hardly talked to anyone and even turned away from Yuri. She didn't want to share her sorrow with him, fearing it might only worsen his own misery. She also didn't want him to know that she was taking whiskey to help her sleep.

She hadn't gone looking to buy the bottle, but when the opportunity presented itself, Britta found herself unable to walk away. The doctor had actually suggested it as a means to help her relax at night. At first, she feared the harm it could do. What if she ended up with a problem like Yuri? Worse yet, what if having liquor so close at hand caused Yuri to start drinking again? But her pain had been too great and the need to forget overwhelming. So she bought the bottle from the doctor and hid it, along with her guilt.

Laura didn't understand the change in their household. She constantly sought out Britta for reassurance and love, and while Britta tried never to turn the child away, there was a fearful edge to the way Britta reacted. What if Laura died, too? Could she bear to lose another child? Added to this was the growing fear of getting pregnant. In her sadness, Britta had shown no interest in Yuri's affections, but that wouldn't last forever. She was his wife and their love for each other was bound to grow. At least if she let it.

"Britta?"

It was her mother. Britta sat up on the edge of her bed and wondered at the time. For the past two weeks when Yuri went to work, he took Laura with him so that she could play with Connie. Phoebe had also started teaching

Connie and Laura their numbers and letters. Play was interlaced with learning, and Laura was proudly displaying her new knowledge of the alphabet. Britta felt only additional sadness that she hadn't been the one to teach the child.

"Britta?"

"I'm in here." She got up off the bed and pushed her hair back. Taking up a ribbon, she tied the mass loosely at the back of her neck.

Her mother opened the bedroom door and smiled. "I thought maybe you would take a walk with me. The day is clear and quite lovely."

Britta yawned. "I really don't feel like it."

"I know, but it will do you good. Come on." Her mother extended her arm as if to draw Britta to her.

She thought of arguing with her mother but realized that it would serve no purpose. Mother was just as strong willed. Britta finally agreed and took up an old jacket that belonged to Yuri. "I don't want to be gone long." She shrugged into the coat.

"Of course not. I have no thought to go far."

Britta followed her mother out of the cabin and up the road that led toward the main house. Beyond this, the path narrowed considerably and headed deeper into the forested mountainside. This trail was well worn from use over the years. Originally it had started as a game trail, but Zee had often used this route to travel to the Tlingit summer village. Britta and her sister had played on this path, while her brother and father used it for hunting expeditions.

"The air is so crisp," her mother began. "Some days feel so wet and heavy, but when it's like this, I find myself invigorated."

"It's chilly," Britta murmured, wishing for her warm bed.

A little side trail cut away from the main path, and it was this that Britta's mother chose to take them along. Britta said nothing. She couldn't have cared less where the road took them.

"I know it's hard to believe, but in time the pain will lessen. You will always miss her, but the severity—the intensity—will diminish."

Britta heard her mother's words but didn't respond. She didn't want to talk about Darya or the pain. She didn't want to think about any of it. Instead, she kept her eyes to the ground and focused on the rocky path that quickly steepened. Hiking her skirt a little higher, Britta struggled to keep up with her mother.

Panting just a bit, Mother continued talking.

"We called him Joseph. Joseph Lindquist had a nice sound to it, and it seemed to fit him well."

It took a moment to realize about whom her mother was speaking. The child born after Dalton. The baby no one had ever talked about. Britta tensed. She didn't want to talk of such things. There had been a time when she would have wanted to know, but not now.

"The doctor said he stopped breathing in his sleep. No one knows why." Mother maneuvered off the trail and motioned to Britta. "There's a small stream over here, if you're thirsty."

Britta followed her mother to the water's edge. The tiny brook rippled over rocks and spilled into a small pool that continued to flow toward the sea. Tall Sitka spruce towered overhead to shelter the meadow, but still the sun found its way through the boughs and sprinkled light upon the land.

"It will snow soon. Your father said there is already quite a bit of snow up high. I wanted to bring you here before it became difficult to traverse." Mother pointed to a rocky wall. "We buried him just over there."

There was a tiny marker at the base. Britta knew it had probably been made by her father. "Why did you bring me here?" she asked.

Mother rubbed her hands against her upper

arms as if the day had suddenly grown too cold. "I suppose I wanted you to see that you weren't alone. That I understood your pain and sorrow. Your loss."

"But you'd already told me that." Weariness overtook Britta. She longed to seek refuge in her bed. "Let's go back."

"Wait," her mother insisted. She went to Britta and reached up to smooth back a long strand of hair. "Burying my child was probably the hardest thing I've ever done. It will probably be the hardest thing you'll ever have to do, as well. There is no simple answer for why these things happen. There is no instant comfort that can be offered. Time is the only thing that will ease the suffering. The days will pass, and eventually you'll find that the wound isn't quite so raw. You'll come to accept that nothing you did or didn't do could have changed the outcome."

"Then why even try?" Britta murmured.

Her mother gave her a sad smile. "Because life goes on, even when we feel it shouldn't. We can't wrap ourselves up in the dead. There are others who need you. Darya is beyond need, but Laura isn't. Yuri isn't. He's hurting, too."

"Don't you think I know that?" She closed her eyes. "I thought I would be stronger— better at this. But I'm not, Mother. I feel as though something inside me is unraveling. I open my eyes in the morning and for just a moment I'm happy, but then the memory of what is real comes back. The house is so quiet, so empty."

"But it's not empty. Laura is still your daughter, and she needs you. Just as Dalton needed me. I did the wrong thing in forbidding your father and Aunt Zee to speak of Joseph's death. I think it was probably the wrong thing to do, because we were never able to share our hurt and pain together. Instead, each person bore it alone, and Britta, that's a terrible thing to endure. Don't bear this pain alone. Don't shut out the people who want to share it with you."

Britta began to weep. "Why would anyone want to share this?"

Her mother took her into her embrace and gently kissed her teary cheek. "Because we love you, Britta. We want to bear your sorrow with you because of that love."

———

Lydia watched Laura play with Connie and marveled at how much the child had changed in less than a year. Laura had come to them looking skinny and sickly. Her blond hair had been lifeless and dull, her eyes circled with a darkness that suggested hunger and exhaustion. She had been afraid of everyone except Britta, but now the world was her friend. The child was blossoming. Lydia could only pray that Darya's death wouldn't cause Laura to regress. So far, it seemed she was taking the loss in stride, but she still asked from time to time about Darya's whereabouts.

Phoebe joined Lydia after a few moments, bringing with her a box of new candles. "The girls helped me to make these." She placed the box on the table beside Lydia. "I thought perhaps you could share them with Britta, as Laura spent quite a bit of time assisting. She seems to have a knack for taking instruction. I think she'll do well in school."

"She's a smart one, I agree. I've never seen anyone thrive on learning the way Laura does." Lydia picked up one of the tapers and admired it. "I want to thank you for helping her get through these hard times."

"I'm glad I could help," Phoebe assured her. "I felt unable to do anything for Britta. She didn't want my company otherwise."

Lydia nodded. "She hasn't wanted anyone's company."

"Is she doing any better?"

"A little. We both know that it takes time. You lost a child to miscarriage, and while you didn't have the same attachments to that baby as Britta did to Darya, the pain is no less real."

Phoebe nodded. "But it is different. I can respect that. Caring for Laura and keeping her busy seemed the best thing I could offer."

"It has been a blessing." Lydia replaced the candle. "I suppose I should load these and get us home." She started to get up when they both noticed Evie coming up the walk.

"I was just about to head home," Lydia said with a smile. "But this is a pleasant surprise."

"Josh told me he'd seen the carriage over here," Evie stated. She looked to Phoebe. "I hope you don't mind my barging in."

"Not at all. Would you like some refreshment?"

"No thanks. I had a letter from Jeannette and felt I needed to share it with you both. It has to do with Marston."

Lydia frowned and retook her seat. "Has he died?"

"Not that I know of." Evie reached into her pocket and pulled out the missive. "He's in trouble again. Both he and Mitchell are apparently on the run from the legal authorities."

"What?" Phoebe and Lydia asked in unison.

Lydia pointed to the chair beside her. "Sit down and explain, please."

Evie opened the letter. "Jeannette says there has been a huge scandal. Apparently Marston and Mitchell duped a great many people through the funeral business."

"How?" Lydia asked.

"From what the letter says, they were accused of switching products, for one. A person would buy an expensive casket, and Marston and Mitchell would replace it with a much cheaper one. They are even accused of robbing the dead."

Phoebe gasped, while Lydia shook her head and said, "They don't care about anything or anyone."

"I had hoped old age would have changed their hearts," Evie said, putting the letter on the table, "but apparently it hasn't."

Lydia found herself feeling rather vindicated. "I knew Marston hadn't changed. He might have said all the right things while he was here, but there was something about his manner that didn't ring true."

"Jeannette says the authorities are trying to find them, but they believe Mitchell and Marston have fled to Europe. I think we need to wire someone and let them know that Marston was here not long ago."

"But he could be anywhere by now," Phoebe said thoughtfully. "Still, why would he come here with his story of wanting to leave you a fortune—of dying?"

"Maybe he really is dying," Evie offered. "Jeannette said he'd been ill for some time. It was actually one of the reasons he wasn't arrested when the news first came to light."

Phoebe continued. "It seems that he would have stayed as far from any of his family or friends as possible. Surely the authorities would first come looking for him among those he knew."

Lydia considered this for a moment. "I doubt they would ever expect him to come here. Obviously even Jeannette didn't figure him to do such a thing, or she wouldn't have written that letter."

"I suppose you're right, Mother." Phoebe looked to Evie. "I agree with you, however. I think we need to let someone know he was here. He might still be in the Seattle area. Dalton had word from the bank there that Marston deposited money into the new account."

"Money he robbed from the dead, no doubt." Lydia got to her feet again. "I agree with Phoebe. We must let the authorities in Kansas City and Seattle know as soon as possible."

"I'll wire them," Evie said, retrieving the letter. "I'll let them know he's been frequent-

the bank and that perhaps they can catch him there."

It had been a simple matter to befriend the bank manager's young assistant, Cyrus Redley. Marston was quite charming when he wanted to be, and the man was a jackanapes. His conceit and overconfidence made him a perfect target for a man as seasoned at using people as Marston Gray was.

He began their friendship by commending the man and boosting his ego with praise. Marston often told Redley that he was in the wrong position—that he should be the manager of the bank given his fine mind and ability with numbers. Redley devoured the words and grew fat on them.

Next, Marston invited the young man to join him at dinner. On more than one occasion, he exposed Redley to opulent indulgence. The man was greedy and longed for the life Marston introduced. So when Marston began talking about his need for a personal secretary, Redley was primed to take the bait.

"I have a vast fortune, you understand," Marston had told the man, "but I have no child, no heir. I would like very much to train up a man to take over my position—to continue the business. I'd like to have a companion to accompany me around the country on my various business trips. Perhaps you could be that man." Redley all but clapped his hands in delight.

Marston finished securing the man's adoration when he handed Redley a wad of bills as a bonus for all the help he'd given. "I reward those who benefit me" had been Marston's comment. Redley's eyes nearly popped out of his head at the sizable amount.

It seemed only reasonable then that when Marston approached the man at the bank on a day when the manager was home with a bad case of gout, Redley was more than willing and able to do anything he asked.

"I've forgotten my account numbers. You know there are several accounts that I'm commingled on. Most are under the name Lindquist, but my sister Evie's account is separate. Her last name is Broadstreet," he told Redley. Marston studied his fingernails as if the matter were of no real importance. "Anyway, my brother has contacted me, saying the time has come for us to make a healthy investment. I need your help, and I'm hoping you might even act as my representative."

"What is it that you need me to do, Mr. Gray?" Redley asked.

Marston smiled. "We are going to withdraw

most of one account. I am to take the money with me to California."

"You're leaving?" Redley asked, visibly upset. "I thought . . . well, we did speak about other matters."

Laughing, Marston enjoyed the man's panic. "Indeed we did. That is why I want you to personally accompany me. In fact, we ought to take additional funds so we can set you up in style once we've arrived."

Redley gave a smile of confidence. "I would be honored."

"Good. Then I will trust you to follow my instructions and meet me tonight at the hotel. We have a ship to catch in the morning and must act quickly." Marston paused and glanced around him. "But say nothing to the people here. I wouldn't want anyone to know that we will have the cash with us. It might leave us vulnerable to thieves."

Redley nodded. "Of course."

Marston smiled. "I knew you'd understand."

Chapter 25

November 1906

*B*ritta, won't you change your mind and come to church with Laura and me?" Yuri asked, his hand on her shoulder. "I could really use you at my side."

"I'm just so tired, Yuri." She pushed back her hair, which hadn't been brushed thoroughly in days. "Maybe I'm sick. I'll just go back to bed."

Yuri frowned. "You haven't been eating much. It's clear you're wasting away."

She slid beneath the covers. "I'm sure it's nothing."

He sat beside her on the bed, and she looked

up hesitantly. Reaching out, Yuri touched her cheek. "I know you miss her. I miss her, too. But Laura misses you, as well. She needs you. Please don't let this sorrow steal you away."

"I'm trying to manage it the best I can," Britta said, her voice barely audible.

"I know, but this isn't healthy. You aren't eating. You're sleeping all the time, and . . ." He looked away. "I know about the whiskey."

"What?" She sounded startled.

Yuri met her wide eyes. "Doc told me about it. Said he'd prescribed it for you to help you sleep. Thing is, he didn't intend for you to do nothing but sleep." He cupped her chin. "Britta, I know the danger you're putting yourself in. It's got to stop."

For a long time, she said nothing. Then in a voice that sounded as though it belonged to a child, she whispered, "But . . . if I don't take it . . . I have such horrible nightmares."

"I'll be here to help you through them," he promised, "but the drinking has to stop. You have no idea how quickly it can take control of your life. I . . . well, you convinced me that sharing my heart with you was the right thing. You knew it would be hard for me, but you stood your ground and in doing so, stood by me. I can do no less for you."

"But what if I was wrong? Wrong about all of this? What if we never should have married?

Maybe you and Laura should just go before I cause you harm, too."

"You're not going to harm us," he countered. "That's what I've been trying to make you see. You have been nothing but good for us. Darya didn't die from neglect; she died because these things happen. Babies stop breathing. Babies get sick. It happens."

"But it shouldn't," she said sadly. "It shouldn't happen this way."

Yuri gathered her in his arms, glad that she didn't fight him. He cradled her for several minutes, saying nothing. Words seemed unimportant. "Please don't give up on me," he finally murmured.

This caused Britta to pull back and look at him oddly. "I never gave up on you. This isn't about my giving up on you."

"Then don't give up on yourself, either," he encouraged. "Life doesn't always turn out the way we'd like it to, but we can't quit trying. Don't give up just because death makes it hard."

"Death is the easy part—it's life that's hard. And frankly, I just don't know if I have the strength to go on."

———

Yuri could still hear Britta's words ringing in his thoughts long after the church service concluded. He allowed Phoebe and Dalton to take Laura home with them, although he thought he probably shouldn't have. Laura needed to be with her own family, but unfortunately Yuri knew he and Britta were in no shape to be a comfort to the little girl.

"May I walk with you?" Lydia asked, coming up from behind him.

Yuri turned and nodded. "Only if I may speak to you about Britta."

She smiled. "I was hoping the same thing."

He extended his hand and took hold of Lydia's elbow. "I don't know what to do for her. She's so lost in her grief. I try to speak to her about it, but she's . . . well, I don't know."

"She's afraid, Yuri. She's terrified of it happening again. She's afraid of losing Laura, you. She's reliving the pain of losing Illiyana and Zerelda. She's faced again with the fact that loving someone can be very painful."

"Is there nothing I can do? Must I sit by and watch her suffer like this and have no recourse—no means to ease her pain?"

Lydia considered this a moment, all the while keeping her focus on the road ahead. "You have to be patient with her. Britta feels she's to blame for Darya's death."

"That makes no sense. If anyone is to

blame, it would be me. I didn't love her as I should have."

"Neither of you are to blame," Lydia said, shaking her head. "There is no reasonable answer for why Darya passed on. We can only accept that it has happened and endure the sorrow that comes with loss. However, as a mother, Britta takes the responsibility upon herself. I did the same. Even though my first husband beat me and caused me to lose the children I might have bore him, I blamed myself. I suppose partly because I kept thinking that if it were my fault, I could somehow control it and never allow it to happen again. Of course that wasn't the case. I think Britta is wrestling with much the same. She probably pores over and over in her mind all the things she could have done differently. The details of each and every day are probably laid out before her like a great puzzle that she must put together."

Yuri nodded. "I would imagine so."

"The only thing you can do is love her, Yuri. Love her and be tender with her. Help her through the sad times, and encourage her to enjoy the good ones. Little by little, hope will return and joy will slip in alongside—when you least expect it."

Marston secured the latch on his suitcase. Redley should arrive most anytime. Pulling out his pocket watch, Marston popped open the lid and checked the time. It was nearly nine-thirty p.m. His plan was to get the money from Redley, then tell him the plans had changed—they weren't to take the morning ship, but rather one later that very night. This would give Marston more time to distance himself from Seattle.

A knock sounded on the hotel door. "Just a minute," he announced, tucking the watch back into his vest pocket. He opened the door and found Redley standing on the other side—empty-handed.

"Come in." Marston looked in the hall after Redley entered the room. He wondered if the man had forgotten the case containing the money. Seeing nothing there, he secured the door and turned to the younger man. "Where's my money?"

Redley met Marston's eyes. "There's a problem. It's more of a delay, really."

"And what would that delay consist of?" Marston tried not to let his anger overcome the moment.

"The account cannot be accessed without Dalton Lindquist's approval. We will have to wire him in Alaska and get his agreement for you to withdraw the funds."

Marston shook his head. "You have the letter of transaction. That gives me authority."

"To deposit into the account, yes. But not to withdraw."

The news hit Marston like a lead weight. "Are you saying that my brother actually gave word that I not be allowed access to withdraw funds?"

"I'm afraid so. There are notations for all of the accounts you mentioned. Not only his, but the other Lindquist account . . . oh, and the Broadstreet account, as well."

"I can't believe this. What madness. He and I . . . we had an agreement. He's up in Sitka, and it's difficult to get in touch with him."

"I know. I tried to wire him. I thought I could clear this up and bring you the money in spite of the situation."

"You wired him?" Marston felt a sense of desperation. If Dalton learned what he was doing, he'd surely have the law on him.

"I tried to, but the line is down. Apparently the cable is broken somewhere along the way. They assured me it happens more often than not. When the line is restored, they will send the telegram."

"This is most annoying." Marston knew he needed to get out of town immediately. All he needed was for Dalton to get wind of this and figure out that Marston was attempting to take money from his account. Money that definitely didn't belong to him. "I suppose I shall have to simply take back my ten thousand dollars and hope that I can still make the proper investments in California. If you have your carriage, I'd appreciate a ride to the bank."

"That won't help you. I mean, I can give you a ride. That isn't the problem."

Marston narrowed his eyes. "Then what are you prattling on about?"

"The money. You can't take out the money."

"I already understood that point. The larger funds are off limits . . . temporarily." He smiled. "It's an inconvenience, but I'm hopeful that the ten thousand I deposited will cover the need. It can act as security until the remainder can be obtained."

Redley looked at Marston as if he'd suddenly grown horns. "No, you can't do that. The money cannot be withdrawn."

The terrible feeling of having been caught in the middle of a prank began to sink in. Marston kept hearing the words the younger man said, but they weren't making sense— until now.

"Are you telling me that I cannot withdraw my own money—the money I deposited a few weeks ago?"

"That's correct. When Mr. Lindquist set up the account, he put the same provision on it that he placed on the others. He would have to be notified of any transaction, be it transfers or deposits or withdrawals. Deposits were to be allowed under any condition, but all other dealings would have to first receive his approval."

Marston thought he might well be sick. Ten thousand dollars was now lost to him, and all because of his brother's lack of trust. He was seething. The cash he'd brought with him was diminishing at an alarming rate, and he needed to be able to access more soon. Now, however, he would have to leave Seattle and do so quickly, or the law might catch up to him.

"I suppose," he finally said, turning away to walk to the window, "that I have no choice but to wait." He tried to sound unconcerned. "I will wire my associates and explain the situation. Perhaps they can even send confirmation to my brother and hurry the matter along."

"I am sorry for the delay," Redley said. Marston could hear the relief in his tone. "It will allow me, however, to give at least a small amount of notice to my manager. I felt rather bad leaving without at least speaking to him personally."

Marston glanced at the man and nodded.

"I will leave you to that matter, then, while I attend to the other."

Redley smiled. "I hope this won't change things between us."

"Of course not." Marston smiled, as well. "We will continue as I always planned."

———

Britta awoke to the feel of Yuri's arms around her. She stiffened and tried to pull away, but Yuri would have no part of it.

"Where do you think you're going?" he asked, chuckling.

"I . . . you . . . frightened me."

He kissed the nape of her neck. "No need to be frightened. It's just me, and it's cold so I thought I would snuggle up here. You're nice and warm."

Britta felt him trail kisses along her ear and jaw. She trembled at his touch, longed for it, but in the back of her mind, her fears resurfaced. Fears of finding herself pregnant—of bearing a child and watching it die.

She again tried to pull away. "Don't. Please."

"What's wrong, Britta?"

Ashamed to admit the truth, she made up an excuse. "I don't feel well. I need to get up."

He let her go, and Britta hurried into her robe. "I'll be back. Don't worry about me."

She hurried from the room and paused momentarily in the hall. Where could she go? What could she do? It was the middle of the night. Slowly, she walked to the kitchen and tried to settle her nerves. Britta lit a lamp and placed it on the table. She then poured herself a glass of water and sat down to think. What was she going to do?

"Are you feeling better?" Yuri asked.

She hadn't heard him, and for just a moment, she wanted to run as far from him as possible. How could she possibly hope to explain her fears? How could she expect him to understand?

"A little," she whispered.

He came to sit across from her. "Is there anything I can do?"

She shook her head and sipped the water. She couldn't even meet his gaze. "I'm fine. Really." She struggled for something more to say. "It won't be long until Thanksgiving, and then Laura's birthday. After that, Christmas."

"True enough, but none of that matters as much as knowing what I can do for you right now, Britta."

She forced herself to look up and give him a weak smile. "It will matter when there's no Thanksgiving feast on the table and you're hungry."

"Britta," he said softly, almost pleading.

She trembled and focused on the glass of water.

"Please let me help you."

She was quiet for a long moment. "You can't."

"I find that hard to believe. I'm your husband, Britta. I want to make this better for you."

And that's the problem, she thought. *You're my husband and you're asking more of me than I'm ready to give.*

"I know you care," she replied finally. "I'm glad you do. It's just that I'm . . . I want to be able to put this behind me. Believe me, please."

"I do. I understand."

She looked at the table. "If anyone can, I'm sure you do."

"You're afraid."

Those two simple words hit her like nothing she'd ever imagined. "Yes." She could barely speak.

He reached out and covered her hand with his. "Me too."

Her head snapped up. "You?"

"Don't sound so surprised."

"But what do you have to be afraid of?" She knew her own fears. Fears of having another child and losing it. Fears of Laura dying.

Even fears of Yuri meeting with an untimely death.

"I'm afraid I'm losing you, and I've only just allowed myself to love you."

She shook her head with great purpose. "No. You aren't losing me. I still love you, Yuri. I will always love you. You don't need to be afraid of that."

"But you've been distancing yourself from me. When I try to talk to you, you want nothing to do with me. When I try to hold you—to kiss you . . ." His words faded.

Britta swallowed her pride and blurted, "I'm terrified I'll get pregnant." Once the words were out, she couldn't stop the flow. Getting to her feet, she knocked over the water glass but did nothing to retrieve it. "I'm afraid I'll have your baby, and that baby will die just as Darya did. I'm afraid Laura will die." She began to sob.

"She could get sick. She could get the measles or some other awful disease. She could die. You could die." Britta buried her face in her hands. "I can't bear this. I can't bear the thought of what might happen."

Yuri was immediately at her side. He took her into his arms and let her cry. He didn't try to stop her tears or to speak words of comfort; he simply held her and waited for the anguish to pass.

Still not speaking, Yuri led her to the couch and drew her down beside him. He sat there holding her, and in the comfort of his arms, time seemed to stand still. Britta held back from speaking for fear the spell would be broken and the consolation would end. Why couldn't they just stay there forever?

"It seems," Yuri said, breaking the silence, "that we are both afraid."

"Terrified," she whispered.

He raised her face to meet his. "God hasn't given us a spirit of fear. The Bible says that much. I think it's in the second book of Timothy."

"I remember that verse," Britta said, nodding. "He's given us a spirit of power, and of love, and of a sound mind."

Yuri smiled. "Seems to me we're going about this all wrong. We're trying to do this all on our own. We need the Lord to help us."

"But I can't talk to God. I'm angry at Him, Yuri. Angry that He would let Darya die."

"I know, sweetheart. But more important, He knows."

She looked at him as the truth of his words sunk in. Of course, God knew how she felt. God knew everything—it wasn't like she could keep Him from knowing her heart. Yet she certainly had tried. The very comfort and hope she needed was in Jesus, yet she was hiding from Him as if she could avoid the situation altogether.

"I don't know what to do next," she said, feeling like a little child. "This is just too hard."

"I know." He smoothed back her damp hair. "Without God, it is too hard for either of us—even if we try to face this together. We need Him, Britta. He's the only one who can help us through."

She nodded and felt her strength give out. But even as she felt overcome by her own weakness, Britta felt a warmth of hope stir deep within. Maybe in giving up her own fight—giving up trying to face this on her own—maybe only then could God step in and heal their hurt.

Please let it be so, she prayed. *I cannot bear this sorrow any longer.*

Chapter 26

December 1906

Despite the stomach discomfort he'd been suffering since Cyrus Redley's announcement, Marston decided the best thing he could do would be to return to Sitka and explain himself to Dalton. He'd simply arrive and tell Dalton that it was all a terrible misunderstanding—that the young clerk had thought Marston wanted to withdraw money rather than deposit. He hated the idea of making the trip to Sitka, but he figured a face-to-face explanation would go a long way to prove his sincerity. After all, who would expect him to show up and face his accusers?

Marston downed a large spoonful of laudanum and waited for the medicine to ease his pain. The doctors had to be wrong about the diagnosis. He simply didn't believe he had cancer—this was surely nothing more than an ulcer. His own father had suffered with such ulcers, so why should he be any different?

The clock struck one and with the chime came a knock upon the door. It was Cyrus Redley, whom Marston had summoned. The man seemed relieved to have Marston's attention once again.

"I feared perhaps you would be unhappy with me because I was unable to get approval for your transaction."

"Nonsense," Marston assured him. "I realize that you are only one man. You can hardly take responsibility for everything that happens at the bank. I was hopeful you could have canceled the telegram to my brother, but it's of no concern. I've decided to go to Sitka myself and explain the situation. I will arrange for Dalton to return with me or send his written approval, and that way, we can expedite my transaction."

"That would be a perfect solution," Redley assured him. "With your brother here, there would be no doubt of his intentions."

"Exactly," Marston agreed. "I'm hopeful you won't mind driving me to the docks. I have just enough time to get there before my ship departs."

"Of course," Redley said. "I would even accompany you, if you wished."

"That won't be necessary. I'll return before you know it. In the meanwhile, keep your job at the bank. It will allow you to keep an eye on my money."

Redley nodded and went to retrieve Marston's suitcase. "I am happy to do so."

———

Nearly two months had passed since Darya's death and Britta was finding the days a little easier to get through. The nights were still difficult, but Yuri faithfully helped her endure the nightmares. He was also considerate of her fears and didn't try to impose himself or his affections upon her, for which Britta was grateful.

Now, as they celebrated Laura's fourth birthday, Britta realized that life would continue just as it had before the baby's passing. Funny, but she had thought at one point that her entire world would end—that she would never be able to surface above the pain. Little by little, however, Britta was finding things to focus on that didn't have anything to do with Darya's death.

Still, Britta couldn't shake the sadness

sometimes. There were moments, even here at her parents' home, where she had first brought Darya and Laura, that Britta couldn't help but feel the emptiness threaten to engulf her once again. She could almost hear Darya crying and remember how it felt to drag herself out of bed at night to see to the baby's needs.

"Look, Mama," Laura said, breaking through Britta's memories. "Aunt Kay and Uncle Ted gave me a new dolly."

Britta smiled at the excitement on Laura's face. "That is a wonderful present."

"I'm going to call her Darya after my sister in heaven." Laura danced away to show her grandmother the doll, and Britta turned so that they wouldn't see her face.

"Look, Grandmother."

Britta took a deep breath and squared her shoulders. She would be fine. She could face this and endure. Yuri immediately came to her side. He didn't say a word; he didn't need to. He laced his fingers with hers and squeezed her hand. It was funny, but over the last few weeks, they had grown closer than Britta had ever imagined possible. Despite the lack of physical intimacy, she had yielded to Yuri many long hours of conversation and dreaming. It was the start of a new future for them.

"We have an announcement to make," Kay

said, pulling Ted to the center of the room. "This is such a wonderful occasion, and we can't help sharing our news with you."

"Do tell!" Phoebe said, laughing. "You and Ted have been so full of secrets lately. I for one would like to know what's going on."

Kay giggled. "We're going to have a baby."

Phoebe's mother and Lydia gave gasps of delight. "What wonderful news!"

Laura stopped in the middle of her doll presentation and joined in. "We need to have another baby, too. I want another sister."

The room went quiet and all gazes turned to Britta and Yuri. Britta froze the expression of surprise on her face, knowing that would be more acceptable than one of terror. Yuri tightened his hold on her hand.

"I think babies are wonderful," Britta's mother said, putting her hand on Laura's shoulder. "They are gifts from God."

"Oh, look Laura," Phoebe announced, "you have another present to open."

Britta was grateful for the distraction they'd created and slipped from Yuri's hold. "I'll be right back. I need to get something from the cabin." She tried to speak loud enough that everyone could hear.

She wasn't but a few steps from the house when she heard the door open, and Yuri called after her. Deciding she might as well wait for him, Britta stopped and turned.

He went to her and reached out to cup her chin. "I know that was hard for you. I'm sorry."

She shrugged. "It's bound to happen from time to time. I'm sorry, too."

He nodded and offered her his arm. They walked toward the cabin. "I think it's time for a change."

Britta bit her lip to keep from asking what kind of change. What if Yuri asked more from her than she could give? Instead, she waited for him to continue. When they reached the porch of the cabin, Yuri drew her with him to the bench.

"I think it's time we moved. We have lived on your mother and father's land long enough. I want to provide us with our own home."

Britta let out the breath she'd been holding. "I can't tell you how happy that makes me. I was just thinking of how there are so many memories here, and while that can be good, it can also be painful."

He nodded. "I know. I've been working on a plan, but it will take a little time. I hope you won't mind waiting a bit longer."

She met his gaze. "When it comes to you, waiting is the one thing I've grown very good at."

Dalton was surprised to look up and see his older brother standing in front of him. "Marston? When did you return?" A multitude of questions coursed through his mind, but Dalton held them at bay.

"I just came ashore this morning. I felt it important to come and explain some things to you—just in case you were misinformed." Marston's countenance bore a look of exhaustion. His complexion was pasty and pale, and he looked thinner than before.

Leaning back in his chair, Dalton crossed his arms. "What type of things?"

"Well, I suppose you received the telegram from Seattle?"

"No, there have been no telegrams. They have had difficulty with the cable and service has been sporadic. What kind of telegram should I have received?"

Marston appeared quite uncomfortable. "Might I sit?"

"Of course. By all means." Dalton waved him to the chair. "I'm sorry I didn't suggest it at first, it's just that your appearance here has taken me by surprise."

Marston smiled and eased into the chair. "I'm sure it has, and for that I do apologize.

It's just that I was mortified when I learned the truth of what had happened."

"And what was that?"

"I went to the bank in order to arrange a transfer into our joint account. I wanted to transfer money from a couple of my other banks and somehow the instructions were confused and the teller thought I wanted to withdraw money. They told me I wasn't allowed to withdraw without your approval and that they had wired you. I assured them that some mistake had been made. I was only trying to transfer funds to your account, not withdraw them."

"I see." Dalton tried to maintain his calm, though all he could think of was that Marston and Mitchell were wanted by the law.

"Well, it was simply a misunderstanding, but all I could think of was the lack of trust we had in the past. I knew you would assume the worst, and I wanted to prove my innocence by coming here in person."

Dalton wasn't sure what to say. It was clear that Marston was upset by the matter, but whether it was for the good purpose of setting the record straight or the less honorable one of cleaning up after the mess he'd made, Dalton couldn't be certain.

"It doesn't appear that any harm was

done," Dalton said casually. "How are you feeling?"

"Oh, my stomach is giving me fits, but I seriously doubt the doctors know what they're talking about. Our father had ulcers for many years. His stomach often grieved him. You probably have endured such things yourself."

"No, actually I haven't. I thought the doctor felt it was cancer—that you didn't have long to live." Dalton knew his statement sounded hard and impersonal, but he continued. "I thought that was the reason you'd come here in the first place."

"That was then. I was worried about my health. I'd just received the news, and it weighed heavily on my mind."

"We had a letter from Jeannette." Dalton's words hung in the air for a full minute.

"I suppose . . . she was worried. She knew I'd been ill while in Kansas City. The doctor was probably frank with her about my condition."

"She did mention you had been ill, and that you had left Kansas City without a word to anyone."

Marston eyed him for a moment and nodded. "I suppose she told you also of the false accusations brought against Mitchell and me."

"She did mention some sort of legal trouble."

"It's all utter nonsense." Marston twisted the rim of his hat. "I can't say it was a surprise. When people are jealous of one's success, they tend to go out of their way to put an end to it. Mitchell and I were simply pawns in their game. However, we did nothing illegal."

"Another misunderstanding?" Dalton asked, a bit more sarcastically than he'd intended.

Marston frowned. "You don't have to believe me."

"That much is true," Dalton agreed. "The authorities are the only ones who have to be convinced. I understand that Mitchell has gone missing, as well."

"I'm hardly missing, Dalton. After all, you know perfectly well where I am, and where I've been. I'm not trying to hide, if that's what you're implying. I'm simply giving my lawyer time to work out the misunderstanding without my involvement. I have no desire to be at the center of a public display of grievances and nonsensical accusations."

Dalton realized his brother was lying, but to press the issue now seemed pointless. He would instead notify the authorities at his first opportunity and inform them that Marston Gray was in town.

Marston grimaced and clutched at his

stomach. "I'm afraid I should leave you for now. I need to take some medicine and rest."

"Would you like me to send the doctor to you?"

Getting to his feet, Marston shook his head. "I'll be fine. I just couldn't take my ease without knowing that things were settled between us."

Dalton rose and came around the desk. "As far as I'm concerned, things are settled."

"I'm glad to hear it. I'll be in touch. Perhaps you would allow me to take you to dinner one night."

"It will depend, of course, on your health," Dalton replied. He could see that Marston's pain was quite intense. The man had grown pale and sweat had formed on his brow even though the day was cold.

Marston took his leave, and Dalton wondered what he should do first. He needed to let his mother know that the man was back in town. Evie too. The last thing he wanted was for the women in his family to be further distressed by this man. After that, he would have to let the authorities know of his brother's location.

Taking up his hat, Dalton went to the workshop to inform Yuri of Marston's unexpected return. "I'm leaving now, but I shouldn't be long. I just need to let Mother know about my brother."

Feeling time was of the essence, Dalton took the wagon and drove out to the homestead. He knew his mother and father were probably both hard at work making gifts for Christmas, as was their way. His father generally made wonderful pieces of furniture for each household, as well as toys for the children. His mother created cushions and quilts, along with clothes for the smaller children and the girls' dolls.

He prayed, silently asking God to give his mother peace about the situation. He knew she would be upset to know her stepson was back in town, but there was nothing to be done about it now. He would explain the reason Marston had come, weak though it was.

"What does he hope to gain?" Dalton questioned, urging the horse to pick up his speed.

The turnoff for the house soon came into view, and Dalton pulled the horse hard to the left. Experience told him Marston did nothing by chance. There was a reason he had come back to Sitka. Perhaps the explanation was valid, but Dalton seriously doubted that was all there was to the circumstance.

He secured the brake on the wagon and jumped down. He was just about to bound up the steps of the porch when his mother opened the door in greeting.

"Well, this certainly is a surprise. I never expect to see you on a weekday afternoon."

Dalton drew a deep breath. "I needed to come tell you something."

Worry immediately etched her face. "Bad news?"

"Depends." Dalton came into the house, pulling her along with him. "Marston Gray is back in Sitka."

"But why?"

"He claims to have come to clear up a misunderstanding he caused at the bank in Seattle."

"What kind of misunderstanding?"

Dalton explained the details and waited for his mother to comment. Instead, she moved to the kitchen and held up the coffeepot. "Would you like a cup?"

"Yes, please. The wind has a real bite to it today. That dampness just soaks through to the bone."

He knew she would eventually say something about the situation with Marston, so Dalton took a seat at the table and waited. Mother brought the black coffee and placed the mug in front of him. She then returned to the counter and pulled back a dish towel from a tray of cookies. "Would you like some of these?"

Dalton laughed. "You know very well that I could eat the entire plateful. Your cookies are some of the best around."

"I doubt they're as good as Phoebe's."

She put the plate on the table in front of him, then went back to retrieve the mug of coffee she'd poured for herself. Dalton took up one of the gingersnaps. "These are my favorites."

Mother took a seat across from him and folded her hands together. "I'm glad you told me about Marston. I would have hated to run into him in town, not knowing that he'd returned. Well, truth be told, I'd hate to run across him under any circumstance."

"I knew you would—that's why I felt it was important to come here as soon as he headed back to the hotel."

"How long will he be here?"

"He didn't say," Dalton told her. "I know the holidays are coming right up, but I don't want you fretting over that, either. I will make it clear to Marston that if he needs any holiday cheering, he can spend some time with me. I won't allow him to ruin Christmas for you."

She smiled and reached out to clasp his hand. "I appreciate you so. I know that you understand the pain that man has caused me."

"I do." He drank down the coffee and grabbed another cookie. "I can't stay. I still have a great deal to get done. Tell Father I said hello."

"He'll be sorry to have missed you. He's off trading for some cedar. He wants to make your Rachel a hope chest."

Dalton laughed. "She's only twelve."

"Exactly. She'll probably marry in another six years. She needs to start making things for her own home and saving them. It takes a good many years to fill a hope chest. It will keep her busy."

Dalton didn't like to think of his daughter growing up so quickly. The very idea that she could be married off in another six years didn't set well with him at all.

"Maybe I'll just lock her in the cache," he said with a grin. "Until she's thirty."

Mother laughed. "I somehow doubt that will work."

Dalton was back home before he remembered he'd need to let Evie know about Marston. He was just starting to turn the horse around when Phoebe came bounding down the walk. Gordon was just behind her.

"Your sister is here," Phoebe told him. "Come quickly."

Dalton jumped down from the wagon and motioned to his son. "Will you see to this?"

Gordon quickly took his father's place on the wagon seat, clearly enjoying the opportunity to drive the wagon. Dalton had once felt the same enthusiasm. He guessed it wouldn't be long before Gordon would ask to borrow their carriage for courting.

"I feel old," Dalton muttered.

Inside the house, Evie was waiting for him. She looked upset, and Dalton knew that she must have had a runin with Marston.

"So you know?"

She looked at him oddly. "About what?"

"Marston being here."

Evie nodded. "I didn't realize you knew."

"I went to tell Mother and then planned to come see you. I suppose Marston came to pester you and beg your understanding?"

"No. He sent for me after he collapsed near the hotel. He must have just left your office. He had some sort of attack, and they've taken him to the hospital."

Chapter 27

January 1907

"T he cancer has spread throughout the body," the doctor told Dalton a few weeks later. "I'm sorry to say this, but it's just a matter of time now."

"How has he taken the news?" Dalton asked.

The doctor put aside the chart he'd been reviewing. "He doesn't believe it's as bad as it is. He's in denial about the entire situation. He believes he simply has ulcers."

"He said much the same to me when he first arrived back in Sitka, the day he collapsed."

"Your brother thinks that his will alone

can keep him alive, and while I've seen such a thing delay death, it cannot hold it off indefinitely."

Dalton got to his feet. "I'll speak to him. After all, he once mentioned that his funeral arrangements were already made. I should inquire as to what that entails."

The doctor nodded. "There is little more I can do for him. We can keep him out of pain to a point, but that's all. Eventually, we won't even be able to control that. If you think he'd be more comfortable dying at home, I see no reason to keep him here."

"He has no home," Dalton said, knowing that Marston would never be comfortable in his care or Evie's. And to be perfectly honest, Dalton wasn't sure he could even bring himself to offer such a thing. "I think it best he remain here."

"Very well. As you said before, you can more than afford to give him the best of care available. I will do everything possible to ease his passing."

"I thank you for that. Now if you'll excuse me, I believe I'll go see him."

Dalton walked down the hall slowly and contemplated the situation before him. Marston's days were numbered, and the man was still without spiritual peace. Dalton wondered how he might help his brother to see the truth.

He supposed the straightforward approach was the best, but Marston had never been one to believe in a higher being. There was no foundation for him to accept God's love and gift of salvation when he'd spent a lifetime disdaining such things.

Entering the ward, Dalton could see the quartered-off area at the far end of the room where they had placed Marston. He would have preferred a private room, but there was nothing of the sort available. He was fortunate there was a doctor to even care for him. Since the government had moved to Juneau, they had lost a number of medical staff.

"How are you feeling today?" Dalton asked as he came around the drawn curtain.

Marston gave him a quizzical look and then gave a hoarse chuckle. "I'm ready to dance."

Dalton smiled. "You look it." He pulled up a metal chair beside the bed. "I was just speaking with your doctor."

"The man is a lunatic."

"I seriously doubt that," Dalton countered. He sat and tossed his hat to the end of the bed.

"Don't you know that a hat on the bed is bad luck?" Marston questioned.

"I don't believe in luck. I believe in the

power of God to deliver me and guide my steps."

The matter-of-fact comment hit its mark. Marston grimaced. "God isn't that powerful."

Dalton studied his brother for a moment. Leaning back, he crossed his legs and relaxed. "I suppose that to someone who has always relied upon his own strength, a time like this would be quite vexing."

Marston looked away. "Age itself is vexing. Life is vexing."

"True. But now you are facing death." Dalton let the words sink in for a moment. "Don't you think it's about time you dealt with it head-on?"

"The doctor doesn't know everything."

"Perhaps not, but I think he knows this much." Marston's clenched jaw told Dalton he'd hit a nerve. He decided to press forward. "You can deny your condition if you like, but it will only make things harder on you in the long run."

"You haven't got all the answers, little brother."

"No, but I know who does. My trust is in Jesus Christ. Yours is in yourself. Now you're dying, but Jesus conquered death. I think my trust is better placed."

"That's all utter nonsense—fairy tales to ease people's fears of life and death."

"Why do you have such a difficult time accepting that there is someone out there more powerful than you?"

"If God is so powerful, then why is it your mother cannot forgive me?"

This question took Dalton by surprise. "I don't understand."

"Your mother claims the same things you do. She speaks of God and the importance of living by His commands, yet she cannot let go of the past. She hates me to this day. I made poor choices, and she despises me. She hates our father, as well. Deny it if you can."

"Time has softened her anger and bitterness," Dalton replied. "She was very hurt by our father, as you know. Then you and your schemes nearly took her life and that of Aunt Zee. You took me from her and had she not suffered the inability to remember at the time, it probably would have left her too devastated to recover. Don't you think she has a right to hold herself at a distance from you?"

"Is that the Christian way? I thought if a person wanted to be forgiven, the Christian was obligated to give that forgiveness."

"Forgiveness doesn't equal reconciliation. That takes time, and sometimes even that is not necessary. My mother forgave the man who shot her, but she has no desire to have a relationship with him, nor to put herself in a position of trusting that he won't do the same thing to her again. Just as she has no desire to trust you not to hurt her again. That doesn't make her less of a Christian. Frankly, I think it makes her wise."

"She doesn't forgive me. She's never tried to make peace with me."

"And if she did, would that prove God's love to you?" Dalton shook his head. "I doubt it would."

"I don't know. I've listened to plenty of talk over the years but have seen very little backed up with action. People are always saying one thing, then conducting themselves in an entirely different manner. Rather like our legal system, where I'm beginning to believe you must prove yourself innocent instead of the other way around."

Dalton considered his brother's statement for a moment. The man had a point. It was easy to declare one's Christian beliefs, and entirely another matter to live them on a daily basis.

"Is there anything I can get for you?"

"No. I don't expect to be here much longer," Marston stated rather casually.

For a moment, Dalton thought perhaps his brother was accepting what the doctor had said, but Marston quickly dispelled that with his next comment. "I hope to be up and out of here within the next few days. You might check on the shipping schedules. I should be getting back to Seattle."

Dalton got to his feet and took up his hat. "I'll check in with you tomorrow. If you think of anything you need, just send word to me. Also, you mentioned having arrangements made for your funeral. It would be good to let me know what those are."

Marston shrugged. "I lied about that. I only said it to put everyone's mind at ease that I hadn't come to impose upon them."

"Then we should make some plans. Perhaps you could write down the things you want done."

"There's plenty of time for such things." He closed his eyes. "I'll concern myself with it another day."

———

"So what is this big surprise you've promised?" Britta asked. She huddled Laura close to her and wrapped her wool cloak around them both.

Yuri drove the wagon up a steep grade, urging the horses to their destination. "We're nearly there." They rounded a stand of tall spruce, and Yuri pointed. "There."

Britta turned to see a large house. "Who lives here?"

"We will, if it meets with your approval." He pulled the wagon alongside the place and stopped. "Come on. I thought you might like to see inside."

"I like it, Mama." Laura pulled away. "I want to see my room."

Yuri climbed down and pulled Laura into his arms. "Run along, then. I think you'll like it very much. Your grandpa Lindquist built this place many years ago." He put Laura down and laughed as she ran to the front door.

Britta allowed Yuri to assist her from the wagon. She studied the two-story house for a moment. "It's beautiful." And it was. She was quite impressed with the log structure. The second floor had a series of three nine-pane windows, while the lower level had even more. Growing up with a man who built houses for a living at one time, Britta knew the expense of glass and the difficulty of getting it to Sitka in one piece.

"Come on. Laura's having all the fun without us."

They strolled to the front door and walked inside to find a large open room. To the left, they were greeted by a massive stone fireplace. Britta noted the beautiful wood floors. They looked as if they'd been laid only yesterday.

Someone had taken very good care of the place.

"Isn't it big?" Laura called out from the stairway.

"Indeed, it is," Britta replied. She looked to Yuri. "Is this something we can really afford?"

"Your brother has made me a full partner in the business. He felt he owed that to me because it was my father's business originally. I told him he didn't—fought him on the issue—but he would hear of nothing less, and so I relented. I figure I'll make it up to him in the long run."

Britta smiled. "I imagine you will."

"It's good to see you smile again." The comment caused her to stop smiling. Britta instantly felt guilty, but Yuri would have no part of that. "Stop it," he insisted. "Just because you find something to be happy about doesn't dishonor your love for Darya. She was such a happy child, and she would want us to be happy—especially for Laura."

"I know you're right. I'm sorry."

"Don't be. Just be happy." He took hold of her hand. "Now come on. I want to show you the upstairs."

They toured through the house, and as they passed from room to room, Laura would announce the ownership of each one. "This will be my room," she said when they came to a small but homey-looking room. Someone had papered the wall in a delicate flower print of pink, green, and white. It was perfect for a little girl's room.

"I think this will suit you quite well," Yuri said. "I thought of you, in fact, when I first saw this room."

"I can have all of my things here," Laura declared. "I can even have my dollhouse right there by the window."

They continued the tour and came upon the largest of the three bedrooms next. Laura took one peek inside and announced, "This is your room, Mama. You and Papa are two people, so you need a big room."

Yuri chuckled. "I like sharing a little room with your mama, but I think you're right. She would like all this extra space. Wouldn't you?"

Britta glanced around, noting the wallpaper. It was done in the French toile de Jouy style with country life detailed in blue against the white background. "It looks like cloth on the walls."

"We could change it," Yuri told her. "I mean if you don't like it."

"It's lovely. A bit . . . well, overly busy in a sense." She shrugged. "But it wouldn't keep me from loving this room all the same."

"I'm glad to hear it. So you like the place?"

She heard the eagerness in his tone. "I do. Very much. How soon can we move?"

Laughing, Yuri pulled her into his arms. "Right away. I just need to finalize the purchase."

"I suppose I'll start packing."

"Come on," Laura called. Her impatience was clear. "You haven't seen the baby's room yet."

Britta stiffened in Yuri's arms. "It's all right," he whispered. "Don't let it ruin this for you."

"It just took me by surprise. That's all." He stepped back and took hold of her hand. "I'm sure a lot of things will do that in the future, but we'll face it together. Deal?"

She nodded. "Deal."

———

That night as Britta tucked Laura into bed, she couldn't help but remember the child's enthusiasm about the house. "I'm so glad you liked the new place your father found for us."

"It's really big. I don't like that Grandma and Grandpa can't come too, but Papa said I could come visit them here."

"Of course. And they will come see us, as

well." She kissed Laura on the forehead and reached for the lamp.

"Mama, can we have another baby soon?"

Britta felt her stomach tighten. She didn't know what to say. She wanted to be able to tell Laura that her heart simply wasn't ready for the risk again, but in doing so she might well steal her daughter's peace of mind. After all, Laura had accepted Darya's absence better than Britta had imagined. Laura still missed Darya and talked about her often, but she seemed at ease with her memories and the fact that these things happened.

"Babies are a gift from God." Britta tried to choose her words very carefully. "Such things are up to God."

"Then I'm going to pray for a new baby." Laura's simple statement seemed to settle the matter. "Grandma says God can do anything. So I'm going to ask Him for a new sister."

"Not a brother?" Britta's nervousness brought a tremor to her words.

"No, not yet. I want a sister first and then a brother." Laura suppressed a yawn and closed her eyes. "Then we can have another girl after that."

Shaking her head, Britta walked to the door. "Good night, my sweet. You sleep well."

"I will when I'm done praying."

Britta stepped into the hall and pulled the

door closed behind her. She drew a deep breath and glanced to her own bedroom door. Soon she would retire for the evening and find herself alone with Yuri. She smiled and thought again of Laura. Maybe it was time to let go of the past and move forward. Maybe having concerns about the future was just the way it would always be. After all, she couldn't predict the days to come. She couldn't tell whether there would be good weather or bad, prosperity or desolation.

Glancing at the ceiling, Britta thought of her daughter's faith. "She puts me to shame. But I am trying, Lord. I am trying."

Chapter 28

February 1907

*D*alton took the opportunity of delivering the mail to his parents in order to speak to his mother about Marston. He'd waited for a few days, just in case Marston was right and on the mend once again. However, his brother's condition had worsened.

"It's certainly a wonderful surprise to see you here," his mother declared. "Your father and I were just making preparations for our trip to see Kjerstin and Matthew."

"I knew you were, and that made visiting you all the more important. There's a letter here from my sister."

Lydia took the missive from him and tore it open. "Oh dear." She continued scanning the single sheet of paper. "She's already had the baby. He came early, but seems to be doing all right." She glanced up at Dalton with a smile.

"What are they calling him?" Dalton asked.

"Orren. Orren Josiah Carson." She laughed. "An impressive name for one so little."

"I'm sure he'll grow into it," Dalton countered. He squared his shoulders and reached out to take hold of his mother's arm. "There is another reason I'm here."

"You heard that I had made a pie last night?" She pointed in the direction of the kitchen. "I have plenty left over, if you're hungry."

"Sounds good, but no. That's not why I came. Please sit with me a moment."

She frowned but allowed him to lead her to the fireplace and her rocking chair. "This must be important."

"It is. It has to do with my brother."

Her frown deepened. "Marston? How can that possibly involve me?"

Dalton waited until she sat down, then pulled an ottoman up close to her. "He's dying—the doctor confirmed this with me."

"He already mentioned that on his first trip here."

"Yes, but I think he used that only as an excuse. He doesn't believe it. He thinks the doctors are wrong, and because of this, he's in denial. He can't face his own mortality."

"Of course not—he didn't dictate the terms. If he's looking for sympathy or someone to care for him now, he's come to the wrong place."

"He's not asking for anything." Dalton tried to think of how he might appeal to his mother's heart. "But I am."

She eyed him for a moment, then shook her head. "If it has to do with Marston, I'm not sure I can help you."

"I've been trying to talk to him about God, Mother. I don't want him to die without knowing and accepting forgiveness. Yours, as well as God's."

She placed her hand to her mouth as if to stop any further comment. For a moment, Dalton simply focused on the rug on the floor, pleading with God to open his mother's heart. He didn't want to upset her, but Dalton knew that, for her own sake, she really needed to lay this affair to rest, once and for all.

He looked up. "Marston will be dead in a matter of weeks. Maybe days. I think for your own peace of mind, as well as to show true forgiveness to him, it would be good to speak to him."

Still she said nothing. Dalton wished his father were there. Surely he could help Mother realize the importance of what he was asking.

"Mother, you once told me that God had allowed you to forgive Marston. Just go to him and tell him the truth. Tell him you forgave what he did. Tell him that he needs to make his heart right with God. Mother, we can't just escort him to the door of hell and say nothing."

She was silent for a moment. "Why me? Why is it so important that I go to speak with him?"

"Because when I mentioned God and His forgiveness, Marston brought up the fact that you hadn't forgiven him—that God wasn't powerful enough to bring that about. I know it's like he's testing us, but what can it hurt to be honest?"

"I can hardly pretend the memories of the past no longer exist. I have forgiven, but I haven't forgotten."

"Of course not, but you can prove to him that they no longer control your life. Mother, you told me long ago that God had allowed you to put my father's actions to rest. That you were able to let go of the past. I'm merely asking you to do the same with Marston—and then to tell him you've done it. I want very much for Marston to make his heart right with God before he dies."

"You shame me," she said, reaching out to touch Dalton's face. "The man has harmed you as much as anyone, yet you are worried for his soul." She drew a deep breath and let it out in a sigh. "Although it will be very hard for me, I will go with you. I will speak to him."

"Thank you. This means the world to me."

"I can see that much. I am truly humbled at the concern you have for your brother. He doesn't deserve your compassion."

"None of us deserved God's, either," Dalton said, "but we are so much better off for it. I want everyone to know that blessing."

———

"What a fine day it is," Britta declared. She and Yuri had decided to take Laura on a hike up the mountain. The weather had been clear for three days now—a remarkable phenomenon in Sitka. The trails had dried, and the sun had managed to warm the air quite nicely. Britta intended to take advantage of the moment.

"In another few weeks, it will be warm like this all the time," Yuri said, linking his arm with hers.

"And we shall be in our new house," Britta added.

Laura ran on ahead of them enjoying the excitement of exploration. From time to time, she stopped and picked up a rock or a piece of wood to examine it. The child reminded Britta of herself at that age.

"I did manage to obtain permission to begin painting and making other changes to the place."

Britta nodded. "I was hopeful you could. There's so much I'd like to do. I want to paint the kitchen—especially the cupboards. The kitchen is so dark. I figure if we paint the cupboards white and maybe use a light green on the walls, it will brighten things considerably. Mother even spoke of showing me how to do some decorative stenciling."

They approached the trail that led to where Britta's little brother was buried. "Let's go this way," she encouraged. She wasn't sure why she wanted to revisit the spot, but it seemed the right thing to do.

"We'll have to be careful of getting too far off the main trail. The snow is still deep in the higher elevations."

"I don't plan to go far. There's a little

meadow up ahead. There's a rocky wall, and it's there that my mother and father buried my little brother."

Yuri met her gaze. "Are you sure you want to go there?"

Britta turned to the path ahead. "Yes. I'm feeling a little stronger every day. My mother told me that time would distance the pain. Visiting my brother's grave seems proof of that. I remember my mother's strength there, and it gives me hope."

The climb steepened and grew a bit muddier. Snowmelt had dampened the trail, despite the dry weather. Laura slipped and landed out flat on her stomach. She got up and turned in muddy misery to reveal the front of her dress.

"Don't fret. We'll wash it up when we get home. Go ahead and play," Britta encouraged. She looked up at Yuri, who was trying to hold back a chuckle, and added, "I came home dirtier than that on many an occasion."

"I remember," he said fondly. "You were quite the little mountain goat, as I recall."

"I was not. I was merely adventurous. I actually considered joining an exploration team to study the vast far north. Did I ever tell you?"

He laughed. "No. I would have remembered that."

"Well, it's true. I went to speak with one of the men leading an expedition out of Vancouver. He was not impressed that I had grown up in Alaska, nor that I was a woman. He did, however, rethink my application when he learned that my parents were quite wealthy. In the end, however, he turned me down. He feared that I might be desperately wounded during the trip."

"I'll bet he was more concerned that you would outshine his men."

She gave her husband a brief shrug. "Who can say? I was disappointed, but I didn't allow it to defeat me."

"I've always admired that about you."

"Admired what?"

"That you don't allow life's disappointments to defeat you. You have a quiet strength that runs deep. You know that little is to be gained by sulking and longing for what cannot change. Instead, you move forward to alter what can be made different."

"Sometimes I feel I used up all of that resolve on things that weren't so very important." She continued to climb the path. "See just over there—that's the place I was talking about."

The small meadow spilled out before them,

revealing patches of snow here and there. The rocky wall where her brother's marker stood caught Laura's attention and she bounded toward it.

"This is a wonderful place. Very peaceful," Yuri commented, coming up behind Britta.

"It is. My mother brought me here and talked of her loss. I didn't really want to hear what she had to say, but now and then I reflect on it. I'm still afraid, Yuri. Afraid of having our own baby and losing him like we lost Darya."

"I understand, but my deepest desire is that we not live in fear. I don't want to constantly be looking over my shoulder for the next bad thing to come."

Britta turned around and met his gaze. "Nor do I."

He pulled her into his arms and planted a warm kiss upon her lips. Britta felt that warmth spread out across her face. She closed her eyes and allowed him to kiss her again.

"I have come to really enjoy being a husband," he whispered against her ear.

"I knew you would," she teased.

He laughed and pulled away as if offended. "Oh, you did, did you? Now, how did you know that?"

"I made it my life's ambition to know you. From the time you saved my life, I knew that we were meant to be together and I worked hard to know everything about you. In fact, I used to follow you around whenever I got the chance. Mother and Father thought I was doing other things, but I would sneak off and find you."

He looked at her in disbelief. "Truly?"

Britta remembered those days easily. "Truly. I got myself into some places that I shouldn't have, but I suppose God was always watching over me. I only did it to be near you."

"I had no idea."

"I remember once I saw someone beat you up. Well, actually he tried. You made the better go of it, but he hurt you and that devastated me. You were bleeding from a blow you'd taken to the mouth, and all I wanted to do was come to you and nurse your wound."

"What happened?"

"Dalton saw me. I don't know why he was there, but he took me by the hand and walked me back home. He never told our mother, and he never chastised me. I think he knew I was only there to be near to you." Britta glanced back over her shoulder. "Where's Laura?"

Yuri turned to look. "I don't know. Laura, where are you?" he called.

Britta had been certain the child would come dancing back into view, but she didn't. Panic welled inside. "Laura!" She left Yuri's side and went in search. She called to her daughter over and over, but there was no response.

"Oh, this can't be happening," Britta said, setting off in the direction she'd last seen Laura. The snowmelt made the trail particularly difficult, and Britta found herself sliding downward even as she fought frantically to climb.

"Be careful." Yuri wasn't that far behind her, but to Britta he sounded miles away.

"Laura Belikov, you come back here right now," Britta called. She heard something and stopped. "Laura?"

It was the distinct sound of giggling. Yuri caught it as well and cocked his head to one side. "It's coming from over there." He pointed to the left. "Laura, this isn't funny. You gave us a fright." He took off across the forested ground, while Britta decided to go ahead and navigate the trail. It was a mistake. Without warning she lost her footing on the steep path and fell face-first onto the ground. She had thought that was the end of her problems, but as Britta struggled to get to her feet, the ground seemed to give way beneath her, and she went tumbling with it.

Her last thought was that her clothes would now be as muddy as Laura's. Then her head struck a rock and her world went black.

Chapter 29

Let me talk to him alone," Lydia told her son. "I think it is better this way."

Dalton stood back and crossed his arms. "If you need me, I'll be right here."

Lydia said nothing. Instead, she marched with purpose across the open hospital ward to the place where the curtains had been drawn to give Marston Gray some privacy. Pushing aside the fabric, she was shocked to see the pale-faced man. He had lost even more weight than she remembered and looked almost skeletal.

"Lydia," he said, grimacing as he struggled to sit.

"Stay where you are," she said, holding out a gloved hand. "You needn't get up on my account."

Marston fell back against his pillow. "I suppose I know why you're here."

"Dalton told me you were dying. He wanted me to make certain you knew that I'd forgiven you the past."

Marston eyed her seriously for a moment. "And have you?"

Lydia could see the tiniest glimmer of haughty pride in his eyes. For a moment, it got her dander up, but then she realized just as quickly that he was beyond hurting her anymore. Especially in his present condition. But more importantly, she felt confident that in her own maturity and peace in the Lord, Marston Gray could no longer cause her grief. She drew up a chair and sat down before giving him a reply.

"I have forgiven you, Marston. Even though I doubt you have ever truly regretted any action you've ever taken. Your entire life was about being your father's son—about controlling what you felt was yours for the taking."

He narrowed his eyes. "Ambition accomplishes much."

She nodded. "So does prayer, but I don't imagine you ever gave yourself over to that."

Smiling, Marston relaxed and his expression softened. "I can tell you now, Lydia, that I've always truly admired your spunk."

Unmoved by his offhand compliment, Lydia shook her head. "I admired very little about you or your father, Marston. But I've not come to insult you or dredge up the past. I'm here to make certain that you know you have my forgiveness. I do not hold the past against you any longer. I turned over my right to retribution long ago." She fixed him with a determined gaze. "Had I not done so, Marston, you would be dead, and I would be in prison—or hanged."

"You would have killed me?" he asked with a weak grin.

She nodded. "For what you did to my aunt and child, yes. I could bear your attacks on me, but when you threatened their lives, that was too much."

He drew a ragged breath. "I know it wasn't easy for you to come here today, but I thank you for the effort. I know you hate me."

"But that's untrue. I do not hate you. I feel nothing but pity for you."

He frowned, and Lydia knew she'd delivered him a hard blow. Marston Gray was not in the habit of being pitied. She got to her feet. "I do hope you'll listen to your brother regarding eternity. You haven't much time left on this earth. Your past deeds are unimportant at this point, but what matters most of all is the condition of your soul. The choice between heaven and hell is yours alone to make."

She turned and walked from the quartered-off area before he could say another word. Lydia felt she had done all that she could to persuade Marston Gray regarding God. She felt guilty for the fact that she honestly didn't care if he accepted Jesus as his Savior or not.

"I'm sorry, Father," she whispered. "I wish I felt otherwise."

Dalton could see his mother's blank expression and worried that things had not gone well. "Is everything all right?"

She nodded. "I told him that I forgave him. I did what I could to persuade him that he needed to turn to God."

"You seem upset. Is there anything I can do?"

His mother shook her head and patted his arm with her gloved hand. "No. I'm fine. I'm going to wait for you at your home. It will do me good to visit with Phoebe and the children."

Dalton let her go. Walking through the nearly empty ward, Dalton tried to imagine what he would say to Marston. He wanted his brother to know that his time was close—that he needed to face his death and let Dalton know what he wanted in the way of a funeral.

"Hello," he said, pushing aside the curtain. "I hope you aren't overly tired."

Marston looked at him for a moment. "If you've come to tell me that I'm dying and need God, I've already heard."

Dalton remembered a verse in the Bible that said something to the effect of people who were ever hearing but not understanding. For all his intellect, Marston could not understand matters of faith—of the heart. His mind could not grasp the logic of such things, for what was logical about putting your trust and faith in something unseen?

"Does that mean you've also chosen to accept the truth of it?"

Marston laughed. "Truth is a very subjective thing."

"Meaning what?" Dalton took a seat, never letting his gaze leave Marston's tired eyes.

"Meaning it's a personal matter as to what is or isn't truth. The doctor believes me to be dying, while I'm not of a mind to accept that. Isn't it entirely possible that a person once told a situation is hopeless then in turn becomes hopeless? I do not desire to give the Sitka medical community that kind of power over me."

"Fighting for one's life is a positive quality, I agree. But your body is worn out. You are seventy years old, and cancer is devouring you. Fighting for your eternal soul would be a better way to spend your energy."

"You mother would agree with you. She said similar things." Marston grabbed his abdomen as his face contorted. "She . . . would . . . argh . . ." He fought to keep from giving in to the misery. "It's nearly time for my medication," he finally said.

"Look, I don't want to make this any harder than it needs to be, brother. The truth is, if you die without accepting God's free gift of salvation, you will be forever separated from Him."

Marston eased back as the pain appeared to pass. "Dalton, you need to give this up. My sin is too big for God to forgive. I have no desire to approach Him, only to be rejected."

"If your sin is too much for God—too big—then perhaps we should worship your sin. Obviously it would be more powerful than anything else."

This actually brought a smile to Marston's face. "Maybe it is."

"You know that's not true."

"Do I? My sin has defined me for seventy years. Call me stubborn, but I can hardly cast aside the very thing that fueled my life, just because I face death."

"Jesus has laid His life down at the very gates of hell in order to keep you from having to pass through. Would you walk over Him, for the sake of being stubborn?"

"I've been walking over people to get what I want all of my life. My tenacity has made me a fortune and given me great pleasure. Being stubborn is not such a bad thing."

"It is when it means you cannot accept any way other than your own." Dalton shook his head and got to his feet. "I used to wonder how a person could ever hear about God—about Jesus dying for all mankind—and still reject Him. Now I see that the devil has a way of blinding the heart to such matters. You scoff at God as you lie here dying. But mark my words, you won't be scoffing when you stand before Him on Judgment Day."

Marston shrugged. "Allow it to bother you if you will, but it seems to me that this is between me and the Almighty. You've made your choice. Now allow me mine."

"I'm glad you were able to go for the doctor,"

Yuri told his father-in-law. "I wasn't sure how I was going to manage everything."

Lydia had only returned a few minutes earlier and even now was deep in conversation with the doctor. Laura, meanwhile, had not left her mother's side. She was so upset that her game of hide-and-seek had caused Britta's fall that she had cried all the way back to the cabin. Yuri had little chance to comfort her at all, however, because he was burdened with Britta's unconscious form.

"She should be fine," the doctor said as he headed for the door. "Just have her rest."

"I'll see to it," Lydia said. She turned back to Yuri. "Laura can stay with us tonight."

"No! I want to be with Mama." Laura took hold of Britta's hand as she stirred and opened her eyes.

She smiled weakly at the child. "I'll be just fine, sweetheart."

Yuri went to Laura. "Mama needs to rest, and you would have to be quiet for the rest of the day. Why don't you at least go play at Grandma's house? Then if you want to sleep here tonight, you can."

"We can make your mama a present," Kjell told her.

Laura looked hesitant. The incentive seemed to work. She let go of Britta and stood. "I'm sorry that you got hurt, Mama. I won't be a bad girl anymore."

"You weren't bad, Laura. It was just an accident. Now have fun with Grandpa, and maybe later you can show me one of your books."

The girl nodded and scurried off to join Kjell. He scooped her up in the air and plopped her down on his shoulders. Yuri smiled at Laura's squeal of delight.

"You'll come for us if you need anything?" Lydia asked Yuri.

"Of course. I'm certain we'll be just fine."

"I'll bring your supper," his mother-in-law declared. "Don't worry about a thing."

He could tell Lydia was reluctant to go, but followed the doctor and Kjell from the room with only one backward glance. Yuri paid her no attention and focused instead on Britta.

"I'm truly sorry about all of this," she told him. "I was so worried about something happening to Laura that I got rather careless."

"Sometimes we can allow ourselves to get overly concerned about things that may or may not ever be."

Britta nodded. "God is truly in control."

"If wishes could make life simple, then you would never have another worry again," Yuri said softly. "Because with all of my heart, I wish only for you to be happy and at peace."

She grinned. "And I'm sure you wish for me to stop falling down the side of mountains."

"Rescuing you is getting to be a habit."

"I would hardly call two events in an entire lifetime a habit."

He chuckled and sat down on the edge of the bed. Reaching for her hand, he pressed her fingers to his lips. "Maybe not, but I do have to confess that I have another habit where you are concerned."

"Truly? What would that be?"

"I love you. I never thought love was possible for me, but I'm happy to have been proven wrong. This is a habit I welcome."

"Hmmm, a very difficult habit indeed. I tried to break it once where you were concerned," she said rather groggily. Yawning, she closed her eyes. "But it was much too big of a task. Loving you is something I am destined to do for the rest of my life."

"Good thing," he replied, feeling his heart flood with love for this woman. "Because I feel it is my destiny, as well."

Dalton was ready to go to bed when a knock sounded on his front door. Opening it, he found one of the hospital orderlies. "I'm sorry to come here at this hour," the man began, "but the doctor sent me. I'm afraid your brother has died."

"When?" Dalton felt as if he'd fallen into a great emptiness.

"About twenty minutes ago. We had checked on him at eight-thirty, and he was still with us. However, the nine-o'clock check proved otherwise. I'm sorry."

"Thank you for coming."

"Doc said you needn't worry about arrangements until morning."

"Thank him for me. I know he did everything possible to make Marston's final days comfortable."

The orderly nodded, tipped his hat, and left without further ceremony. Dalton waited until the man was well up the walk and headed back to the road before closing the door. He then leaned against the fireplace mantel. Marston was gone. Just like that—his life was over. It was harder still to know that his rejection of God had been so complete. Dalton would have liked to have comforted himself by believing that Marston would have reached out to God at the last moments of his life, but that didn't fit Marston Gray's style.

"I heard someone at the door," Phoebe said, crossing the room. "Is everything all right?"

"My brother has died."

"I am sorry, Dalton. I know you wanted so

much for him to make things right with God. Perhaps he did. You planted the seeds. He could hardly ignore the truth completely."

"If anyone could, it would be Marston."

She considered this a moment. "You did what the Lord called you to do. You were there for him. You offered him comfort and the company of family. Given the things he did in his lifetime, I would say you went far beyond what he deserved."

"Perhaps, but I don't understand why he would face death in such a manner. God's Spirit could have offered him a more perfect comfort. Marston would have known real peace had he only accepted the truth."

Phoebe touched Dalton's arm. "I'm really sorry."

"It's just such a waste. Marston's entire life was a waste. He was greedy and selfish, longing only to do what would gain him the most benefit. He never extended help to anyone else or even tried to make life better for those around him."

"He was blind to the truth, but only because he chose to be," Phoebe replied. "You once told me that such choices are at the very heart of free will. God desires us to come to Him willingly. He won't impose himself upon us." She shook her head. "You could not impose

God on Marston. He had the right to choose for himself."

"You're right of course, but there is still pain in his passing. He is lost to us forever, and I can't help but wonder if I had tried harder to show him God's blessings and benefits . . . well, perhaps he would have accepted the truth."

Phoebe raised a single brow. "Who can say but God? For me, I'm almost angry. Angry that anyone could be shown the truth and still deny Jesus."

"But Marston didn't believe it to be truth. He thought his past to be too much for God to forgive."

"Of course, that could have just been an excuse," she said, then immediately looked sorry. "I didn't mean to speak ill of him. It's just that people are full of excuses when it comes to repentance."

"You know, you're right. And that gives me a certain sense of relief. I lived an example of God's mercy in front of Marston. I forgave the past and tried hard to build a relationship with him when he declared such a thing was important to him. He had every opportunity to change and chose not to. The waste of it all—of a human soul—well, that grieves me. But I did all that I could. The rest was up to Marston."

"But it's all right to be sad, isn't it?"

He gave his wife a nod and reached out to find comfort in her embrace. Death was never easy to face, but given Marston's defiance of God, Dalton couldn't help but feel deep sorrow—the sorrow of losing something that was never intended to be lost.

Chapter 30

June 9, 1912

Yuri waited impatiently for Britta to deliver their third child. Laura played checkers with her little sister Elsa, age four, but from time to time would seek to engage Yuri in conversation.

"When will the baby come?" she asked for at least the tenth time.

"Should be anytime now," Yuri replied, hoping that somehow his comment might be true.

Elsa looked up from the game. "Papa, why is it so dark?"

Yuri got up and went to the window. A few

days before, the town had received word from the navy that Novarupta—a volcano in the Alaskan peninsula northwest of Kodiak—had erupted. Ash had progressively darkened the skies, and now it was even wreaking havoc with the livestock.

"Remember I told you about the volcano?" Yuri explained. "The air is full of the ash that came from the eruption."

"When will it go away? I want to play outside."

"Me too," Laura said with exaggerated frustration. "Grandma said we would go look for wild rice."

"Well, there's no way of telling how long it will be like this," he continued. "The word they brought from Kodiak said it was so dark and the ash so thick that a person couldn't even see a lantern they were holding out in their own hand. They were fortunate to even get the ship out of harbor."

"That's really dark," Laura said, giving a shudder. "I hope it doesn't get that dark here."

"I doubt it will," her father replied.

"Will the volcano get us here?" Elsa asked, coming to crawl up on her father's lap. "I'm scared."

"No, the volcano is far away. It can't do us any harm here . . . well, except for the ash."

"I would like to see it," Laura said, sounding braver than Yuri knew her to be. She had asked about the volcano's ability to harm them only two days earlier. "The lava sounds so wonderful. I've never seen lava."

"Me either," Yuri told her, "but I don't really think I'd want to see it. It burns everything it touches."

"Are there volcanoes in hell, Papa?" Elsa asked, her eyes wide.

He shrugged. "I would not be surprised if there were."

"Mama said that Mount Edgecumbe used to be a volcano. Will it erupt, too?" Laura asked, frowning. She got up from the checkerboard and made her way to Yuri's lap. "It can't erupt now, can it? It has snow on top."

"No, it won't erupt. It's a dead volcano."

A cry of agony broke from Britta. The trio looked to the stairway. Laura spoke for them all. "How much longer will it take?"

"Well, it took quite a while for Elsa to be born. If I remember right, it was about twelve hours."

"But Mama has been hurting for a long time." Laura shook her head. "I don't think I will ever have a baby. It must hurt a lot."

Elsa nodded at her sister's comment. "She was hurting yesterday, too."

Yuri smoothed back his daughter's hair.

"Your mother says that the pain is worth the joy that comes when the baby is born. She was so happy when you were born that she quickly forgot about all the work to get you here. The baby will come in due time. You have to be patient. The doctor said it shouldn't be too much longer. Grandma will let us know when the baby is born."

"When will Grandpa come back?" Elsa asked. "He promised to play checkers with me."

"He had to go to Uncle Dalton's house to pick up some things for the baby. Be patient."

As if on cue, Kjell Lindquist came into the house without so much as a knock. He wore cheesecloth tied around his head, with a heavier kerchief around his mouth and nose. Both were stained from ash. He also held a gunnysack and looked much like a homeless traveler.

Peeling off the contraption, he smiled down at the girls and Yuri. "I shook as much of this off as I could outside, but it seems the stuff just clings to everything."

"It's fine. The girls and I can clean up any mess you make," Yuri said, motioning the girls from his lap.

"Phoebe sent cookies. She figured you might need something to bolster your strength."

"Mmmm, Phoebe makes the very best

cookies," Yuri declared, then glanced at the stairs and smiled. "Just don't tell your mama I said so."

"Mama said so, too," Laura told him. "She told me if I wanted to learn to make cookies, I needed to have Aunt Phoebe teach me."

Kjell laughed. "Your grandmother feels pretty much the same way, and I know she can make a good cookie." He turned to Yuri. "Dalton had a chance to talk to one of the naval officials. He said the ash is killing fish and animals, and has even caused clothes to disintegrate on the line. The man advised Dalton to keep anything of value inside."

"What about the horses, Grandpa?" Laura asked.

"I put them in the shed and closed the door tight. Then I covered the window to filter the dust and ash. I think they'll be fine."

"You and Lydia should probably stay with us tonight," Yuri encouraged. "That way you won't have to go back out in this."

"Sounds all right by me. I know the horses will be happier."

Yuri took the sack from Kjell. "Did they say anything else about the eruption?"

"It's finally stopped, but Kodiak is taking the brunt of it. The ash has collapsed roofs, and people are dying from respiratory complications. I'm certainly glad Kjerstin and her family moved to Nome last year. I was heart-broken to have them so far away, but now I'm glad. It would have been a terrible thing for them to endure. Bad enough that so many others are suffering."

Yuri put the sack on the table and motioned to the stove. "Coffee's fresh. Should I pour you a cup?"

"Thanks, but I can get it myself." Kjell went to the cupboard for a mug. Just then the sound of a baby crying broke the silence in the house.

"The baby is here!" Elsa exclaimed and began to dance around.

Yuri felt the blood rush from his head. He grabbed the back of the chair. *How foolish is it to get light-headed now?* he thought.

He looked to Kjell, who just chuckled. "It's rather like taking a blow to the stomach, isn't it?"

"I figured I was an old hat at this."

Kjell shook his head. "You never get used to it. It's shocking and wondrous every time."

"Is it a boy or a girl?" Elsa asked her father.

Yuri shrugged. "We don't know yet. We'll have to wait until Grandma comes to tell us."

"It's a boy," Laura declared matter-of-factly. "I asked God for a boy this time."

hat if God decided that you needed r sister?" her grandfather asked.

Laura seemed to consider this for a moment. "I suppose I would have to say all right."

Yuri and Kjell laughed and Elsa clapped her hands. "I want to see the new baby."

"Patience, darling," Yuri told his daughter. "I want to see the baby, too." But mostly he wanted to see Britta. He wanted to know that she was all right—that she had survived the birth without any complications.

After what seemed hours, Lydia appeared at the top of the stairs to announce that they could come see the baby. Yuri went first, taking the stairs two at a time. The girls followed at a giggling run, while Kjell brought up the rear.

Across the blue-and-white room in a bed that Kjell had made for them the previous Christmas, Yuri could see for himself that Britta was fine. She looked tired, but very happy. "Come see our new addition," she urged. "The doctor is just finishing the exam."

"Is it a boy?" Laura asked.

Britta nodded. "Yes. You finally have a little brother."

Laura smiled up at Yuri. "I told you it would be a boy. God always listens to my prayers. Mama said so."

"But I also told you that sometimes God says no or wait," her mother added.

"I know. But I didn't think it would matter to God this time," Laura replied. "We needed a brother. We can have another sister next time."

Everyone but Britta laughed at this. Yuri caught her rolling her eyes instead. "I think your mother has done more than enough for a while. We will let her rest and not worry about giving you another sister just yet."

"What will we call him?" Laura asked.

Lydia looked to Yuri and then Britta. "Yes, what will you call him?"

Yuri smiled as Britta gave the slightest nod and urged him to speak. "We're calling him Morris James, after the man who brought me to the Lord."

Lydia nodded in approval. "How marvelous. I think that's perfect."

"Here's your son, Britta." The doctor deposited the baby in her arms. "He looks healthy and strong. Congratulations."

Yuri sat on the bed beside Britta and studied the now-quiet baby. "He's so tiny. I think he looks even smaller than Elsa when she was born."

"He's the perfect size," Britta countered. "A perfect fit for our family."

"And he looks very much like Britta did when she was born," Lydia threw out.

"And only Britta would dare to compete with a volcano for such attention," her father added, putting an arm around Lydia. "You probably should have named him Novarupta."

Everyone laughed heartily, but despite the noise, the baby slept on. The earth might well be in turmoil, Yuri thought, but here there was peace and joy.

———

The days turned into weeks, and Britta found herself once again amazed at how quickly a baby could change. Morris was already growing and taking on a distinct personality of his own. Britta still found herself fretful that something could happen to the infant, just as she had worried with Elsa, but she tried hard not to let it ruin her happiness.

Morris was a delightful child whose nature made him quite easy to handle. He seldom cried and most generally waited patiently to be tended. Now as he slept, Britta couldn't help but gently run her finger over his soft brown hair and marvel at the gift God had given.

"Is he asleep?" Yuri asked, entering the bedroom.

"Yes." She straightened and went to Yuri. "How about the girls?"

"Dreaming away."

Britta embraced her husband. "So finally some time for us."

Yuri held her close and stroked her long hair. "If I haven't told you lately how happy I am, you should probably hear it now. Especially since you are at the very heart of such feelings."

Britta pulled away just far enough to gaze into his eyes. "I'm very glad to hear you say it, Mr. Belikov. I feel the same way about you. I cannot imagine any other life than the one we share together."

He put his hand to her cheek. "You don't regret losing out on the travel and excitement of being a world-class violinist, playing for kings and queens? You don't miss the music?"

Britta shook her head. "The music never left me. You and the children are my music."

Yuri cupped her chin and kissed her ever so gently. "And you are mine. Like a beautiful serenade."

"Funny you should say that," Britta said. "The oldest type of serenade was actually a composition to honor or express love for someone special. I like very much being a composition to express love for you."

"You've always been my serenade and more," he said, gazing at her in wonder.

"And you are mine," Britta whispered, leaning her head against his broad chest. "So much of the past was just God's various interludes to bring us to this moment of perfection. I have no regrets."

Yuri's arms wrapped around her and held Britta tight. No orchestra could have made music as beautiful as his contented sigh. She closed her eyes and smiled.